Just a few comments that this Book

'I told 'em that it should be entitled 'The Re-Write' rather than the 2nd Edition but they was having none of it. Mind you it is has most definitely been very well re-written in every single aspect.'

..............Chris Ellison
Acclaimed Actor & Accomplished Artist

'My Stephanie Marchant collection is now complete.'

..............Dave Day
The Golden Lion Group

'Can't wait for the TV interviews.'

............Mallett
A 'Cockney Red' Friend

I'm actually in these stories under two different identities!

..................Derek Le Warde
Ex-Knockerboy and Local Jeweller

'I really love the books, but the extra '*Romantic*' bits in this 2nd Edition make it so, so much more special.'

...................Kimmy Dawes

A few years ago I worked alongside Stevie in the 'Hospitality' industry. He encouraged me to follow my dreams and have self-confidence in my own talent, for which I am eternally grateful. Things have worked out okay for me since then!

..................Celeste

A few more comments; 'Once one starts they all want a go!'

‘Well worth re-reading for all concerned, I loved it.’

...............Mike Holland
Local Philanthropist

‘I missed ‘Brighton’s Knockers’ first time round so feel very privileged and glad to get a second opportunity with this Edition.’

................Yael Breuer
International News Reporter & Latest TV Presenter

‘The Audio version will be available soon.’

...............Jack Bowman
Producer & Director with BBC
& Worldwide leading Audio Book Pioneer

‘Keep Writing ’em and I’ll keep Printing ’em.’

...............Mark Tulley
Gemini Print

'We quite like our bruvver and are also quite proud of him. He ain't heavy...'

.............Sisters Tracey & Lisa

Dedication

This book is in the honour of one of Brighton's Greatest Sons.

Micky Dawes.

A True Blue Brightonian Legend.

He single handedly revolutionised the Antiques

Business back in it's heyday.

Folklore hints that he was in fact the instigator of the 'Brighton

Knockerboy' tradition that still thrives in the City to this day.

He certainly nurtured and encouraged it!

Here's to you mate. Cheers'

Also to the rest of Brighton's honest Antique dealers

Both of 'em!

Previous Publications by these Authors:

'Brighton's Knockers'
Published 2014 ISBN# 978-1-63452-341-7

'A Lovely Pair of Knockers'
Published 2016 ISBN# 978-1-78280-943-2

'Knockerboys' Love'em or Leave'em
Published 2018 ISBN# 978-1-64370-904-8

'Absolutely Knockered' Parts 1, 2 & 3
Published 2019 ISBN# 978-1-78972-626-8

stevieboybrighton@live.co.uk

Front/Back covers designed by Stevie Martin

'Brighton's Knockers' 2nd Edition.
Published 2020 ISBN # 978-1-83853-536-0

Printed in Great Britain by
Mark Tulley@ Gemini Print Ltd
Shoreham-by-Sea, West Sussex

Humble Thanks To Tracey

Foreword by Stevie Martin.

It is true to say that I only get a couple of brief and seemingly inconsequential mentions in this book. The first instalment of an anthropological Trilogy that charters the legendary History of 'Brighton's Knockerboys'.

My involvement will become more apparent later in the series. Please be patient, because, as we all know, everything comes to those who wait.

I tell you now that Stephanie Marchant was, is, and will forever continue to be one of the great loves of my life.

It is with immense personal pride that I can reveal that the following stories capitulate every pore of her heart and soul. She reveals in a stark nakedness, a truthful catalogue of sometimes comical, yet always entertaining events, that were conveyed to her by just a few of the many Brightonian rascals that decided to 'Go On The Knocker'.

These mesmeric characters then proceeded to somehow or other shape and influence her life in a most interesting, intriguing and enjoyable fashion.

We may never have actually met ourselves, had it not been for her fateful involvement with some of the colourful characters and loveable rogues that we now refer to as 'Brighton's Knockerboys'.

I beseech you to hold her, and then myself if you like, close to your heart with reverence, because of our candour and honesty beyond reproof or question.

On top of that, I am quietly confident that you will experience a vast array of emotions not usually regarded, expected or associated with the simple pleasure of reading a few books, dedicated to the same enterprising subject, in such an unorthodox and original fashion.

I should mention one other little factor.

There are indeed a few contradictory matters betwixt the whole compendium of the 'Knockerboys' story, but where's the surprise there then? Dealing with such a bunch of toe-rags, conniving slippery little sods that they were, why would you expect anything else?

See what I mean?

Finished with three questions and no reasonable or responsible answer to a single one of them.

Magical!

Enjoy......... *Stevie Martin*

Please forgive me for including an extra little personal story, right at the end, but sharing another unbelievable coincidence was just too hard to resist!

It all comes at no extra charge, so where's the harm?

Knocker Boy Town
1 Market Diner
2 Waggon & Horses
3 Kensington
4 Basketmakers
5 Bardsleys
6 Horse & Groom
7 Cobden
8 Albion
9 Dover Castle
10 Derek's
11 Jack Balls
12 Pavilion
13 Il Bistro
14 Cricketers
15 Coach House
16 Hippodrome Bingo
17 Linden Club
18 Conquerors
19 Bow St Runner
20 Esquire Club
21 Pullingers
22 Brighton Tavern
Kensington Place
22
3
North Rd
Church St
Esquire Club
Upper North St
Western Rd
North St
Holland Rd
George St
Church Rd
21
20
19
18
17
16
15
BINGO
linden club
Brunswick St West
Brunswick St East
Waterloo St
Middle St
Kings Rd

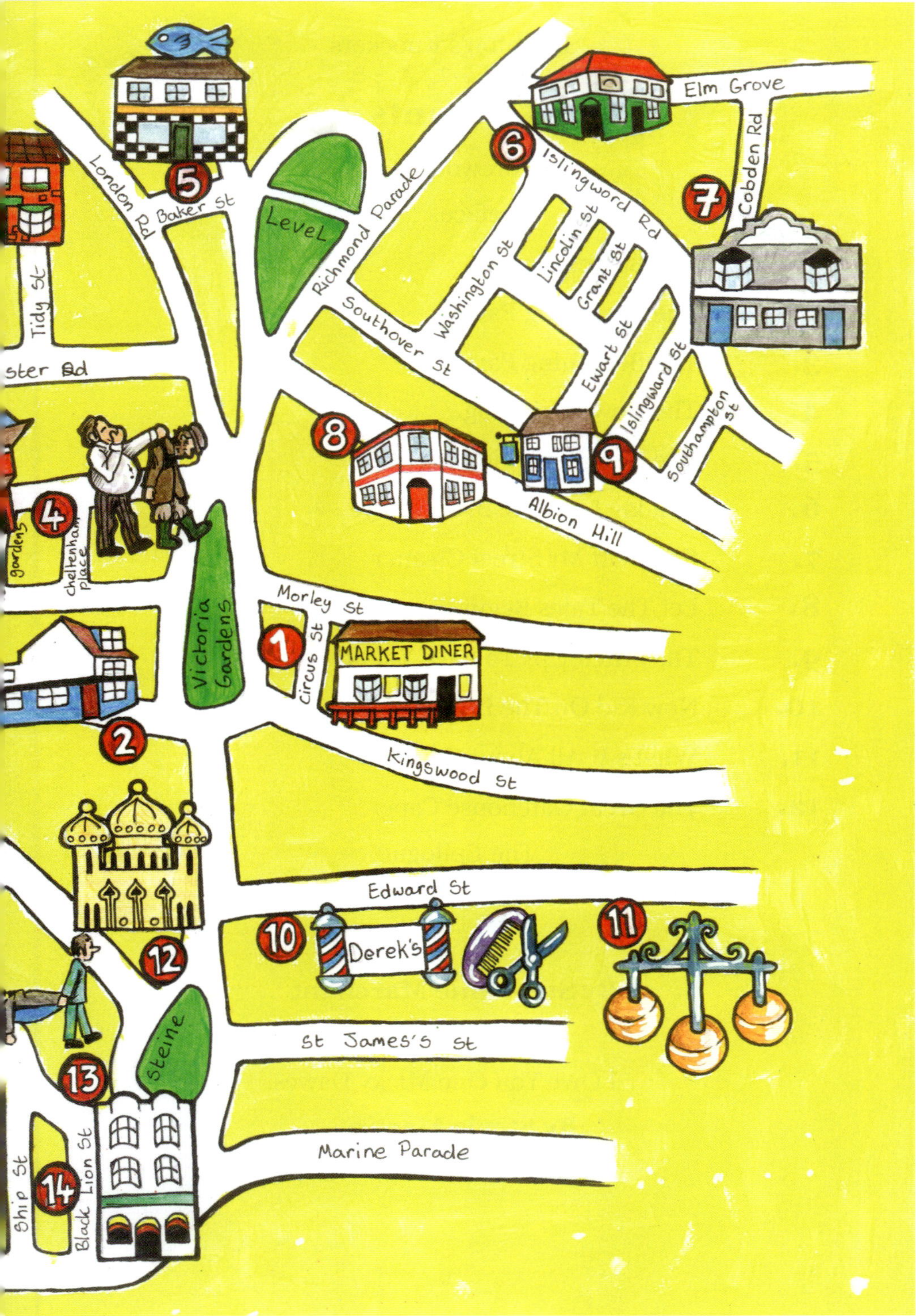

Elm Grove
Cobden Rd
London Rd
Baker St
Level
Richmond Parade
Islingword Rd
Lincoln St
Grant St
Washington St
Southover St
Ewart St
Islingward St
Southampton St
Tidy St
ster Rd
Albion Hill
gardens
cheltenham place
Morley St
Circus St
MARKET DINER
Victoria Gardens
Kingswood St
Edward St
Derek's
St James's St
Steine
Marine Parade
Ship St
Black Lion St
1
2
4
5
6
7
8
9
10
11
12
13
14

Contents

By Stephanie Marchant

I Owe You One Micky Dawes.

By Stevie Martin

Preface.

I sincerely hope that you are reading the Preface, as it is essential to your enjoyment of the following pages, much more so than any other piece of literature you may have ever read before.

The whole reason for this is to direct you to a few pointers and help you to enjoy and appreciate the book in all its full glory. As a rule it would be appropriate to nominate in ‘Bullet Point’ categories, but the whole thing is far more laid back than that, and rules don’t really apply to this piece or any of its’ contributors.

The number one factor is the inclusion of so much ‘Bad Language’, but the characters that helped to make this a readable and believable piece, just so happen to talk like this in every day life. There is no intention to offend, or impose anything sinister on the people that they are talking to, or any dramatic intention, it’s just the way they are.

Once you take this on board it makes for easier reading, but to omit the expletives would dilute the whole scenario in every aspect, and deny you of the true reality as to how they conducted themselves at work, leisure and home alike.

There is not, however, any Racism, Homophobia or Sexism, even though we are going back to the mid sixties, it just wasn’t their style.

Another, yet essential factor for you to understand what the hell is going on at certain times is ‘The Glossary’. Now this is not a part of any book I personally would normally be interested in, but in this particular instance, please believe me, it is necessary. Many of the phrases and words quoted are in ‘Cockney Rhyming Slang’.

However, most important of all, some are completely made up by the characters in this book, relating only to events that they themselves instigated. One example being ‘A Haggerty’, this refers to a house clearance, and only by reading the relevant story could you possibly be any the wiser, I rest my case, m’lord.

You will also probably pick up on a different attitude from myself, as the book develops, this is because the whole experience was in fact life changing for myself, and a huge learning curve. This is something I would like to think you will also empathise with, as things unfold.

The same applies to certain repetitive phrases, it’s not laziness, they are there for a reason, but to reveal why would only spoil the fun, now wouldn’t it?

All the stories are true, with just a few names, places and descriptive items altered slightly for legal purposes, reasons that will become perfectly clear as we go.

I also tend to inadvertently slip in Film and Song titles, see how many you spot.

Oh, and by the way, if you contemplate making the drastic mistake of browsing through the Epilogue before finishing the whole book, you are guaranteed to ruin the page-turning journey altogether.

I therefore suggest, that you now rip out those pages immediately to avoid the temptation. Not only will you enjoy the read much more, it will also double the book sales when you go searching for ‘The Lost Pages’.

I truly hope you enjoy yourself, love always **SM**.

1. The Beginning.

To introduce myself, my name is Stephanie Marchant, I am quite pleasing to the eye some say, and reasonably educated. I should be able to claim ‘well educated’, but the establishments that produce such results could not quite contain my unruly behaviour and attitude. As such, despite promises of huge financial investment or ‘anonymous donations’ by my Father, they chose to rusticate me on numerous occasions, much to his despair.

From an early age, mischief was my chosen subject, at which I excelled. If St. Trinian’s were an option in my younger days, they would have welcomed me with open arms, and Head Girl classification would have been mine for the taking, unchallenged. As it was, the world renowned, Roedean School for Girls, ascertained, after two fun filled terms, that I was healthy and physically fit, mentally fit, fit for anything and for goodness sake, “fit off” somewhere bloody well else. Charming, I must say. What a way for such an esteemed establishment to carry on.

Dad proceeded to sue them for defamation of character and slander, but upon production of confirmed evidence by the local constabulary, sworn affidavit by local clergy, teaching staff and a number of Licensed Victuallers, decided to stop proceedings. Wise move under the circumstances, hee hee, what can I say, I was only having a laugh!

My Mother died tragically when I was just two years old, and Dad, bless his heart, would often reflect, at vulnerable times such as Xmas, Birthdays and Holidays, when having had a few champagnes and brandies too many, that he may have taken his own life, had I not been about. This always upset me, instilling a little guilt, but expressed his undying love of the woman, thus, enabling me to be the centre of his world.

Not benefiting from the support of an extended family network, enabling him to raise a fine high-spirited young girl. But, let me tell you right now, he certainly did his damn best.

He always said I was a proper little Minx, affectionately nicknaming me 'Minnie', something that I accepted in the loving way in which it was proposed, my closest friends all tag me the same.

At certain stages of my life, with puberty being a major contender, fatherhood became slightly stifling and embarrassing for him. I was accordingly introduced to such institutions as the ‘Girl Guides’, to help out with the “Girlie” developments of life, as he referred to them.

Poor sod, I was well ahead of my time, as this continued through my teenage years to young adulthood. By this time I did in fact find it necessary to educate the teachers myself, and explain how to infiltrate and manipulate the minds of the weaker sex (men of course) in ways they could never have possibly imagined. By sixth form and University, my frequent excursions to Harrods, Selfridges and Harvey Nichols saw to it that my underwear, shoes, perfume and clothing were second to none in the seduction stakes.

Store cards were in there infancy back in those days, but my Dad was well aware of what a young lady required to take her chosen place in society. Bless him.

The thing is though; this book is not really about me, it is mostly dedicated to another subject, which I stumbled across completely by chance one summer evening, back in 1986, in one of the dingiest and most unexpected locations you might ever imagine. But, in actual fact, the following is a collection of stories, tales, fabrications and most unbelievable stone bonking lies. They will for sure, keep you spellbound from beginning to end.

Furthermore you will be completely satisfied that every little scam, rip-off and diabolical liberty has been explained in its entirety with absolute and very precise truth. To a hedonistic degree of perfection, they were perpetrated by a bunch of complete and utter rogues, both individually or collectively, in military style sync.

Here's a question; Do you believe in fate? Your answer, is in fact, quite immaterial, whether you do believe in it or not, it does exist. When life pans out in its most mysterious ways, there is not a single soul on this planet who could deny that at one time or another during their brief stay in this world, that some strange unexplainable things occur. I am not talking about weirdo, out of space, alien type of things, just inexplicable situations that could never have been imaginable, without some overpowering force that made it so.

*

Here the story begins. At this time (1986), the best Club in town was 'The Kings II', in Circus Street, behind Grand Parade. Which was also the location of all the wholesale fruit and vegetable businesses in Brighton & Hove. It was a great location for a club, as, when throwing out time came, the revellers had somewhere else to go within 50 yards.

As with all reasonable sized towns, I later learned, this was the epicentre of the working man's trade. For those who didn't actually have a trade to speak of this was the aforementioned Fruit & Veg supplier. They would get up early, 5:30am, check out what was hot and what was not that day, and make a reasonable bid accordingly, to try and get a few quid, by loading up a barrow with as much stuff as possible.

To explain in layman's terms, if there were to be 4 or 5 pallets of tomatoes unaccounted for, instead of 15 shillings each, old man Griffiths (T.G. Fruits) would gladly get rid of them for four bob a go rather than throw them away.

Every day there would be some young ne'er do well willing to give the shittiest bit of fruit or veg a try on a barrow. This would then be loaded up like the Eiffel Tower and one of the more lowly types was instructed to push it to the delegated pitch of the day, with the understanding that at least two shillings would be coming their way at the end of the shift, usually about two-ish.

This, therefore, led to the conception of the 'All night café'. As the delivery drivers would have journeyed from all over the country, loaded up with all sorts of produce. Originating from Covent Garden, Newhaven, Shoreham, Portsmouth or even Southampton Docks. Plus of course all the local Farms from surrounding areas, and would arrive from between midnight to 5:00am.

It was generally accepted that a facility to meet their needs was necessary, after driving for five hours or so; you surely need or fancy something to eat. Just around the corner on Grand Parade, The Northern Pub, was also allowed a distinctive license to accommodate those who had worked all through the night and were on different time scales. They had slept all day worked all night and were ready for a shant before going home, 'simples' (as the meerkats say).

Hence, due to this conception, anyone coming out of The King's II around 2:30 am, if not with the desired company, would be only too happy to get some greasy sobering up grub down their neck before venturing home.

Note also, that there were always a few opportunist cabbies lingering around to catch a nice pissed up punter who just wanted to get home immediately and prepared to pay top dollar, bearing in mind the Club was top notch and only entertained a high earning clientèle.

Sorry to blag on a little boringly, but sometimes you have to explain the lay of the land, or else it doesn't make sense how things occur later on.

Brighton's Knockers

My Dad had always enjoyed his own rendition of Guy Lombardo's 'Enjoy Yourself', and so as not to disappoint, I had endeared myself to that philosophy, however this one particular night I had made a bit of a ricket. My chosen beau for the last couple of months had turned out to be a right arsehole, and to top it up his best mate was an absolute wanker, he had kept pestering me for a quickie or a snog on numerous occasions.

I can only surmise that it was down to soppy bollocks Nigel, who had probably given him the impression that I might be game, or he was in fact just a complete tosser altogether, who didn't give a monkey's about anyone.

Nevertheless none of this is relevant to the whole scheme of things and it all pretty much finished on that night anyway. Thank God.

I proceeded to the All Night Diner with my pal Tracey, and after I had ordered my food, went outside with my mug of tea for a ciggy. It wasn't actually necessary to go outside in those days, but simply prevented the next table starting some irrelevant moaning and groaning about 'personal space', and just plain decent manners, as all the tables were crammed so close together.

Sitting on a bench outside was a sorry looking old soul, who was one of those blokes, who had those big doe eyes that I knew meant he was alright. He would possibly welcome a little company, so I half pulled a cigarette from the pack to assure him he was welcome to take one.

"You're out late Granddad, you should be wrapped up in bed. What's your name then?"

"Don't do me any favours darlin', 25 years ago I'd have you tucked up right next to me my little treacle, and to answer your question, my name is George." This unexpected sharp and quick-witted retort took me completely by surprise.

Accepting one of the offered tobacco sticks, he paused momentarily, and then continued.

“Wasn’t that long ago I would be buying a little beauty like you champagne down on the French Riviera, rather than slurping a poxy mug of jamboree outside this delightful little establishment.”

Thinking to myself that he had never bought a bottle of decent bubbly in his life, I humoured him with a little hug and a delicately placed peck on the cheek.

“What was your chosen profession back in the day, then?”

“Me, my little darlin'? Well, I was a dealer in Fine Art and Antiques sweetheart.” The only antiquity here was the old fellah himself as far as I was concerned.

“Oh that must have been interesting George,” I replied mischievously.

“Oh yes, babe, ‘The Knocker’ was the greatest game ever, and it all started right here, many moons ago.”

There was a mysterious yet affectionate way in which he said this, accompanied by a cloudy look in his eyes that totally transformed his face, suddenly glowing and with a smile reminiscent of Steve McQueen or Paul Newman on the big screen, totally unforgettable and mesmerising!

He had what we like to refer to as a ‘worn in face’, resembling the state of Captain Cook’s face on his intrepid journey back from the South Pole, quite wrinkly but with a steely reserve, a slight twist to his nose and the similarity of bloodhound bags under his eyes, reminding me of old ‘Deputy Dawg’ himself. I still say to this day that he had his house slippers on under his tracksuit bottoms, but Georgie in true style, vehemently denies the possibility.

My number was called for the needy bacon sandwich and chips I had ordered, and it was quite a wrench to even bother with it, but bother I did, all the while hoping that my new acquaintance would still be out there once I'd finished. With half my sandwich stuffed in a napkin, I popped my head out the door and much to my relief he was still plonked on the bench. In a vague conversation with a smartly dressed lad, who made his excuses and left as I approached.

I asked if he fancied a cuppa, he looked up fondly, winked and waved at his pal in one succinct gesture, and then the cheeky old rascal beckoned me towards him and whispered in a totally posh silver spoon accent, as if passing on state secrets from behind the Iron Curtain:

"At this particular moment, I think I may be partial to a nice mug of Maxwell House, taken white with two sugars if you please, if it is not too much inconvenience to you young lady, if you please."

Well, I was quite perplexed, this was a complete transformation from the sorry looking chap I had encountered just 15 minutes ago, and although I had obviously had a few sherbets that night, was still well aware that something had occurred, to which I was not privy to.

The thing was though, this situation wasn't about to end here, so I promptly popped my head back in the Café, and ordered as requested, doing as I am told by a complete stranger, something weird going on but totally at ease and in no way offended or threatened.

We started chatting once again, and he began to fill me in on his past, reflecting on the better days when he and his mates could always earn a nice few quid by going around 'Knocking Doors' and getting a decent day's work, meaning in a financial way.

It seemed like a just a couple of minutes, yet Tracey emerged from the Café saying she thought I had left her posted, and that I had actually been conversing for some fifteen minutes. I was incredibly intrigued how a chance meeting had totally captivated my attention and imagination in such a meaningful way.

Whilst walking back home I could do nothing but repeat some of the things George had been saying to me, much to the dismay of my companion, who questioned why I had wasted my time with some silly old git and simply disregarded everything I spoke of as 'Bullshit'. Yet for some strange reason I was totally spellbound.

*

I had obviously not made any plans to meet or see him again, but before I had even opened my eyes the next day, I was reservedly determined to find him again and get to the bottom of this unheard of 'Great Days of The Knockerboys'. How Brighton was 'The Finishing School', for all and sundry that desired to be involved in one way or another, and hence, get up to a few bits and pieces of skulduggery that had never been witnessed before.

He had talked about a nice few faces from 'The Smoke', had tried to set up in Brighton and been fleeced unashamedly in one way or another of their ill gotten gains.

'Just coz' you can stick a shooter in the face of some poor Post Master General or Bank Teller, up in London or somewhere in Kent, don't mean you can pull a fast one on any true blue Brightonian, I can assure you.' This was just one of the little phrases that were starting to haunt me.

I resolved to find him again, and proceeded to pop into the Diner a little more frequently on the off chance of seeing him again, and making a concerted effort to attract his attention. What I had in mind was an exciting little project for my own personal gain and amusement.

*

It turned out that I bumped into him one afternoon, completely by accident once again, in 'The Waggon & Horses' in Church Street. I was just about to leave, after a sumptuous lunch with a good friend, Julliette, from Uni.

He came sauntering in like he owned the place, and was quite simply three sheets to the wind and a little red-faced. He was wearing a smartish suit, his shirt was open at the neck, collar askew and his tie was wrapped half-way round his neck, where he had started to take it off, but failed miserably and given up, leaving the job undone. No house slippers today, his Brogue shoes had a shine all of their own. He also had perched on his crooked nose a pair of Geppetto style half-glasses, over which he glanced in my direction.

"Hello my little darlin', now where do I know you from?"

"Couple of weeks ago at the all night café. I am so glad to see you again." I purposely wanted to use the wrong name, so as not to show too much interest:

"Funnily enough Brian, I was hoping to bump into you again. You might be able to help me with a little project I was contemplating undertaking. Would you believe it, I'm a poet and didn't know it." Another one of those silly little rhymes that had got my attention on that first encounter.

"Actually, young lady, it is George, 'Gorgeous' to my pals, friends, family and veritable acquaintances."

He caught me completely by surprise with his superior command of the Queen's English, and once again I was compelled to take stock of what was actually occurring. It was of course totally appropriate at this time for him to convey his accrued status.

Giggling to myself, I offered him my hand, 100% certain it would be cradled in his, and promptly kissed.

“I am still Stephanie and this is my friend Julliette.”

He of course, did not disappoint.

He then introduced me to his companion, Morry Hughes, this was carried out in an exaggerated cordial and gentlemanly fashion. This pantomime-like greeting, was something I would witness many times by many like-minded folk in the months to come.

Without further ado, or the slightest hint of hesitation he proceeded to explain that they had just had ‘A Right Result’ round the corner, in the Magistrates Court and were celebrating accordingly. Something to do with Customs and Excise not knowing their arses from their elbows, and deserved everything they didn’t get.

Julliette quietly but distinctly whispered to me that she had to get back to work at American Express, or she would get fired. Our last lunch had taken three hours and she was now on a probationary period for 6 months for such irresponsible behaviour. Her promotion hopes were now certainly in the balance, so very politely she bode her farewells both to me, and our newfound friends and left me to it. As she departed, George volleyed:

“See you again soon Jules.” He’d only just met her for three seconds and was already using terminology normally associated with a long-term friendship, the bloody cheek of it!

Of course I knew only to well, that it was this turn of phrase and instant knack of having known you forever and a day that had captured my imagination that first night, and I was certainly not about to let this meeting go amiss, for sure, that's for dam sure.

We had a right laugh for some three hours. I was not permitted to put my hand in my purse, and both of them were complete Gentlemen. The time absolutely flew by.

A tirade of various different people came and went during this time, all of whom insisted buying all three of us a drink and point blankly refusing to accept anything in return. This was actually a display of admiration and full respect for the pair of them, whilst also displaying good manners and courtesy by including myself, who none of them had ever set eyes on previously, without so much as batting an eyelid.

One particular fellow caught my attention, he was of a younger generation, mine. He looked familiar but I couldn’t quite put my finger on it. His name was Steve, seemed quite attentive but did not share in any ‘Knockerboy’ tales. After telling a couple of silly Tommy Cooper style jokes he bought a round of drinks, said he had to get back to work, bade farewell and disappeared like Zorro.

Champagne, was ordered for all and sundry, slightly shaming my first impression of ‘Gorgeous George’, and before I knew what hit me I was quite sozzled. But feeling so alive and excited about the way things were going. I knocked a couple of drinks off of someone’s table whilst visiting the Ladies, so while brushing my hair, I got my act together and decided it was time to make tracks.

Both Morry and George insisted paying for my Taxi, which had been ordered by a click of the fingers, but I assured them I was quite capable of sorting it myself.

Not prepared to let this episode be the last, I checked with George when we may be able to meet up again, as I was interested in some more of his antics 'On The Knocker', a few of which I had heard that afternoon, from both of my compadres and visiting associates.

"Try The Kensington, about seven on Friday night," he advised.

"There's usually a few of us playing pool and having a lark in there then. Take care honey and I look forward to seeing you soon." He pressed a fiver into my hand, and gave me a pretty little wink, indicating that I should not protest. I concurred. As I got in the cab, I heard him remark to Morry:

"What a nice girl, she's got that something about her, but I can't quite fathom what it is, or put my finger on it."

*

At this stage it is only fair to explain a little more about my situation and personal circumstances. Raised in Epsom, Surrey, I had come to Brighton to attend Sussex University on a three-year course in Journalism & Media Studies. When I discussed this with my Father he had simply replied:

"Can you just leave me to think about it for a couple of days Minn?"

I had seen no problem with this, as he had never been one to make instantaneous decisions, something I had learned to respect. He invariably came up with exactly the same conclusion but under much better terms and circumstances, and always with my best interest at heart.

My intention of renting a small bed-sit whilst studying had not impressed him, although he commended me on my committed intentions of self-sacrifice. He was none too keen with the kind of residential areas in the Town that provided such accommodation, as they often harboured unsavoury characters and as he described them: 'Too many petty criminals, junkies and no-hopers.' His solution could hardly instigate any argument from me.

"This is my proposal," he began, in quite a serious mood. His forthcoming monologue was not to be interrupted until complete. We did know each other ever so well.

"I have been looking at a more substantial type of property down on the coast for some time now, and I do know a few people down there, and so I have decided to go ahead and purchase a place in Hanover Terrace, it's quite substantial mind. It's a nice area, pleasant park called The Level, right opposite, central for all amenities and a decent property that won't lose value for sure. It is also very convenient for Public Transport to and fro from the University."

"The thing is, an old buddy of mine from when I did my National Service, moved down there with his wife a few years ago and we always kept in touch. Well, he died of Cancer three months ago, and they were pot-less, and Grace, she has had to move in with her Mum, on a Council Estate."

"The place is well overcrowded, too many of their offspring celebrating that 60's summer of love bollocks, and therefore she is not too comfortable, to say the least."

"The fact of the matter was, old Barney had a bad case of the mumps when he was a kid and this rendered him impotent, this doesn't help poor Grace with all the kids running about all over the place, so here we go."

"You can have the Upper Ground, and the 1st floor, for yourself and a couple of well-selected roomies, as you call 'em. I will take the top floor as my Holiday Retreat and office, this will be self-contained, in a sociable manner, just a little rope across the staircase to indicate privacy expected. So, when I come down I won't intrude on your personal life, but we can still spend some time together if not too inconvenient."

"Grace, well she will have the Semi-Basement Flat, which will also be Self-Contained, with its own entrance, and as part of our agreement she will also be the Housekeeper. That means she will do routine chores such as washing up, laundry and hoovering, plus a bit of cleaning and polishing."

He sensed my pure unadulterated pleasure, then continued:

"But, I don't want anyone taking the fucking piss out of her, and if people start taking liberties we will have to review the situation. Grace is under strict instructions not to stand for any nonsense and will report back to me if necessary. Now is that clear?"

What could I say? Well the thing is, I am my Father's Daughter, so I replied confidently, now that it was my turn to speak:

"Well, what is she like this Grace? Am I going to like her? She is not going to be like a wicked stepmother or something is she?"

His bellowing laugh made me feel so good. We had our biggest hug for years, and of course Grace turned out to be nothing short of a Fairy Godmother. Not only to me, but also to all my friends, who had the pleasure to enjoy her company over the next five years or so. She was a gem!

She even mentioned once, when we had a glass of wine or two, that my Dad and me had transformed her life. Better than a win on the Pools, as per standard of life and friends you could trust. It was to become, and I confidently maintain, continues to be, a lifelong friendship and trusting relationship second only to my Dad.

Our first meeting was all three of us enjoying a lovely lunch at The Grand Hotel, which was quite formal, but they were 'Old School' of course, and things were always done in the proper fashion. She was a little more elegant than I expected, a smart woman, would best describe her.

Her fine lacy dress was just off the shoulder and past the knees, with some delightful pearls round her long swanlike neck. The shoes were certainly not common a garden high street jobs, resembling hand-made couture worthy of The King's Road, a lovely soft suede, four inch heel in a tangerine shade, matching her small handbag. I coveted them immediately and could not resist asking where she got them.

"I was really spoilt on one of our anniversaries, and my husband Barney, you know of course he's no longer with us." I nodded sadly, with pursed lips.

"Well, he had them hand-made for me at a terrific little cobblers up the King's Road."

The stone was set.

She had spoken unexpectedly, with such eloquence and serenity, that at first had me slightly baffled, but of course, once things were put in place, my Father's judgement would never be questioned or doubted ever again, not for a single second.
He was quite a clever old sod, my Dad.

We then had the unenviable task of choosing all the soft furnishings for the new residence, as we liked to call it, and this was just divine! Local department stores such as Hanningtons and Vokins were duly visited. They had great bedding and quality towelling for one and all. Carpets and curtains were all colour co-ordinated to our taste.

Although her quarters were private, I helped Grace pick out plenty of things for her place. This little spending spree, with no restrictions, bonded us together. Dad had sorted out any relevant building alterations and fitted kitchens were subsequently picked out with ease.

It also became customary for me to have coffee early one morning at the start of the week to fill Grace in on the latest pieces of gossip or set the world straight on some Political standpoint, we didn't take ourselves too seriously though.

I dare say if I ever meet the love of my life and settle down, it will surely be with Grace's blessing, as without it, I should be wary. It became apparent that she knew 'Gorgeous Georgie Balcock' also, and this spurred me on, especially during one hesitant stage, as I knew she approved of our little arrangement.

*

It turned out Dad had more than a discerning interest in Brighton. During the late 60's the local Corporation (now known as the Council) were in the process of selling off a large percentage of their social housing properties. First offer went to the Tenants, at a considerable discount of the market value, providing they could show due diligence to pay the mortgage, and place a minimum 5% deposit.

With so many of the tenants being of middle age or older, and practically none of them able to provide 3 years of books and earnings, they were caught in a wicked spider's web. Not only had they just come out from the era of post-war rationing, the majority, regarded the position of a fully fledged home-owner as out of their league or class even, far too much of a commitment and beyond their means. Most of them still considered butter as a luxury; it was still many years short of the ridiculous notion of every home having a fridge or washing machine.

Not averse to pulling a stroke or two and bending the rules a little bit, when it suited, my old man was certainly no shirker. So when a chance of a lifetime came across him, he had gone right to work, big-time. Once aware of the opportunity at hand, he had immediately pounced on a few properties, and then been drawn into the more sinister, yet alluring world, of backhanders and bribery.

This led to, what they call, a Pirates fortune, one that can be nurtured, examined, admired and treasured. In your heart and hands, yet never to be shared with anyone else, for fear of being discovered. Bestial bastards would want a piece of the action, unnecessarily and undeservedly, like the tax man for instance.

'Every Tom, Dick and Harry think they are entitled to a share of the pot, ‘So Fuck Em’ as in the words of Captain Blood.' was a favourite saying of his.

He grafted all the properties on both sides of Elm Grove and Islingword, such as Grant, Ewart, Southampton, Jersey, Cobden, Washington and Lincoln Streets, building up a substantial portfolio of potential clients that needed independent financing that no Bank or Building Society would even look at, let alone validate or give any serious consideration.

His proposal was simple. He would purchase the house at the reduced rate that the tenants were entitled to, around about £400-£600. On completion of Deeds, they would then sell him the property, plus an extra one hundred pounds for themselves, whilst he footed all the costs entailed.

They were of course unaware that the fees, estimated at around £50 were non-existent, as they were included in the purchase price. Not one single client objected to the included extra amounts that covered the ‘Complimentary Refurbishments’.

He cut a nice few cute corners along the way, as there were usually about 40-50 properties up for auction on any given day.

It was not too difficult for a particular civil servant to overlook whether or not the buyer was resident or not, and a Five Pound note in those days was enough to let such innocuous detail to go unscrutinised.

To top it up, he was also aware that there was in place, another Government Funded process that allowed the new owner to apply for a grant. This was to re-roof the property, re-design the interior and install an inside bathroom, so upgrading the habitation to a more acceptable standard of living, befitting a homeowner.

Once this process had taken place, he drew up contracts that permitted the tenants to sign a document agreeing to pay a fixed rent till they no longer wished to reside at the property.

All payment of rates, however, (now known as council tax) which were subject to increase at the discretion of the Council, and inflation, would be their responsibility. This may seem quite draconian, but in actual fact, the increase of rent was usually from £2.50 a week to £5.00, but this, in their eyes was forever. Doubled but fixed for life.

He never, ever, I don’t care what anyone says, reneged on one single solitary deal made on this arrangement. Mind you, why the heck should he, it was a match made in heaven for all concerned.

Some of them, however, flatly refused to allow the modernisation, insisting that he had already saved the family home, and there was no need to spend more money on them.

That was of course until they saw next door, with the shiny new MFI kitchen and an actual bath ‘fixed to the floor’ with a shower attachment, something most of them thought was only available in posh hotels.

His own particular favourite, which he disclosed to me on one occasion, was Grant Street; as it allowed the easiest, yet most impressive change. The majority of folks in those days only used the ‘Front Room’ on special occasions, but they never had any such moments worthy of its use, so once the two rooms were knocked through they felt their home literally was now their castle.

These were the rooms that needed clearing out of bookcases, dining tables and chairs and display cabinets. They had contained all those useless old tankards; vases and figurines handed down by Mum or Gran over the years, needing just more tiresome polishing and dusting.

*

The only bone of contention, raised years later, was why didn’t their own family play a better or bigger part in these matters. One time we were enjoying a nice Sunday Lunch when he went into a right old rave;

“You know. These clever little fuckers that had just started ‘The Knocker Game’. The answer was simple. They were all just a selfish load of flash, cocky, little fucking bastards, who didn’t give a toss about anyone else but themselves, to the hell or the high road. And, may they all rest in shit!”

His face had suddenly changed, with no reasonable evidence or expectation, and gone a dark shade of purple and his blood was definitely boiling.

Beads of sweat were cascading down his temples and his rage was quite simply unatonable without reproach.Beads of sweat were cascading down his temples and his rage was quite simply unatonable without reproach.

I had never seen him get so het up, and on the verge of losing his temper, alongside his ever-increasing blood pressure. Not one of his finest statements, I must admit, but everyone to their own, he was my Dad after all!

Anyway, I would give things a shot, and go to 'The Kensington' on Friday night and see how things panned out.

*

2. The Beginning Part II.

Once again I had these niggling thoughts in my mind, that were telling me I could be on to something big and that if I did not act on these thoughts I may well live to regret it, and Dad's advice of 'Enjoy Yourself while you can, because tomorrow may be too late'. Something along those lines. It never seemed to come out the same two times running, this factor in the back of my mind was also egging me on to follow my instincts.

There was also this slightly captivating image of George and his bunch of merry men embedded in my head, plus the anticipation and excitement of what might be coming next, this affected me in an uncanny way.

Once they all started to reel off time and again the specific details of their exploits, in such an animated fashion that seemed quite unique. Of course, it was all 'absolutely God's honest truth', 'I swear on my Mum's grave', 'may I be struck down where I stand so help me God', and of course, surely someone should write a book about it.

The Friday soon came around, but this time I had a plan. I was aware that 'The Kensington' was not the type of place that the wives would accompany their husbands, not on a Friday night anyway, that's for sure. Saturday's and Sundays was an unwritten Golden rule, 'Always look out for your Family' often announced by one of the motley crew but rarely followed through, till absolutely unavoidable.

The mistresses and girlfriends only rule, applied to Fridays, on top of the odd midweek liaisons, depending on the depth of the relationship, on top being the operative words.

This I had picked up on at 'The Waggon & Horses', in a none too questionable fashion.

Don't think for a minute WAGS only materialised when dinlo footballers started earning disgusting kinds of money, these Herbert's had been 'Larging It' for years and there has always been a bit of skirt ready willing and able to do a turn for an easy life.

"What the fuck" one of them was later to remark to me, "I know he's an ignorant twat, but all I have to do is cook a bit of Lilly & Skinner on a Friday night, give him a blow job, or lay on me back for five minutes. Half the time he don't come anyway. I'm a spitter not a swallower, by the way, nudge nudge, wink wink, say no more."

"He carves up every month for a blinding two bedroom flat in Kingsway Court, between First & Second Avenue that is, plus a couple of hundred quid a week as moving about money. The building has got a Gym and a Sauna, some lovely little old dear comes in and tidies up twice a week and I can still have a bit on the side whenever I fancy."

"If I pop into any boozer in town, they all know who I am wiv, so I don't have to bother with paying for drinks and invariably have a bit of lunch thrown in, into the bargain. My old Dad always said it was rude to say no, to any kind gesture and I promised him on his deathbed, no word of a lie, I would never let him down."

"It won't last forever of course, but then they'll always be some uvver prat ready to jump in and take his place. Beats walking the streets or sitting in a shitty little flat waiting for the next Tom to pick you out. If I meet my knight in shining armour along the way then all's well and good, 'Que Sera Sera'."

This certainly educated me about the type of girls with whom I may be associating with, in this newfound particularly unrefined circle of society. It seemed that everyone knew one another, and I thought some of the funny looks that some folk received was simply a figment of my imagination

As a ruse, my routine would be simple; I had had some nicely designed, Gold embossed Business Cards printed. Only 50 of 'em, great value from the guys at Brighton Print Centre, Preston Road, Phil & Dale, always happy to oblige, still going nowadays and happy to sort out all my printing needs. They just had my name and phone number on. I would meet George briefly, make my excuses for not being able to stay long and proceed to arrange a future rendezvous and just ask him to call me if he needed to cancel.

When I entered the pub I was glad to have made the plan. The first thing I heard, in the smoke filled Public Bar, with not a friendly face in sight, was 'Oy Oy, Saveloy, look at the Eartha's on that'. Bloody charming, I thought to myself. Mind you, what would you expect with a load of blokes, playing pool and having a drink with the lads, after a hard week's graft. Now plotting and scheming some new way to con people out of their treasures, and inherited wealth that they would now never be able to reflect on, nurture or benefit from.

George chirped up from the back:

"Hold on a minute boys, this is a dear friend of mine, Stephanie, with whom I have a little business to discuss and attend to. If you will excuse us."

An aura of complete nonchalance and aloofness that Scarlett O'Hara had originally displayed, when she starred in 'Gone with the Wind', yet George had seemed to have perfected, with due diligence. Then gently, taking my arm and leading me through to the Saloon Bar, he looked back over his shoulder and barked:

"Be sure to watch your fucking language in future, you dirty rotten scoundrels."

Winking at me, then adding, 'what can you do, eh?'

At that point some other twat, that I later found out was a saucy greedy little upstart, with a horrible nose by the name of Peter Lombart commented:

"For Thirty Quid she can be a friend of mine an' all, Georgie Boy."

George ushered me through to the Bar and indicated he would just be a moment. Whatever he said to the runt with the bad mouth was never ever mentioned, but for a good five minutes it was eerily silent round the other side.

The thing was, my Dad often mentioned that 'Revenge, was a dish best served cold.' Not exactly the most original statement. In the not too distant future, I would be in the position to enjoy a very nicely chilled dish at the expense of Peter Lombart, and would thoroughly enjoy making him squirm, and then making him suffer anyway. Tough luck, 'Titchie Willie'.

George began, "To be fair, I didn't think you was all that serious, to be honest with you. Now what can I get you to drink?"

"Just a small glass of white wine, if that is okay George?" I replied, whilst taking the seat he had offered me.

"Large white wine please, Monsignor" he instructed the barman, "A large V.A.T. for me and whatever you want for yourself, my good man." It was my turn to speak once he sat down opposite me.

"Well the thing is this George, I do actually have a little proposal to make to you."

"Go ahead my little sweetheart, fire away, at your service, Madame." The twinkle in his eyes was really cute. If ever the term 'lovable rogue' was appropriate, 'Gorgeous George' fitted the bill. While talking he gesticulated a great deal, in a rather effeminate way.

"Right then, here we go," I began, "I propose that, as many acquaintances of yours and you yourself, may well agree, (slow pause to exact ultimate effect and also to encapsulate his attention away from the loud heckling and barracking going on in the other Bar) that, all these little escapades and trysts that you've all had over the years would make a great book."

"The term 'best-seller' has been bandied about from time to time, and yet nobody has bothered to attempt the task at hand."

He was pondering with his hand on his chin, clearly showing due accord and attention, indicating respect to what my proposal may involve. I knew, at that immediate instant, I had caught his attention. I was now being taken seriously, exactly what I had in mind intention and desire, was not yet clear to my adversary, as he now appeared to be.

"Go on," he said. I continued in a quieter and secretive tone:

"Well, I have nearly finished my degree in Journalism & Media Studies, as you know, or don't know. Whatever! Anyway, the point is this: part of the curriculum is that one has to produce your own private piece of work or project, that has never seen the light of day before. This is called a dissertation, and at the end of the procedure it becomes part of your synopsis and goes towards the final tally of your achievement. Thus becoming an essential component towards you achieving a P.H.D. (slight pause) do you understand where I'm going with this, George?"

"I think so babe, carry on."

Now, the thing is, and this is the absolute God's honest truth dear reader, (it's catching already isn't it) I had spent quite a bit of time preparing this little pitch, being sure to include a few words, I thought may not be within his vocabulary, hopefully, anyway, so I was slightly agitated when he came back with his answer.

"You will have to give me a couple of days to think about that sweetheart, as it is not quite as simple as you may think."

I would expect this from my Dad, but George, what the hell is this all about?

He knew instantly that I was not impressed with his reply, but immediately attempted to justify his answer and placate me, hitherto steering me back to his way of thinking and explain his position.

"Here's the problem," he began, whilst indicating to the barman to replenish our drinks, "Another one over here please Jimmy. The thing is this: even though there is not one single solitary sonofabitch in this town, what has worked on 'The Knocker', who could ever be capable of putting pen to paper for so much as writing a Christmas Fucking Card."

"If these little stories, even though of course, they are not stories, but true to life experiences of course. 'God Be My Judge Mind You', if they were to get out in the press or some soppy little magazine, there would be absolute fucking murders."

"World War Fucking 3 would break out and half of the Town's money earners, including many of those respectable shop owners, and a couple of the Towns most reputable Dealer's and Jewellery shop keepers, would be banged up within a fucking fortnight. They probably wouldn't see the light of day for God knows how fucking long."

"So how could you possibly ask me to be the perpetrator of such information that could potentially render the 'Knocker Game' redundant for all time, and those concerned? I couldn't do that to me own Mum, not in a month of Sundays, or for all the tea in China, not for the Crown Jewels or..."

"Alright, alright George," I interrupted, "I've got the message, you don't have to try for an Oscar just to put me in the picture, pun intended."

I knew for a certainty that I would be changing that kind of dysfunctional loyalty somewhere down the road, but I'd cross that bridge when I came to it. I knew exactly where this was going and had come fully prepared for such news.

"You know me George, I'm 'Old School', I wouldn't do that to you or anyone else. Anyway, you will have an absolute guarantee, and it will be in writing if you so desire, drawn up by a brief of your own choice of course. No true identities will be disclosed, locations will all be altered, and everybody will be protected by a disclosure clause."

"This means, should there be any comebacks, on any information divulged in the mentioned capers, that might possibly or by any stretch of the imagination, be connected to any relevant event, or alleged wrong doing, on the part of any person or persons in question. The said subject could only be verified as conjecture and hearsay evidence, by some vindictive, bitter and twisted, jealous little toe rag or toss-pot competitor."

I felt that I had him by the short and curlies, so continued in the same convincing and earnest tone.

"Received in an anonymous fashion that cannot, and will not, under any circumstances, be confirmed by anyone connected to the Publication and therefore, rendering them completely immune to prosecution or investigation. So what do you think now then, my old son?"

I then just added the little sweetener:

“Don’t forget sweetie, it could well be worth a nice few quid to both of us as you say, and it’s strictly down the middle 50/50 remember.”

Of course no financial commitments had been discussed up to this point, but I was already learning fast how the ‘Knockerboys’ worked their magic, and why shouldn’t I board the gravy train?

He drew a big breath, sighed and then displayed the broadest smile, Zippy himself would have been proud of.

“Well,” he ventured, “It seems I may have underestimated you young lady. Please forgive me for the oversight. You have certainly done your homework, and if I may say, this is much more important to you than what those ignorant prats next door, may fink, or surmise, if they give a flying fuck in the first place. (He took another deep breath) Soo, with that in mind, how do you propose to go about it, my dear?”

My moment was upon me, “Well,” I began in earnest, “How about, we set aside a few little sessions at various points of the week, meet in a place, convenient to both of us, and you relate in decent and precise detail, some more of the stuff taking place in those ‘Good Old Days’, and I will try my best to convey it from chat to paper.”

“I don’t wish to be coy or prissy, but I basically think that it would be much more productive if we shied away from Licensed Premises for these meets. You know me Georgie, I like a drink as much as the next person, but this is a job of work, and should be respectfully treated as such, for the greater good.”

I would like to think my convincing smile and good-natured pat on his forearm was worthy of Knockerboy status. Getting a seat in the next Volvo leaving town, to, ‘Get In, Some Gaff’, and ‘Get As Much Gear Out, As Possible’ with whatever bunch of toe rags would let me jump in with them.

George was not slow on the uptake, his reply went like this:

"That, pretty much sounds like a goer to me, consider me in. Mind you, all that stuff you said about protection must be in place before I say a dickie bird, you do understand that don't'cha sweetie?"

I just nodded diligently, trying to contain myself, and to help myself resist cuddling the old bastard, I'd cracked it!

My short lived education had already armed me with the knowledge that once I gave George 'The Top Up' by mentioning the matter of vast amounts of money by way of 'Consultancy Fees' he wouldn't give a flying duck who came unstuck, this was really getting to me now, I was as bad as any of them, within reason of course.

"How's about, I come round to you this coming Thursday, with some Fish & Chips."

Bardsley's of course, the best Chippy in Town for donkey's years, and something we had both agreed upon on the 'Waggon Trip', as we now referred to it. Everything had a tag to it, 'First Meet' at the café, next one in the Waggon and now 'The Kensington Kafuffle.'

"A few cans of beer, not too much mind you, and we start at the beginning with the old barrow boys stuff. Then I will try to get some sort of structure to the piece and we'll just take it from there, whaddayasay?"

"It all sounds good to me," says George, and just at that moment a big fat prat shouted across the Bar,

"Georgie Boy, come on unload the Rattley matey and get yer score out, you're up, and don't bother trying to ponce the poxy little fifty pence for the table again on yer way round, we're onto you Ballcock."

Continuing in the same derogatory tone, the fella carried on:

"Now referred to in educated circles as, Ballcocks Bollocks, and everyone has been informed that the betting on this game is strictly cash. My money is on Bertie Collins, 4 games on the spin and just waiting to get you by the balls, no pun intended. Sorry mate."

The big fellah turned out to be Bubbles, actually a really nice bloke, lovely missus Beverley, and in possession of one of the best memories ever witnessed in the 'Knocker Game'.

The fact he was about thirty stone, winner of any Billy Bunter contest that ever took place with an arse the size of two beach balls, taking up half the Bar at which he stood, still did not impress me.

He had in my opinion, not shown the slightest bit of respect, or deemed any admiration from the group of inadequately educated onlookers and talked down to my pal, and would, mark my words, pay the price at a later date.

All the while though, he was also someone I was longing to gain confidence of, as I had already heard many tales of his knowledge. He possessed unchallenged admiration of his fellow 'Antique Dealers & Purveyors of Fine Art and Objay D'art'; his remarkable memory for fine detail or hallmarks was second to none in most people's opinion.

To be fair, as I followed George round to the Pubic Bar, as I now liked to call it, Bubbles immediately straightened up, tucked in his shirt and asked if I would care for a drink, and then proceeded to apologise for his ranting and raving. He was unaware Georgie had such delightful company in tow. He wasn't red faced due to any embarrassment; he constantly gave the impression that his blood pressure was going through the roof. My low opinion of him ebbed away in seconds and he was now my second best friend in the world of 'Brighton's Knockers'.

It was uncanny how one moment it was possible to despise someone you had never even met before, and the next bloomin' minute you are drinking and dancing with them like you had known them all your bloody life.

This was the ever-unattainable addiction, as well as attraction that had somehow drawn me into their world, yet it was all totally harmless really. Brighton was literally just a tiny little Village, in actual fact, everyone knew everyone, and they all knew everyone else's business, whether they liked it or not, this is still apparent today, and will continue to be so for evermore!

George was setting the balls up for the next match, in the background Bubbles was laying three tenners to one that George was the 'J. Arthur Rank Outsider' and was only taking cash bets.

I slipped up beside him, having already explained I was meeting a friend in Town, and proceeded to wish him all the best for his next game. A couple of wolf-whistles ensued of course, with some ignorant prick commenting on my 'Eartha's and 'Bottle' so I simply said in a private moment, for all to see:

"Catch up with you on Thursday Georgie, about 6:30pm." He nodded accordingly, and as far I was concerned, the deal was done.

*

When our next meeting was due, there was a slight tinge of nervousness and anticipation.

George had called to confirm our meeting, and I had stuck by my word and agreed to foot the bill for our dinner. We met in the Bat & Ball for a quick half, just to break the ice. It's always weird when you meet someone for the first time and it is apparent that you are both aware the pair of you are going to be totally sober.

To date this had never been the case.

We made our niceties, and exchanged formalities in the now understood exaggerated fashion.

*

It was quite amusing in a perverted kind of way. Nobody else within earshot was aware that this was a total falsehood of breeding and status. What with the bowing and over polite mannerisms, that were being publicly displayed in front of their very eyes, and accompanied with no remorse or guilt whatsoever. It was pure pantomime.

I suppose you had to witness it to appreciate it.

We both agreed that this was just a trial run and if we were not both totally comfortable, with the situation, the whole thing would be written off as a good idea gone bad, with no hard feelings.

As far as I was concerned that was as likely as George telling someone that the geezer Siddy Berman who runs The Esquire Club, Holland Road, wasn't really Jewish and was a shit Pool player. Prepared to lose a few quid, the one eyed yid was quite tasty at the game, and would stitch you up at every opportunity if the game wasn't going his way. His sister Bobby, however, very much disapproved of any financial commitment relating to the outcome of any games on the table, so he was constantly distracted during a game in case she tumbled gambling was occurring.

I must apologise for going off on a tangent there, but these buggers had started to really get into my head, and now I have already begun to take a leaf out of their book, and change the topic of conversation on a whim, without even knowing why.

He, Georgie, fancied a nice bit of Huss, with chips and a gherkin; I selected the special of the day, which was fresh caught monkfish with chips, and mushy peas. I found it so amusing that, as soon as I had paid, George remarked:

"Those Gherkins look a bit on the small side tonight Roy." Roy simply replied:

"Yeah, they do a little bit don't they, I'll stick two in for you Gorgeous, is that alright? As it happens, can I include a couple for you also luv?"

I nodded in agreement, and gave a conspiratorial nod to my partner in crime. At it all the time, is there never a let up on this continuous conspiracy to get as much out of anyone for as little as possible and still not look like an absolute shit all the time? Evidently not.

Whilst we waited for our supper, I kicked things off with the suggestion that we could possibly stay put in the chippy.

George confirmed that a deal was a deal,

"Make a plan and stick to it Minnie, one of the golden rules my little darlin', one of the golden rules" and that as we had agreed, even if not in writing at this stage, we were to dine in his residence, all was prepared and I should not be wary. How could I decline such an ambiguous invitation, given with such panache and grace?

We took our take-away just round the corner to Bromley Road, where George's Council Flat was. It seemed kooky that he only actually lived five minutes walk from my place, and that during my time in Brighton our paths had never crossed.

Of course our paths had indeed crossed now!

That's that all-important piece of Fate, sticking its great big nose in again!

We enjoyed unwrapping our food, with George checking whether or not I needed any condiments, and then surprisingly emerged from the kitchen with pre-heated plates from the oven, and what appeared to be brand new cutlery, at this stage I changed my mind and requested a little mayonnaise if possible.

"It's not the fucking Ritz yer know," was his reply, which made me splutter slightly and nearly choke on my gherkin. Waving my hand up, I started to apologise for being fussy, but he simply disregarded my efforts and engaged on an historical monologue about Bardsley's from whence we had just came.

"Did you know? Old man Bardsley was a Blacksmith from Burnley, came down South and opened his first chippy in Shoreham in 1926?" He was off on one:

"Then, after opening in Upper North Street, by Russell Street where the Tax Office is, a couple more in Portslade and then Hove. 'Old Curly' Davis opened the gaff over the road in Baker Street in nineteen sixty fuckin' free, he woz Muriel's Dad."

"In 1970, a few years later, Roy Brown joined the team, and then by 1989 straight out of school at 14, Neil, who was Muriel and Roy's son joined them. Really and truly they're like True Blue Brightonian Royalty when you fink about it."

At this stage I really felt the need to nip things in the bud, so I jumped in a bit with:

"Ok Ok, that's all very well and good, but I'm not here for a History lesson. If I wanted that, I'd have done a different course at Uni." I then rose from my comfy chair, continuing.......

"Come on I'll wash these plates up and then we can get on with the case in hand. My time is money you know, and 'There ain't no taste in nuffin', as you keep on bloody well telling me, what do you reckon?"

As he looked up at me, I realised he had already slipped into his own little world, oblivious as to whether or not anyone gave a toss what he was saying. This reminded me of the moment he told me about his kids never listening to his worldly advice and just doing whatever they fancied. One of the penalties of bad parenting, or, for just not being there for that Christmas Nativity Play or School football match, those precious moments that your kids yearn for, and long for your attendance and recognition.

This was also close to my heart, as even though I was no ideal candidate for a Prefect position at any of my many Educational establishments. I had always wormed my way into any School performances at festive times. I was never out of Netball, Hockey or Athletic Teams wherever I managed to remain for more than a fortnight, and there was not one single solitary time when my Dad was not present to witness my efforts, and congratulate me afterwards with a loving hug.

He also often treated the whole team to a nice tea at some posh place (including the teachers) to help with morale, really and truly he just loved being part of my life and would never consider for a second missing out on one little bit of it, not if he could help it.

This is where George had missed out, and he knew it. By being out with the Boys, those times that can never ever be recaptured, and I was now fully aware how much it saddened him.

"You are quite right, Stephanie" he said, in a forlorn and reflecting manner, "Let's get to it. Now, where would you recommend or suggest we begin?"

My reply was quite simple and obvious: “Well, Georgie Boy, I, would recommend that we start at the beginning. What do you say?”

He began “I am gonna make a nice cup of tea, you are just the one sugar aren’t you, and then I am going to reveal how, the whole jolly story of how ‘Brighton’s Knockers’ all began. Wait there my little darlin’ I shall return forthwith.”

He crept off to do his duties and returned within about four minutes with two mint condition Victorian china cups and saucers adorned with sterling silver teaspoons, full to the brim with lovely fresh PG Tips brew, with six Rich Tea biscuits on matching side plates.

Then were to follow the first of many glorious stories, that I trust, you will find as enchanting, interesting, and utterly mesmerising as did I.

Hopefully I will be able to describe to you my dear listener, in a similar fashion that captivated myself, in the delirious, delicious and continuous comical fashion in which they were portrayed to me, as by my mentoring storyteller.

Then, and only then, you my friend will receive them and take them endearingly to your bosom with pleasure and joy, to be held close to your heart for evermore.

LET THE GAMES COMMENCE!

*

3. The Beginning Part III.

"Right then," began George, "Here we go. It all started when I had just been slung out of the Merchant Navy. It had been about three weeks or so, and I was absolutely fucking skint. I'd started to feel a bit of a ponce on my old dear, and married life wasn't exactly what I had expected."

"We lived up Scotland Street at the time, my Dad worked on the Railways, fuck knows what he actually did, but he went off to work at 6:00am and came home about 5:30pm. That was just how it was in them days. Ask no questions, told no lies, 'But what the fuck is it to do wiv you anyway you soppy little prat?, had a way wiv words my Dad."

"My problem was not much different to anyone else's. I had met this nice little sort called Shirley, up the Regent one time, and she was quite keen to take things further. I wasn't the worst catch in the world even if I do say so myself, and things were ticking over reasonably well. I had a job down Woolworth's in London Road and we had planned to save up and get a place of our own."

"Things woz different in them days, and you have to remember, this is the same sort of time as 'Heartbeat' and 'The Royal' woz on the telly, nobody had a great deal and we made the best of things. We lived day to day, from hand to mouth, and were only really just coming out of the rationing system, so no one expected much of anything; jam and butter on yer toast was still regarded as an unnecessary luxury."

"Anyway, we had a couple of ciders one night in The Elephant & Castle, London Road, and then went over to the Fair at The Level. It was the right old bees knees in them days, The Wall of Death, fantastic great big giant cuddly toys to be won on the darts and rifle range to impress the bird. You always thought you woz Sterling fucking Moss on the old dodgems."

"Humongous candyfloss on a stick to share, and then you could still muck about and have a laugh with all yer mates. They even had the old Boxing Booths where you could get a Fiver if you lasted three rounds with the resident Champ. Not that any poor fucker could, they always got a right pasting, mind you they came unstuck one time and that turned into a right bloody scramble, I'll tell you about that another time."

"Anyway, we got a bit frisky, you know what I mean, got carried away a bit, and we ended up making out, so to speak, behind the Coconut shy of all places, on this occasion Shirley was none too shy at all. It was all over before it got started really, and I was none too sure of myself when Shirley remarked 'Is that it Georgie? I 'aven't even finished me chips yet!'"

At this point I did have to laugh, because he was being so honest and forthright, there was a bemused look on his face when I did so. It was very refreshing and there was a kind of kindling of spirits going on, with his frank attitude and candid openness. He continued in earnest:

"So the turnout was no great fucking surprise. Six weeks later I'm sitting indoors having a cup of tea, when all of a sudden there's a knock on the door. Mum shouts out to me that I have visitors, bearing in mind this was in the tone that meant, at the door there was the, 'not fucking coming in' type of visitor. I had not done anything wrong recently, as far as I could recollect, especially anything that deserved a visit from the 'old bill', so I ventured to the door to see what the problem was."

"Just my luck, I've only got someone up the duff' who happens to have three of the biggest fucking bruvvers you could ever imagine, the Missin boys of all things. They were none too pleased and looking for some kind of solution or retribution to their poor little Shirley's plight, as it appeared I was the perpetrator of some ungodly deed that needed to be sorted out, lively!"

"With bullying bastards like that on yer doorstep there was not an awful lot one could do, so I accordingly agreed to do the right thing."

"To be fair wiv you Steph, in my day, the first sexual encounter you had was more than likely to be your last, partner that is, coz you would have to be a bit of a bastard not to marry the girl. If you got her in trouble, you also got her up the aisle and then you got it in the neck for all eternity, that's just how it woz in them days, Que Sera Sera, whatever will be will be."

He then began to serenade me in an embarrassing way;

"Que Sera Sera, whatever will be will be, the future's not ours to see whatever will be will be. Oops sorry about that my little sweetheart, I got a bit carried away there. Let's get back to the point, shall we?"

"Anyway, I really wasn't up for this sort of predicament and lifelong commitment, despite the bullying fucking Missin brothers. So I devised a cunning plan, and declared that I had joined the Merchant Navy. Well, the reception to this news was quite relieving, coz they all said how admirable it was, and that I would be doing the right thing. To my amazement, however, within two fucking weeks they had arranged the wedding, booked a honeymoon for two nights in Camber Sands, near Hastings somewhere down the coast and that was about it!"

"Soo, off I go on me travels, and proceed to send home half me pay for the next year or so. I managed to wrangle a lovely number as a Waiter come Barman and so got to mix with all the punters, in them days the old cruise ships were just floating Hotels, not like these floating Holiday Camps they have today. Bit of Bingo in the afternoon, a few stop off's that people would never get to see as a rule, most of them was getting on a bit, but fancied a bit of a laugh and half the time the couples went their separate ways once they was on board, so it was all quite sociable."

"I went to South America, most of the Mediterranean and was on my way to the West Indies when the Captain called me to his quarters at the port in Portugal, can't remember the name of that piss-hole for the life of me. It turns out, some snotty nose passenger has accused me, me of all people, of shagging his missus while he was in the Casino. I swear to you, I never saw him, so how could he have seen me. I still reckon to this day his missus confessed. Oh well, what can you do?"

"So anyway I was slung off the boat, held at the local detention centre, just a local Police Station holding cell really, and then got picked up a couple of days later and plonked on a cargo ship bound for Southampton where they would drop me off and leave me to my own devices."

"Shall we have a little break, George?" I interrupted. It seemed an appropriate moment, as I knew I had to try and take this all in, always trying to get back to the subject I was most interested in, but then realised he was just filling me in on the basics. I knew I had to give him some leeway, or he wouldn't spill the beans on what I was after. My tactic of comfy surroundings was working well, and we were now just a couple of old pals talking about the 'good old days', absolutely ideal, after a lovely meal. (Poet Know It!)

"Sure," said George, "I'm not boring you am I?"

"Oh no, of course not, just thought we might have a cuppa or something."

"Spot on luvvy, I'll stick the kettle on, won't be a minute," and trundles off to do the honours. We settled back down and he proudly placed the tray between us, announcing he had made a nice Carrot cake this afternoon in honour of my visit.

"You lying old git," I said jokingly and he just smiled and replied:

"Course I never, what do you take me for, some old fairy? No. I did think it was a nice touch though and I'm chuffed we are getting on as well as I had hoped. I was a little bit nervous to tell you the truth. I don't have too many guests to speak of, as a rule, and had to borrow a Hoover from Doris next door to spruce the place up a bit."

"Aah, you didn't have to bother with all that nonsense," I said smiling.

"You gotta be kidding. It fucking well needed it, and once she knew I had company tonight, she went to town and gave the place a right proper spring-cleaning and told me not to let it get in that state ag'in. Nice old girl she is, but not quite my type, if you know what I mean. She gets a bit lonely since her old man Bert passed away and so we have the odd cup of tea and cake together, and she knows I love her Carrot cake."

"Now, where woz we? That's right. I got sent back home and jumped the train to Brighton from the port and headed back to me mum's to face the music and see how the land lied on the home front."

"Can't say as I was particularly looking forward to things, but there was not an awful lot I could do about it. Frosty and precarious would be an understatement to say the least. The Missin Boys were on the warpath as far as Mum could tell, and young Garth, the son I was yet to meet, had not been too well by all accounts."

"As I had not been in regular contact, it had come as a bit of a shock to Shirley when she contacted the Navy about no money coming in, and was right pissed off when informed about my missing in action, so to speak."

"All sorts of stories were being bandied about, and my whereabouts was a right bone of contention, with all concerned, as you can imagine. Well, I just sort of shrugged me shoulders and decided to go and face the music."

"Well what a right result that was. When I knocked on her Mum's door, up The Highway, in Moulsecomb. Lo and behold Shirley opens up, wiv this bright eyed little kid on her hip and just gives me the biggest smile and sigh of relief that made all the apprehension and worry just melt away in a minute."

"'Where the fuck have you been Georgie, I've been going out of my mind wiv worry aboutcha'. She says, puts the little un' on the floor and throws her arms around me like I had just come back from the dead. She shouted over her shoulder, 'Mum, it's only George come back to me, I said he wasn't what you Arnie and Timmy said he was. Come in my darlin' and tell me all about it.'"

"That was it really, I was home, had a family, and it was time to try and get back to a normal life and sort things out."

He took a slurp of his tea and more crumbs than you would think possible cascaded all down his shirt as he bit a chunk of his cake.

George assured me there was not more of his personal life to speak of relevant to our project, much to my relief, and that we were now at the stage where things began to turn a little bit better for him.

Quite unprofessionally, I'm sure I gave a loud sigh at this time, expressing my impatience, but he chose to ignore it all the same. Always the gentleman was George.

"Soo, there I am," he began. "Noo job, noo money and no prospects to speak of. I was having a cup of tea one morning, about 11 o'clock, in the market café, you know, where me and you first met.

In walks this right cocky looking kid, about 5ft 9ins reasonably smart, but one of those types that could have a whistle made to measure in Savill fuckin' Row and still look scruffy two weeks later, he was just that type of person."

"Anyway, he starts jabbering on about how Benny Weakes had fucked everything up for everyone in the whole Town. 'All he had to do was keep an eye out for the cozzas, how fucking hard is that. There I am wiv some right cushty tomatoes at the top of St James's Street, doing a right roaring trade we woz."

"It was our second load up, coz we had a blinding deal wiv Denis at TG Fruits first thing this morning, and all of a sudden PC Nobby fuckin' Clark is on us like the bubonic fucking plague, and I has to have it on me toes and leave six poxy boxes of prime Tommie's on the Barrow."

"I dunno what the bloody world is coming to, Jesus H fuckin' Christ'."

"He hadn't noticed me sitting in the nearest corner behind the door, but he glanced down at me and went 'Oops sorry mate, I hope you aren't religious are you? And subsequently offended by my totally unnecessary blasphemous behaviour?"

"My dear old Mum keeps reprimanding me and pointing out it is not essential to continue taking the Lord's name in vain, I do apologise most sincerely'."

"Well Stephanie, that was the first time I ever met Mister Vincent Nearly, and I can still remember word for word exactly what he said. Of course I just looked him straight in the eye and said, 'I'm not quite sure what the H in Jesus' middle name stands for, is it Horace, Herbert or Hector, could you possibly enlighten me?'"

"Vince, well he just laughed out loud, and told me he thought that he found it quite comical, complementing me on my quick wit and sharp rebuttal, and whilst he laughed smugly, proceeded to spill his tea all over my table. Let me get you another one he said, I said no, but he wasn't having none of it and ordered me some toast with dripping as well, one of the House Specialities."

"We got chatting, and I told him all about my desperate plight and present awkward predicament, he agreed that being on the wrong side of the Missin clan was no picnic and he didn't reckon a single one of the pricks."

"He then told me to have whatever I could afford on the favourite in the 3:30 at Plumpton that afternoon. I told him I didn't have a dinar to spare, so he says to me, 'Well how about if we go up the road in Kemp Town at half-past twelve, and try a little bit of totting. I've already paid the hire for the poxy Barrow anyway, and if we get a bit lucky we can both have a little wager on the 'Hot Tip', how does that sound Georgie Boy?'"

"Well, obviously I wasn't gonna turn down an opportunity like that, what has just fallen out of the sky like an angel from heaven, so I agreed. He shows me where the Barrow was, just round the corner and says to me, 'There you go, meet me at the top end of Bedford Street, on the corner of St George's Road, at 12:30 and we'll give it a go'. He always had his hair slicked back did Vince, he was a proper Brylceam boy, and as good as his word, he was standing there waiting for me as I arrived with the empty Barrow, right on time."

"As we walked up towards Freshfield Road, he began to explain that he had heard a whisper of someone karking it recently and he (Vince that is) had previously tried to get a load of Brass and Copper stuff that the bloke had stashed away in the shed. 'I am pretty sure that his missus is not aware of how much shit there is in the shed, and so if we can catch her at the right moment we may well get a decent days work out of it'."

"There was only one place we were headed that day, but just out of sheer politeness he felt the need to cry out 'Rag'n'Bone, Rag'n'Bone, any old, Rag'n'Bone' in quite a tuneful manner. A couple of people tried to get our attention but he completely ignored them, but more than likely making a mental note for another day."

"We arrived at the house, in Hereford Street and a frumpy lady came to the door, with a scowl to scare a cat out of one of its nine lives. This was the same fuckin street that Tom Sayers the famous bare-knuckle fighter was born, what a tiger to fill yer tank he was, any way where woz I ?"

"Oh yeah, she asks us what the fuck did we want, not the nicest greeting I have ever experienced, but Vince did not flicker or flinch for one solitary second, completely disregarding her rude manner as if it were the proper and normal way to greet someone at your door."

"He began his oratory in a right posh tone he did, it went something like this; 'I was talking to the man of the house a few weeks ago, madam, and he said he would consider offloading some of his old bits and pieces that are taking up too much space in his shitty old shed at the back of your delightful garden. Now would it be possible to speak with him, if you please, the thing is, it was a few weeks ago and I did promise him l would come back when it was more convenient'."

"Well she did not know quite what to say at first, but after some consideration, and running her fingers through her hair she replied, 'Well, unless you are one of them clairvoyant types that think they can talk to anyone, not a bloody chance, the old bastard died four days ago and I couldn't give a flying fuck what's in the poxy shed, I've got too much other stuff to take care of. What's in there anyway? I never go up the back garden, that was his little bolt-hole, wassannit?'"

"Vince was in like Flynn, 'Ooh, I am so sorry to disturb you at this tragic time, please forgive me,' he then starts to back away from the doorstep, still facing the old girl but obviously no longer interested in doing any business with her, like she's got the plague or something."

"She takes the bait like a Greyhound after the Hare, 'Well don't go running off like a scared Rabbit sunshine, you're here now, you may as well take another gander and then tell me what it's worth, if anything.'"

"'Are you sure?' says Vince, 'I think maybe we should leave it for the time being.'"

"'Stop fannying about sonny', she says, 'Come on in and let's see what we can sort out, I'm bored to tears at the moment, and I haven't even got anyone to moan at, now he's pissed off upstairs. Mind you, if I had my way, he'd be headed bleedin' downstairs the stingy old git."

"So, down we go. The woman can't even be arsed to come with us, and sends us down the garden on our own, the place was chock a block with old brass and copper kettles, coal scuttles and a few old prints. 'This is handy', says Vince, 'Look 'ere Georgie, you just start loading up the Barrow wiv all this brass and copper gear, and I'll sort the old trollop out as best as possible.'"

"So there I am traipsing in and out of the shed and just slinging it all over the fence, then loading up the Barrow, in them days it was all derelict buildings on the front of Eastern Road and it was just like a dirt track out back only used by the 'Bin Men'."

"Whilst back inside, Vince is letting her know that it seems her Husband must have sold off the best bits since he had last been here, however what was left we would gladly take away for her at no charge whatsoever."

"Due to her unfortunate circumstances and as a gesture of good will, we were prepared to donate five pounds towards funeral costs or flowers, whatever she wished."

"The old girl was chuffed to bits, the old man only ever gave her thirty- five bob a week for housekeeping, and so she was in her element. Soo, we was off to Hicksies scrap yard, down Richmond Parade to cash up. I was quite good at loading up and after everything was weighed and paid we shared the princely sum of £26 between us."

"I could not fucking believe it, this was a decent weeks money to anyone and it was still only half-past two, still an hour to go before the big race at Plumpton."

"We had just missed last orders for the Pub, coz they always closed for the afternoon, so we both poodle along to the bookies. I hadn't had that much money on me since I could remember, but I wasn't about to get too excited, as I did not wish to seem over impressed."

"Vince had done five quid by the time the big race was on and was watching me closely, so as to suss me out I reckon, but I was aware of this and none too bothered."

"Soo, the race comes up, and the horse opens up at 7/2, that's three and half to one, I writes out me ticket and Vince enquires as to my stake."

"'Well Vince, me old china, this is my most honest and sincere opinion. I woke up this morning with fuck all and even less to fuckin' look forward to, we had a cup of fuckin' tea and smashing bit of holy ghost, you forced me to work my absolute fuckin' bollocks off for a total of two measly hours, and I am now in the possession of a decent weeks wages."

"Soo, I am having eight fuckin' pound billy goats, on the nose, and that still leaves me with a fuckin' ching to go home wiv if it don't cop. What am I supposed to be fucking well worried about, it's only a game anyway, innit?'"

"A friendly smile comes over his soppy bloody boat and Vince copies my betting slip and has the same eight-fucking-poxy pound to win bet. He then advised me to stop fuckin' swearing so much! The fucking horse pissed it, I can't remember for the life of me what it was called, but we both copped for just over thirty quid apiece after tax, and that my dear is how I met Vincent Fucking Nearly."

"Vince put his arm around me when we came out of the bookies and declared, 'You know what Georgie boy me old son, it is unlucky not to be superstitious and I think you are gonna be lucky for me.'"

"This was to be the beginning of a lifelong friendship that I will never regret or forget for a single solitary minute, swear to god. We had a few drinks that night in 'The Constant Service', 'The Beaufort', 'The Cobden' and 'The Dover Castle', his last profound statement in 'The Albion' was, 'I shall just have one more drink. Before I have another one.'"

"And as we parted company Vince told me to meet him first thing down the Market Café, that was to be about 5:30am. I was most certainly not gonna let this opportunity slip away through me fingers, so promised I would be there 'El Pronto'. Bearing in mind as well, mind you, that more than one person that night had told me that young Vince was a grafter, good money getter, had ambition, and anyone working with him would always earn a shilling, and never go without."

"It was not the most joyful or promising of receptions when I got indoors, but as soon as I had plonked a tenner on the dinner table, Shirley had nothing but nice things to do or say in the bedroom that night, altogether a most successful day, might I say."

*

At this stage George, stood up from his armchair and asked:

"Now, would you care for a little glass of wine, I know you don't wish to do all this lark in the boozer, but I know you're a bit partial, so yes, or no?"

"Well, if you have something available I suppose it won't hurt." I ventured to his expectant rapport. He walked back in with that all too familiar Cheshire cat grin on his boat, then, fondly cradled in his hands, he had a lovely delicate crystal wine glass and a well chilled bottle of Chablis.

Spot on!

"How will this suit you then my little Minnie?" he enquired, fully aware that he had swam the channel with this type of service.

"Yeah, I s'pose it will suffice for the time being," I commented. He went back to the fridge and then returned, clutching a couple of cans of Best Bitter and plonked himself back into the armchair, ready to continue with his pearls of wisdom and tales of daring-do, by some of the most endearing and captivating characters that ever walked on this planet.

*

"Right then, where was we? Oh yeah I know. Well when I get there at 5:30am, as requested, next morning, there was a terrible row going on with Vince and some fella from one of the wholesalers. It seemed that a deal had been done over some of those lovely juicy Greek peaches, fucking great big bastards they woz, and when they were nice and ripe they had the most tantalising smell you've ever seen, absolute belters."

"The bloke who had done the deal, had done it without the knowledge that the other porter had already sold em' to Roy Yeates, quite a big player in the Fruit and Veg game in them days. So this George geezer was saying that any deal done by him was not valid, Vince was having none of it and was demanding to see the Guvnor'."

"The fing is, sometimes they would make a deal, realise they'd made a ricket and try to renege by saying it was someone else's fault and there was nothing they could do about it. Let me explain."

"For instance, if there was ten sacks of potatoes going nowhere they would grab hold of someone like Benny Weakes and say something like, 'Go on fuck off with them and give us two bob'. It was all fine and dandy, but then if someone offered sixpence a sack they would have a sudden change of heart, this bit of loose change was always going straight in their own sky rocket of course."

"This was, however, not going to happen to Vince, and it looked like someone was gonna get into serious trouble if things were not agreed upon before someone in management upstairs was made aware of what was going on, and this was certainly not conducive to the way things went at this time of day." (George had a lovely knack of introducing an exquisite unexpected piece of terminology at times. Cheeky little git!)."

"So as I turn up, Vince looks at me and says 'There you are George, where have you bloody well been all Sunday morning, I bet you've been giving that Shirley bird a right seeing to again behind the bicycle shed again haven't you, you dirty little sod. Well let's not worry about that for now, let's get on with the serious business to hand. Will you please tell this man that I handed over £46, you saw me count out the cash, didn't you?'"

"'Yeah course you did. For all them 92 boxes of those Greek peaches that are loaded up on the Barrow, just 5 minutes ago and Horace said he would be back shortly. Look, for crying out loud, I've got the fucking receipt right here in my soddin' hand'."

“I got straight into the act and said ‘Aahh nhooh! Not that old fucking chestnut! I've never heard such a disgraceful accusation in all my born days! Of course you did Mr Nearly, who would ever in their right mind doubt it for a single second. What sort of a place is this, where a man’s word is not his bond? It’s a diabolical fucking liberty, where’s that fucking Horace gone then? He woz here just a fucking minute ago.’”

“The porter just shook his head in disgust and decided that any chance of snatching the peaches back were long since gone. Then Horace turns up, and what I thought was a big row when I turned up was nothing compared to what followed.”

“George steamed into Horace, telling him he wasn’t worth the trousers he stood up in, just coz you’re family don’t give you the excuse to be a useless piece of shit, it’s coming out your wages, don’t bovver coming back tomorrow and all kinds of ‘orrible crap.”

“It would have been funny if it wasn’t so bloody serious. Still, when you think about it, four quid was like fifty today and that was all bunce, and it wasn’t like Roy Yeates was just gonna say don’t worry about it, he still wanted the peaches he’d already paid fifty quid for.”

“Then there was the continued berating about the fact that Roy was one of their best customers, and they got all their fucking decent money from him and not these two-bob-bit chancers that came in once a fuckin’ fortnight, them soppy little prats, did not take preference. At this point, Vince realised it was best to leave them to it and make haste with a timely departure, with said goods, no longer in danger of being repossessed.”

“Vinnie summoned young Morry Hughes over, and of course he was only too pleased to be included in the forthcoming day’s events, and so he pushes the Barrow just around the corner where we were to have a quick sort out. There was 38 peaches in a tray so after about twenty minutes we had 87 trays instead of the original

92. He then gave strict instructions to go no further than the Café before we set off to our pitch for the day, and keep em' covered in case that Roy Yeates spotted us and starts having a pop."

"Fucking hell Steph, I'd only been there thirty seconds and I was now a star witness for the defence. 'Aah well, it's only a laugh' said Vince when I asked what the hell had been going on. He then explained how he had done the deal with Horace and then cottoned on to poor old Horace's plight, and during the interim of him getting caught selling short and being fired, Vince and Morry had jumped straight in and loaded up the barrow with the Peaches."

"When this other prat came down to take over, in his newly promoted position, he wanted to see a signed document before the goods left the warehouse."

"Vinnie had done a right good deal before anyone twigged that these particular beauties usually went for a shilling each in the shops."

"My haphazard and unexpected appearance had only helped the situation, once there was a witness, 'I told you we'd do well together didn't I' said Vince."

"'Them two prats need to brush up a bit on their communication skills'. Then he just fucking started laughing to himself, like he was the only one that got the joke, fuckin' classic."

"Like I said, we got to work on sorting the Peaches. The last fuckin' thing you needed was someone coming back wiv' a dodgy peach, that would just fuck the whole day up, so you was just simply stock-checking as they say, to-day, ta-da."

(With fluttering of the eyes and splaying of the arms like the great Al Jolson himself, no need to say what was said next).

"While we did this, some smarmy git mentioned about trying to get hold of Sylvie up in Accounts. 'Fuckin' hell, if she offers you a lift in that Triumph Herald Convertible of hers you are on your way to fuckin' heaven, I'll tell ya'. I told him he was talking out of his arse, cos I knew Sylvia, she was pally wiv my Shirley, and even though she had been left in the lurch with a kid, she was no tart and there needed to be some sort of decorum and sense of respectability set in place."

"He was a Cousin of the Missin brother's but it just niggled me that day, that he, fucking muggy little runt that he was, with no rhyme or reason, could just, be so disrespectful of a bird, Woman in fact, and get away with it with no comeback. I never get into rucks as a rule, being a bit on the short side, but it pissed me off and I shoved a right rotten peach straight into his boat and squeezed it till he fell down to the deck."

"'You are such a muggy Missin little runt, now why don't you just fuck off, here's sixpence for your troubles you soppy little prat. Now, think yourself lucky to get that, don't bovver poking yer nose round here again coz you ain't welcome, yer Cousins can go fuck 'emselves an' all so don't bother trying to stir things up, coz I ain't bovvered'."

"Vince took a step back, and raised his eyebrows at my sudden show of passionate aggression, but did not protest and I sensed there was a glimmer of respect in his eyes. Morry was in agreement, and remarked, 'can't make you wrong there Georgie boy'."

"To be fair wiv you Steph I was quite surprised yet also proud of myself, and even though I didn't exactly get away with it altogether, I'm glad I did it. Shirley heard about it, so did Sylvie, and, I suppose everyone fucking else. Didn't do me any harm in the long run though, that's for sure."

*

“As I said there were a few over-ripe peaches, on average two to a tray. So we now had 87 trays to get rid of and so the famous old sales pitch was about to be severely tested. We could quite easily go for three for a shilling, but today Vince was going for Gold. ‘What we are gonna do,’ he said, once we were up at the pitch in Cranbourne Street: ‘Is the old classic, that may not have long to live, due to inflation and the greedy fucking bastards at the Market, this may well be the last time that we hear this historical cry of the working class.’”

“With a huge bellowing voice, he started to cry out: ‘Eachy Peachy Sixpence Eachy. Come on girls get yer peaches here today, come on then, join the queue. Hold on there madam give everyone a chance. Come on then girls here we go. Eachy Peachy Sixpence Eachy.’”

“It seemed that within minutes we had a queue of over thirty fucking people, it was normally just the women, but on this day there was blokes buying a couple just for the sheer entertainment value and ‘keep the missus happy factor’. Oh I’ll tell you what Steph, it was bloomin’ marvellous.”

“As they was queuing up, we hit ‘em wiv the old closer: ‘Cum on darlin’, ‘ere we go. Six for half-a-crown. There you go. Yer old man’s gonna love these. Make sure you eat ‘em while they’re nice and ripe.’”

“‘These are grown to eat in the bath my lovely’, was another phrase bandied about that day, but other great reputations were made that day also. They smelt irresistible and of course we ate a few ourselves and took a nice bag each, for indoors.”

“We were sold out by one o’ poxy clock on the nose, so we had a grand total of £174: £46 for the stock money and £4 for young Morry. Vince announced that this left £120 so we had £60 each.”

"'What about the odd four quid then Vince?' I enquired. 'Are you fucking sure of yourself Georgie Boy?' he quipped back at me and we just laughed at each other. Both fully aware that this was one of those Golden Moments that we would repeat for years to come. Funnily enough, Vinnie even remarked: 'You mark my words Georgie Boy. They'll be writing books about this type of thing one day.'"

"So, there we was, wiv another pocketful of money. At one stage that night, when we were having a drink in 'The Albion', near the bottom of Albion Hill, we both said in unison 'It's only a laugh anyway innit.'"

"Vince told me to have the next day off, as he had some other plans to attend to, but to be ready for eight o'clock Thursday morning, as we were going to start something new and exciting. I was hooked on this young fellah, he had plenty of energy and wasn't scared of a bit of graft. He had certainly changed my state of mind and finances and now I was actually looking forward to things."

NOW THINGS WERE REALLY GONNA START HAPPENING!!

*

I said to George that I thought we had covered plenty of subjects for the time being, and that I would now take this information and inside knowledge back with me and write some of it up. He agreed it was enough to get on with, but assured me we had only just scraped the surface and there were so many more things to talk about. I assured him that once I had written a couple of pieces, I would show him the results, and then discuss the finer details of 'His End'.

Telling him:

"The thing is George, if some of this stuff gets picked up by the right people there could be a nice few quid in it for you, you know that don't you?"

At which he seemed surprised, but I knew better of course. Although we were getting on well, I was after all, dealing with an old scoundrel and should not let that slip from my mind for a single solitary moment.

"I'm sure everything will work out fine," he replied. "My first instinct the uvver' night, you know, about it maybe leading to a bit of bovver, well that has slightly evaporated darling. I trust you now, and I am confident that pretty soon the others will be feeling the same way. Take care sweetheart."

With that, he helped me on with my coat, gave me a tiny peck on the cheek and bade me farewell. There was certainly a conspiratorial feeling about what we were doing, which added that touch of excitement to proceedings, after all we were just reminiscing old times. As I walked home I had a euphoric feeling all inside me and could hardly wait to get started, but I had promised to let Grace know how the meeting had gone, so would start in the morning.

Once Grace had got the jist of things, she advised me to take it slowly and from time to time show a little disinterest:

"Keep 'em all dangling, from time to time and be sure not to give anything or too much away. Oh yes, and for God's sake, do not under any circumstances, tell your Father about any of this."

"I don't know why, but for some reason, whenever 'Those Brighton Knockerboys' are mentioned he gets in a right funny mood."

She would never steer me wrong, so I would bear this in mind when he next came to Town. I had never kept anything from him before, but this was my business and so I just had to resist the temptation, till the appropriate time of course.

As I put the key in my door, the phone began to ring and as it was 10 o'clock I realised it may well be urgent. Julliette was in a terrible state when I answered.

"You won't believe what's happened," she said through her tears. "That prick Nigel, has only told Tracey, that I was sleeping with him, whilst you were still seeing him. I have to tell you, it's all a pack of lies, I would never do that to you."

"Calm down, calm down, darling," I said. "That really doesn't surprise me. Why the hell I stood that from him, for two months, I'll never know. Where are you babe?"

"We are in 'The King & Queen' at the moment. I know it's late, but can we come and see you?" she replied.

"Of course you can. Why don't you get it together, pop in the offie for a couple of bottles of wine and we'll sort it all out?" I advised.

"Oh Min you're such a good friend and person, we'll see you in about fifteen minutes."

Then the pips went from the phone box and I hoped she had heard my last words. She had. They were both with me within ten minutes and we all just hugged each other for a while, slagged all men in the world for half-an-hour and everything was resolved. We were the famous three female musketeers as far as anyone was concerned and some bitter jealous ex-boyfriend would never come between us.

I then proceeded to tell them about my recent exploits with Georgie and his associates. They were slightly taken aback at first, but as my intentions unfolded they became mesmerised and even astonished at my future plans for the information I was gathering at a breakneck speed.

When I revealed that I was planning to put it all together in one piece, they congratulated me and assured me that if at anytime I needed a bit of back up, they would both be there for help and support. We ordered Pizza, washed it down with five bottles of wine and had our first sleepover for ages.

My new coffee percolator helped tremendously with our hangovers in the morning, but Jules could still not risk taking a ‘sickie’ as she was still on probation at Amex.

Tracey hung about for a couple of hours and Grace was on hand to hear all the latest news and events. A girlie morning was in order.

*

4. The New Beginning.

As part of our new arrangements, George had given me his phone number and I was to call him once I had a sample of my work to show him. Consequently I was ready to meet up with him within the next three days. The thing was however, I had shown Grace some samples of my notes first, just in case I was barking up the wrong tree and was not up to the task.

After all, I had for the time being, been accepted into a world where only birthright gained automatic entry into the 'Brighton's Knockerboy' community. Or, as in my case. 'Special Guest' category, and I did not wish to 'mug myself off' as it were.

She was a complete revelation, and showed a side to her that I never knew existed. After reading my few pages she said she had some important opinions and that I was to come down for a nice meal and she would reveal her suggestions. Well, I was quite fascinated by her seemingly covert plans and air of secrecy, or was my imagination running away with me and I was just getting paranoid that everyone was up to something dodgy?

Well, it was nothing of the sort of course, but exceptionally cunning and would be my greatest asset in the months to come. She suggested two lots of material, the one that I showed George and the one, which was to be my masterpiece as she had named it.

She thought that it was all brilliant, but as a safeguard I should not reveal all to George, as he was sure to start mouthing off to all and sundry about what was being perpetrated by him and his new best friend: 'The Stunning Steph,' or whatever sort of nickname he had surely concocted. I was at first a little disappointed in her pessimistic attitude, but within just a few seconds when it sunk in, I realised she was without a doubt, right on the money. Not one of this little fraternity could be trusted and to err on the side of caution was paramount.

So many of these Herberts would prefer to do you a bad turn rather than a good one, and anyway it made perfect sense.

What George didn't know about wouldn't harm him, and if a Publisher wanted to print any of it, they would be entitled to the full story and not get the sugar-coated version. This also meant that I would be at perfect liberty to reveal, whatever I wished and only disclose to George, what he wanted to see.

This in turn would also negate, the still yet to be signed agreement between us, on the possibly incriminating facts that he first pointed out. Even though this had dissipated at this stage and he really wasn't that bothered if it meant an earner for him.

It was a bit like 'The Top Up' he and Vinnie had been using for so many years, so why worry about it? After all, if they did get the hump, I could always threaten to reveal all the correct names and places of interest and that would really put the shits up 'em. That was Grace's excuse anyway.

Also, she pointed out, I had the edge at this stage of the game. Just because I had a nice figure. attached to a great pair of legs, carried myself well and could still have a laugh, didn't give them any reason to not show me respect. It was after all, to be my creative writing talent and skills that would string it all together, plus my nosey parker, investigative nature that would make it all possible. 'Don't sell yourself short,' she told me, 'coz you can bet your bottom dollar, not one of them greedy gits would think twice, given half a chance'.

It also, to some degree, in my mind anyway, protected George from any repercussions, as he would not be party to any of these unauthorised revelations. He would be provided with his own copy to prove that any discrediting on his part was invalid.

With my abridged version of events I made my way to George's place on Thursday afternoon.

Evidently he had had a nice little tickle on the ponies and had finished early that week. He suggested that if it wasn't too inconvenient, to pop round his gaff for an hour or so. This was perfect as I had been chomping at the bit to see him, but refrained from doing so on Grace's strictest instruction. It was like we were now both on a mission, and George was the prey, but in a nice way, that is. He would certainly get looked after one-way or another, whatever the outcome, and the worst way in the world, he would have had the pleasure of meeting me, and what's so bad in that?

*

He greeted me warmly, and informed me I was right on time, and the kettle had just finished boiling in the anticipation of my prompt arrival. He went straight into one:

"So glad you were on time, them Nearly Brothers used to drive me up the fuckin wall, if Vince or his kid brother Harry was driving, whatever time they said they were coming, you could bet yer sweet arse they would be knocking on the door twenty bloody minutes earlier. What with the Navy and all, I was good wiv' me timekeeping, so if I said I'd be ready at eight, I woz. So it drove me absolutely crazy wiv them coz you'd just be straightening yer tie and there'd be all sorts of tooting car horns, door bell going and banging on the windows."

"This usually meant I would forget one thing or another, because of the rushing about, impatient couple of sods they woz. Then, if it was Dick or Jimmy, they would always be twenty minutes late, with some sort of pathetic excuse and you'd have been sitting around twiddling your thumbs and drinking too much tea. Then we go and meet at the Café or somewhere and they wanted a drink coz they woz behind schedule, and hadn't had time for a cuppa, and you were already full up and just wanted to start work and get down the road."

"There was no point in trying to remember who was supposed to pick you up: 'Early Nearly' or 'Lately Nearly', because they never stuck to the plans anyway. So it was never a smooth start to the day, at the beginning of the week."

"Once we woz away it didn't matter, because we all got up the same time for breakfast and that was it. If someone decided they wanted a lay-in, that was their problem. But when it came time to divvying up the readies at the end of the week, this type of behaviour was severely punished. We would all agree that the said lazy bastard was hit where it hurt."

"Harry Nearly actually refused two days money to Dick the driver one week, because he had not delivered any bills one day. Dick had a right whinge about it but Harry would not back down, needless to say Dick never skived off too much after that incident, and still got docked the breakfast money even though he never had it!"

"There were always a few silly things to bicker about, but on the whole it was alright, the thing was, 'It was always only a bit of a laugh, anyway,' as we used to say. Poetry my best subject at school, you know that don't'cha Steph."

"Anyway, how goes my little Enid Blyton, how's the writing coming along?"

Not having seen him for a week or so I had completely forgotten how effortlessly he could rabbit on so much about nothing without coming up for air. Without any consideration or intention of letting me get a word in edgeways. Brilliant. He didn't have the faintest idea why I was smiling.

"Everything alright doll?"

"Of course Georgie, why don't you have a butcher's and a little browse over my first draft. I will just get my pen and paper out, I should have done this before really. So that I can jot down a few things, while we go. If that's alright with you?"

"Yeah sure, just let me settle down and we can carry on." He slipped his half-rim glasses on and began to read. Smiling to himself and having the occasional chuckle. This in turn, gave my confidence a lovely boost, and after about fifteen minutes he was finished.

"Well," he declared, "I think we can safely say that I am happy with things so far, and more than willing to carry on with your proposal. How do you want to go on about it, do you prefer the more private locations or out and about?" He had given some consideration to my thoughts, after all. Once again he had tried to catch me off guard, but this one I was ready for.

"Well," I said, beginning my prepared reply: "We can certainly get a lot more done when indoors, but I also appreciate the fact that you enjoy being out and about, so I reckon we should do both. When we have some important factual things to take care of, we stay home. But if it's just a couple of the more comical tales that can be shared with others, as they all know about these true incidents anyway, we will meet at some Pub or somewhere. Then it doesn't become so much of a chore and I will also get to meet some more of the culprits involved."

George straightened himself up in his chair, and was about to say something, but I raised my hand and insisted, "Hold on a minute, let me finish before you jump in."

(I was fully aware he wanted to butt in but it was imperative that I kept myself in a controlling position, let these slippery bastards get a grip and who knows what could appertain, another pearl of wisdom and gem of advice from my beloved Grace.)

"Once I know a few more of them, when you mention who's involved, I can put a face to a name. It is highly likely the story will turn out better that way, what do you think?"

Rubbing his chin and raising his eyebrows with a knowing grin, he simply said:

"Well, I was saying to someone the other day, that you were no dummy, and what you have just said right there, proves my point. A couple of faces have already pulled me up, asking about you. I've told 'em if they don't wanna talk to you, they don't have to. But as far as I'm concerned, this is between me and you. Any other information that you may gather in my company, is totally none of my concern."

"Still, as you have probably already gathered, once someone starts explaining or going on about some caper or whatever, there's no fucking stopping 'em. So who am I to judge where and when we meet, and who to, and who not to listen to?"

It amused me, how sometimes when speaking, he would use the same words two or three times in the same sentence, it was like he was a kid who had just learnt a new word and wanted to repeat it as much as possible. This slightly unhinged my 'A' Level Education, where it is frowned upon to do such things in well-written English. This would be more betterer! But I am sure you would wish to hear it, as it should be: 'God's honest truth that is'.

"So, to follow on from where we finished. Good job we've got written down where we left off last time, or I would start to get things jumbled up. Mind you it's funny how I can remember so clearly how things went really, innit? Seeing as I'm getting on a bit now."

He was still as sharp as a tack really, but I thought I may as well play along with this little charade, it was only a game anyway, wasn't it?

"Vinnie only turns up, dead on time, driving an old Commer Van. One of them with the column gear change and proudly announces this is the new company vehicle. 'Well, we're off to pastures new today me old kiddie', he says, 'Wotcha think of our new calling cards?' Shoving a small box into my lap, containing our new flyers. As he did this, a momentary lack of concentration nearly ended the day right there and then. He had nearly gone straight into the traffic lights at the bottom of Elm Grove, and swerved right across the other side of the road, causing a 41 bus to screech to a halt."

"I had to laugh though, as I witnessed about seven or so people, all falling over each other on the Lower level of the new Double Decker Bus. The white haired Bus Conductress, leaned out of the back of the open plan platform at the back and enquired to my driver: 'Have you got a license young man? It really is required you know.'"

"I can't remember her name, but she was a right peach and worked on the old ticket machine for years. She was always caked up wiv make-up and it was funny to see all the young boys lusting after her. Many a young kid, had her in his thoughts, when in the privacy of his bedroom at night, I can assure you. She was like the Queen of the Buses and was based in the old Bus depot in Park Street, next to Queen's Park school, where they filmed 'Wish You Were Here', with Emily Lloydd in."

"You know, where she does the mock striptease for the boys on the office desk showing all the old stocking and suspenders. Then she gets up the duff and strolls right through the Bowling Green in Queen's Park with the baby in the pram, and don't give a monkeys'."

I raised my eyebrows slightly at this stage to indicate my lack of interest, and George took it on board.

"Sorry about that Babe, but I do get a bit side tracked sometimes."

“I’ve noticed that from time to time, come on get on with it we haven’t got all afternoon, and you said you had plans for this evening.”

“Yeah, I did as it happens, but my friend changed his mind, at the last minute and has left me posted, don’t suppose you fancy a game of Bingo do you?”

“I don’t go in for gambling, myself.”

(Then, in the exaggerated accent of Foghorn Leghorn)

“Oh, don’t be silly, it’s not gambling. It’s just a social fing. Come on, you’ll enjoy it, and there’s usually a few faces up there an’ all. Go on Steph, whaddayasay?”

“Let me think about it. We’ll see.” I had arranged to meet with Grace after this meeting so didn’t want to commit.

NOW. TO GET BACK TO THE STORY AT HAND!

“So, he pulls up outside the Diner, as if he was a Chauffeur delivering The Duke of fucking Edinburgh himself. Course everyone piles out, looking and pointing wiv comments like ‘Gone into retirement boys?’, ‘Started a removal business then?’ and other various sarcastic old shite.”

“Vince just waves them aside, like a person of too high a position in society to even notice them. ‘Just local peasants and riff-raff Georgie Boy, pay no attention.’ He had a great aloof tone when required, did Vincie.”

The pride in his voice when he said this was quite commendable, and I realised that everything Georgie was telling me came right from the heart, and I therefore felt duly privileged. It was right at that moment I vowed to make sure that everything I would reveal in future publications would honour and display only respect and due diligence to 'Brighton's Knockerboys'.

"Once we had ordered tea and toast, Vince proposed the new order of things. 'Well, after that nice little tickle up Kemp Town, I thought we would give another area a go, where maybe they haven't seen our type of Entrepreneur before. There must be loads of all that Brass and Copper about.'"

"At this point Johnny Wadey (later to be referred to as 'The Judge' due to his vast knowledge of gear), lent over his shoulder and said: 'Do you know that Tommy Barnes, he's got a gaff in town. You know the Old Coach House in Middle Street? "

"Well he's paying good money for some of that stuff like you had on the Barrow the other day. Ten bob them candlesticks, thirty bob the fire fenders and all sorts of stuff like that. That scrapping bollocks is a fucking mug's game, I tell yer.'"

"Charlie was now on the firm. He looked a bit peaky (I later found out this was due to the unnerving driving lessons he had given the youngster, the day before). We didn't pay much attention to 'The Judge'. On finishing our teas, Vince announced we were headed for Shoreham, armed with the new bills I had yet to see. It's not like any of us had ever pushed a Barrow that far for sure."

"Okay, okay. Well, we heads off towards the Pier while I look at the flyer that reads something like 'Dealers Ready to Pay Cash for all Artefacts, Furniture, Brass and Copper, Fine Art & Objects D'art. Top prices paid for all Watches, Chains and Jewellery'."

"I tells him, we don't know fuck all about any of these things. 'So fucking what' he says, 'It's only a fuckin' laugh anyway innit? Come on boys: we're off to See The Wizard, The Wonderful Wizard of Oz.' We all chimed in together: 'Because Because Because Because, The Wonderful Wizard of OZ there Woz'."

"This was actually to become one of our great songs, which we liked to steam into when things were going well and that just reminded me of that moment."

"I'm not getting all soppy on you Steph, but it just tickles me when I talk about some of them early days."

He then, transformed once more and had that lovely tender look on his face, that a new Mother or Father has, for their newborn baby. The subject matter at hand of course, was hardly that of an innocent child. That's for sure. But we were suddenly starting to get somewhere in my eyes, and it gave me a sense of progress. There was still something about George I was not so sure about, and it wasn't anything bad.

He continued: "Well, the coast road was not too busy in them days, but the journey was still none too pleasant. It was more like a ride on The Dodgems, but without the actual collisions, although we were actually very lucky. In fact it was some of the pedestrians that were even more fortunate. Vince had a kind of problem recognising what a Zebra crossing was for, and insisted in shouting at, at least, half-a-dozen of the poor sods to 'get out of the fuckin way you moron, can't you see I'm driving' on more than one unfortunate instance. We did, however manage to arrive in Shoreham in one piece by about 9:30am."

"What we gonna do now? I enquired to Vince, who seemed to have become the uncrowned Prince of Thieves, as it were. It certainly didn't feel that we had come all this way, to help some old dear with her gardening."

"'Whaddaya fucking think we're gonna do?' he's gone: 'just as per usual, we will spend a couple of hours dropping off these notices of intent, find a Café for a nice little bit of bish-bosh and then pick em' up after lunch. What did you think we was gonna do, go fucking swimming? Now come on. My old man always says 'Time can waste itself, so no need for you to do it for it. Let's go. You go down there

Georgie, I'm going up that road and Charlie you may as well go up there.' Pointing accordingly in each direction."

"'It's gonna take a couple of hours and then we'll get at it. It's only a fuckin' laugh anyway innit? Oh, and by the way, don't bovver running back to the motor if it starts raining, coz' I have the keys and no-one's stopping till all 600 of those bills have been dropped.' It seems a funny number I know, but of course Vince had ordered 500, paid, and then asked the printer for another ton to help the new business get off the ground, typical."

George paused slightly, and said: "It was quite funny really Steph, how he sort of took to the role of Master and Commander in his stride. We never really questioned his instructions, but they never felt like orders either. He was only 16, but also he never really came across like he thought he should be in charge, it just seemed to happen that way!"

Georgie sighed, finished his tea, picked up my cup and saucer and said:

"And that's about it really, that's how it all started," and then just casually walked into the kitchen and started doing the bloody washing up. I was perplexed and speechless for at least twenty seconds.

"Well, what happened next then?" I exclaimed. "What the fuck happened next George, for fuck's sake, what happened next?" I could not refrain from swearing. I was to find myself using expletives more often nowadays. Mixing with these guys was going to change many of my normal traits in the months to come.

He stuck his head around the corner and with 'the cheekiest grin you've ever sin.'

"Oh, did you wish to hear more about it, it's getting on a bit you know, (looking at his wristwatch) you sure you don't wanna go to the Bingo. There's a Link-Up tonight down the Hippodrome in Middle Street. I can show you exactly where we sold all the gear that we bought that day, whaddayasay?" He sounded like the Lion from the Wizard of Oz this time.

Who is kidding who here? I thought to myself.

"Oh well it's only a laugh, innit?" I assured him, I was going to join him for Bingo. But I needed to go home first and change so said I would meet in 'The Cricketers', as suggested at 6:00pm, for a drink then round the corner for Bingo. As it was 'Eyes Down Look In' for seven o'clock.

I quickly popped into see Grace to let her know everything was okay, and she was so supportive, with that soulful look in her eyes, and just wished me all the best and have a good night.

We met as arranged and once again George surpassed all expectations, as he had made a concerted effort with the old Blazer and flannel trousers, with nice white shirt and tie into the bargain. I had my suspicions though, that his adoring neighbour had pressed and ironed the shirt. I didn't think for a minute, that people actually dressed up like this just for Bingo, but it was within seconds I realised why he had made such a special effort.

"Please let me introduce you to, Bonzo, a good friend of mine and a very good judge of a bit of Myson, various kinds of period furniture and one of the countries leading experts on early Staffordshire Pottery." Georgie smiled at this point in time, just like a kid who has been accidently locked into a sweetshop and no-one else knows about it.

He knew he had my full attention and a knowing grin came across his face. As I offered 'Bonzo' my hand, which he took delicately in his, and proceeded to regally kiss it gently, like he was Charles the bloody second.

“Pleased to meet you young Stephanie. Georgie mentioned you might be able to join us. Glad to make your acquaintance, I’m sure.”

He was definitely a player this one, with his comb over hairstyle, Crombie Coat, Pin Stripe Suit, button down collar with a tie-pin and Liberty Tie. Not for the first time I noticed a sparkling pair of Oxford shoes you could brush your hair in with precision.

All this, just to go to the fucking Bingo! Do me a favour.

We took a seat, and Bonzo picked up on my hesitant nature immediately. I was also waiting to see what sort of character George was introducing me to, and whether or not he had spilled the beans on our little project already, without my knowledge. This character was certainly not cut from the same cloth as most of the other Herberts I had so far come across. He had an air of suave sophistication about him, but in a completely natural and unreserved fashion, dissimilar to the trumped up amateur dramatics I had previously witnessed.

Grace had already pre-empted me to disappointment, and warned me that even though George and I seemed to have a working relationship at this time, I should not place too much faith in one of these Herberts once a few quid was involved.

She had then resorted to the old Fred the Frog and Sid the Scorpion tale, where Sid the Scorpion asks Fred the Frog to give him a lift across the river. Well, first off Fred the Frog says no, because Sid the Scorpion will sting him. Sid the Scorpion says of course I won’t, what do you take me for?

Fred the Frog believes him and agrees to give him a lift, turns out Sid the Scorpion knows about some pretty little froglett on the other side of the river that fancies Fred the Frog, and he can make an introduction.

So, they starts across the river, Sid the Scorpion is not too much of a burden on the back of Fred the Frog and all is going well. Then all of a sudden, half way across the river the Scorpion stings him, and they are both doomed, for evermore, and Davey Jones's Junior's Locker is their only destination, as they fall to the bottom of the riverbed. Fred the Frog says, 'Why the fuck did you do that? You prat, now we are both gonna die'. Sid the Scorpion replies, 'I can't fucking help it, I'm a Scorpion'.

This she told me, was the way of 'Brighton's Knockers' and they just could not help themselves. So just be careful, keep your guard up and be wary, at all times. Always have your guard up, and don't believe for one single solitary moment any single one of 'em. Because for sure, his name is definitely Sid, and he will always, without a second thought, treat you like your name is Fred!

Back to the case in hand.

As nice as 'The Cricketers' was, and still is today, at that time it was not so private. Nowadays they even have the most lavish of private function rooms upstairs 'The Green Rooms' which feels like your own private club in the middle of town, but in them days it was just a Pub in The Lanes.

So, when George started to explain how we met and that we had a little project we were working on, I shied away a bit. This did not go unnoticed, but no harm done. Bonzo suggested getting off so he could get his 'Lucky Table' at 'The Hippodrome' and also see where Tommy Barnes's yard used to be. Straight down the alley by the side of the Pub and then across the road down the next alley, Ship Street Gardens and hey presto we are in Middle Street.

This three-minute walk also included a quick fire History lesson, as the first right, Black Lion Lane was the narrowest lane of them all, measuring just 2ft 10 ins in width, and the next one harboured what used to be Barnes's yard, 'The Coach House', on the corner.

It was actually a former coach house dating back some three hundred years, and will crop up in various tales yet to come your way.

I could say more but will not succumb to the temptation of going off on a tangent on this occasion!

Even I can manage to control myself sometimes.

Once in the Hippodrome, things changed slightly. The place actually had an eerie air of nostalgia about it, without having that horrible musty smell of a building on it's last legs and on the way out, just waiting for the demolition crew to do it's worse.

The Steward welcomed both my suitors by name and took our coats to the cloakroom for us. No sign of a ticket, but that was hardly worth mentioning. They were on their own turf here and nothing needed a second glance.

Word for word dialogue would be far too boring in this sort of instance, so to cut a long story short, we bought our Bingo books, six each for the boys and just three for me.

Before we started playing, George had finished telling me about the first big day on the knocker. I had obviously been gagging to hear about it, so as to finish the story from earlier that day.

George explained, in a secretive whisper that sometimes drove me to distraction and brought on a headache, from the concentration needed to absorb what he was saying:

"So, we're back in Shoreham, had a light lunch and Vince says that we will each take a different Street this time and go pick up the Bills where someone else had dropped. Showing we were no one man band and a different face from earlier in the day. Coz you can bet yer life we had been spotted through the curtains on our first foray."

"If any of us 'Gets In,' we were to just concentrate on the Brass Candlesticks, Fenders and anything else to scrap. It's not like we didn't know what we were up to, but should there be anything we were unsure of, simply tell the person that this was 'Not my area of expertise, but my colleague who is at present on another appointment, locally, would be available very shortly.' This seemed reasonable enough, so off we go. Well, it was un-fuckin-believable, Steph!"

"Within three doors, I had bought: eight pairs of candlesticks for a shilling a pair; two fenders for 12/6 each and twelve copper kettles for four bob apiece."

"On top of that, I had made an appointment for my area manager Horace, to see a lady at number 32 for 2:00pm, with regards to an oil painting and some other various copper and brass items. Back at the motor, Vince had already loaded on 20 pairs of Candlesticks, 7 fenders, some copper kettles and a fucking great big bronze bust of Winston Churchill."

"How the fuck did you get that down the road? I asked him. I just gave Charlie a little whistle, he said. Nice one Charr, you woz bang on it there."

"Charlie had also bought some odds and sods which included some candlesticks, 3 coal-scuttles and 3 copper bed-pans for three bob each. So we was nearly full up already and we'd only been at it for 45 maniacal minutes."

"We decided it was best not to be too greedy and, leave it there. Then I would escort Vince to the lady in question for the arranged appointment. We would arrive on time while Charlie waited in the van. He was quite happy with this. He bought The Evening Argus, early edition, pointing out that 'Garth', on the back page, was in serious trouble with some Germans at the moment. A sly dig at my kid really, but he always was a snidey runt, leave him to it."

"So I knocks the door. When Mrs Haggerty answers the door, I introduce my associate 'Horace' and advise that he would be interested in the picture I had seen earlier. She led him through to the sitting room and he simply turned to me and dismissed me with a wave of his hand, 'My man will wait outside for the time being Madam, whilst we conduct our business, go wait in the vehicle. Thank you Hector. I will call if you are needed. Now Mrs Haggerty, this painting...' A heavy depressed sigh followed by: 'oh dear, is this what all the fuss is about?'"

"I just scarpered and awaited the outcome, feeling a bit foolish for wasting the kid's time. How was I to know the picture was no good? Anyway, we definitely had a fair bit of scrap to be getting on with. (Haggerty was to become one of our secret passwords that indicated a particular situation that no one else would recognise)."

"After about twenty minutes, he stuck his head out of the front window, and sang 'Give a little whistle, that's me' then whistled at me, indicating I should come to the door."

"Just as I got to the door, it swung open and clutching a huge luggage trunk was the lady of the house with beads of perspiration streaming down her cheeks. ' Here you go Hector, cop for this son.'"

"She had a desperate look about her, like she'd just seen a ghost or something, and instantly I recognised, that she couldn't wait to get the thing out of the place."

"Now Stephanie, you know me. I'm not slow on the uptake, so I grabs it with both hands and shot off down the garden path with it. Heavy bastard it was, but there was no time to mess about. Vince follows me down the path with the Painting under one arm and what looked like a thin suitcase under the other."

"'Look lively Georgie-boy. We've got another two trips each and I wanna get away sharpish.' We both loaded up again, as he had said, then sped off down the road without saying a single solitary fucking word. Charlie didn't have a clue what was going on but was just told 'shut'cha mouth,' by his kid brother. We gets to Lancing and Vinnie pulls into the Car Park by the main green and just let's out a huge breath like he'd been diving for pearls or something."

"'Well boys, I think we have just had a blinding day's work. Let's have a butcher's what we got.' Once we had a count up, Charlie and me reckoned it was a good four Barrows' worth of scrap, and asked Vince how much we had laid out and what he reckoned it was worth."

"'Gentlemen, we spent exactly twelve pounds and three shillings before number 32 came into play. Bearing in mind I have made a follow up appointment for further discussions, at that particular address, and there is, for sure, much much more to come out of that fucking door. I reckon that little lot would all scrap for about £16.'"

"'That however, is inconsequential to how things are gonna pan out today lads, have a gander at this lot. Let's all have a butcher's'."

"He dragged the first big trunk out the back of the motor, flips up the lid and there is two fuckin' great shiny Deep Sea Diver's helmets. 'What the fuckin' hell we doing wiv that load of old shit?' asks Charlie. Vince begins to reveal his intentions."

"'Well,' he goes, 'That Johnny Wadey, is no fucking mug. He may be having a laugh at our expense, but we are gonna take a chance and go see this Tommy Barnes bloke and check him out. If I'm not mistaken, we could have a right result here. There's loads more stuff we got out of the old girl's place and plenty more to come if we play our cards right.'"

George then took a big swig of his Beer and carries on:

"Well, we pulls up outside that yard you just seen down Middle Street, and out comes Tommy, about the same size as me, wasn't he Bingo?" Bingo puckered his lips in agreement and nodded, not wishing to interfere with the man in the chair, so to speak.

"Out jumps Vince, shakes his hand and tells him that he and I have some things that may be of interest. Tommy just casually informs us he is always interested in acquiring stock, and if 'The Judge' had sent us he was certainly interested."

"He had a confident way about him did Tommy Barnes, yet still had an that of decorum and a sense of nonchalance that would never cease to amaze me. I loved him from day one. But not in a funny way of course."

I myself already liked the sound of Tommy Barnes, but of course had never heard hide nor hare of the bloke. Such was George's way of involving you and making you feel part of the story. I truly hope that you too my dear reader are being cajoled into this forever captivating and enticing world of what happens next.

"The next ten minutes changed our fucking lives forever. Vince first started trying to bring out a couple of pieces at a time. But Tom was no Toby-jug and demanded, but not in a bullying way mind you, that we should just get everything out and then we could have a proper deal."

"'Come on boys, reverse the motor into my yard and just fucking get it all out and then we'll know where we stand. You buy for cash and so do fucking I, but I'm gonna do you a right favour here, and don't you ever forget it.'"

"He was quite well-spoken, was Tommy Barnes. Charlie chirped up, 'You ain't even seen anyfin' yet.' and that was when Vince slipped him a Ching and told him to fuck off round the corner to ‘The Victory’ in Duke Street, then adding, so that everyone heard, ‘And don’t bovver coming back. We’ll see you later.’”

“An instant respect was confirmed. Tommy took a good look at what we had, then asked Vince what we were looking for. Vince began: ‘I am well aware that the candlesticks are twelve shillings a pair and on that I am happy. The fenders are one pound and sixpence, copper kettles vary on condition at eight shillings each, the coal scuttles are negotiable, bed pans seven and six and the rest of the stuff we will have to talk about. Of course I may not have a great deal of experience in these matters but I have it on good authority that you are a fair man to do business with.’”

“‘Nice one son, I like your style,’ said Tommy with a wry smile. ‘You’ve got the right attitude for this game. Now let me tell you what the price is and what you are going to take, how does that sound, my son.’”

“Vince sort of winced inwardly because he was now dealing in a man’s world and had to show respect, without coming across as a soft touch or on the other hand, in any way intimidated. ‘Go on then, show us your best.’”

“So Tommy begins our education. I’ll tell you what Steph, we should have paid this geezer money for what he showed us that day. But you know what it’s like, if you like someone, you help ‘em, and Tommy instantly liked us, that’s just how it was in them days.”

“So, he starts doing the old circling trick, stroking his chin and rubbing his forehead. A little look here and a little prod there. Very enlightening it was. We would use the same tactics so many more times over the years to come.”

“'Right,’ he says, ‘Candlesticks are ten bob, fenders a nicker, copper kettles seven and six, Coal scuttles two bob. Don’t bother with them again unless they are in mint condition. Them bedpans ain’t too clever at the moment but I’ll still give you ten bob, as a favour.' (Tom always included a favour when he done a deal. Even if it was just one piece, he was always doing you a favour.)"

"'Now, that is just for all that run-of-the-mill crap, that anyone can get, any day of the week. We all know that, don't we?' Yes, we nodded, but not wishing to stop him in full-flow, the same way we didn't wanna be stopped when we was doing it. Respect, see. 'So that, if my maths does not fail me, comes to £33, do you agree?' Vince replied: 'You're ten bob short really, but I think that's alright.' Tommy just grunted a laugh out loud and said he'd play darts for it later."

"Bearing in mind this was twice what we would have got for scrapping the whole lot of it, things were looking good. But we didn't let on our excitement, of course."

"Tommy started again, after indicating to one of his lads, to cart off all the gear. 'Right then, all that other shit over there,' pointing to some brasses, Charlie's contributions and some other stuff, 'Well that can all go back in yer motor and end up down Hicksies scrapyard, or junkyard, whatever you wanna call it. Where it fucking well belongs.'"

"So beginneth the lesson: 'So young Vince, let's have a closer look at the real deal of the day. Now this Bronze, what sort of readies are you looking at?'" George stopped for another slurp, and then continued in a more subdued tone.

"For one of the only times I ever saw Vince hesitate in his whole life. He just sort of froze. I think it was because he knew he was onto a right winner. So he simply said to Tommy, 'Well, I think it is a masterful piece of craftsmanship, worth every bit of whatever you think you can sell it for. Of course I know there are expenses, in running a fine establishment in such a prestigious location such as this, and of course you do need to turn a profit also, plus find wages. Just make me an offer and I'll think about it.'"

"Giving me the all-important wink, that confirmed we were on a winner. Tommy said he would give £80 for the Bronze because it was slightly damaged. Neither of us could see fuck all wrong with it, but as it had cost £4 it was neither here nor there."

"The smudge was of no-one of any consequence to the Art world, but he'd take it anyway, because he liked landscapes with cows in. Cost £6 sold for £25. The trunk containing the helmets was very common but £22 anyway. Here Vince put his foot down and said the Trunk itself had to be worth ten-bob, Tom conceded."

"Then we came to the linen bag of costume jewellery, as Tom referred to it. This would be nice for his two little girls (Delia and Tracey) to play with. For a fiver. Then it came to another little gem: a small mother of pearl inlaid musical jewellery box with a dancing ballerina as the lid was opened. There were a few pieces in it still and Tom said he liked it, and was quite happy to 'Take a Chance' for thirty quid."

"Vince had already casually slipped me the £33, and calmly let Tommy count out the £162 in cash. This made us a fucking pound note short of two hundred fucking quid."

"Vinnie remarked 'It has been a pleasure doing business with you Tom, and I'm sure we will be coming back to see you soon, when we have some more things of interest.'"

"'Before you go,' says Tom, 'come back in here and I'll show you some more of the stuff I can use.' Back we goes and it was like an Aladdin's fucking cave, wiv stuff piled right up to the massive ceiling. 'Anything here you find on your travels I'm interested in, and as you already know, I don't fuck about and I'll give you the money straight away.'"

"Vince and me had a quick shifty and then shot off round the corner to tell Charlie. He was nowhere to be found and the Pub was closed anyway. 'Sod him,' said Vince 'we'll catch him later.'"

George then took a quick look at his watch indicating Bingo was about to begin, which absolutely cattled me. I'm thinking fuck the bloody Bingo. But what could I do?

The caller came out amidst rapturous applause from the players and then all of a sudden I had become invisible and they were both concentrating on the game at hand. Any attempts on my part to hear the rest of the story was met with deep frowns and fingers on lips from the pair of them, plus the loud tut-tut-tuts from neighbouring tables. I was once again left in a state of frustrated anticipation. Oh well, what can you do?

During the first interval I tried to get him to finish how the day ended. But George was having none of it, and then Bonzo started to explain that it wasn't being rude, but if you can't finish what you've started saying, it's best to wait. This totally fell on deaf ears where I was concerned.

I then proceeded to make my excuses and asked George to call me next day and maybe we could have a coffee somewhere to cap off the end of the story.

He was encroached in conversation with a middle-aged woman whilst playing the £200 jackpot fruit machine, and merely nodded nonchalantly towards me as if I was an unwanted nuisance niece he had had to drag along with him, and an obvious burden, so it wasn't really worth it.

I now seemed like a bit of unwanted luggage not worthy of the excess charge, the bastards. Once I stepped out of the Bingo Hall, I headed back towards 'The Cricketers' for a much-needed calming down drink. I suddenly had a surge through my body of complete hypertension, such as never before. How the fuck had I let these two Herberts get into my head so easily? They had no sense of urgency whatsoever. Why was I experiencing this intense feeling of frustration and anxiety?

So as not to be selfish, I am prepared to share this sensation with you, so you will have to wait till the next chapter yourself to see what happened next.

Still, it’s only a laugh anyway innit!

*

5. The New Beginning Part II.

So, that evening did not end particularly well, and despite my constant glancing at the doorway in expectation of George and Bingo making a glorious fun-filled entrance, that was the last I saw of either of them for a good week or so.

Grace tried to comfort me. Saying it would all work out in the end, but as much as anything, I felt a little used. One minute this was the best thing since 'The Rubik's Cube' and the next it was not worth so much as a fucking phone call.

Then comes the guilty truth once again. I'm just getting the old Saveloy, half-portion of chips and a Gherkin from Bardsley's, about 1:00pm on Friday and Roy beckons me to the rear of the counter, where he's frying the fish. He says quietly to me:

"How's Gorgeous George bearing up? What with his Mum an' all."

I replied sheepishly: "Oh, you know Roy. As best as can be expected. You know he's an old trooper, is Georgie"

"Yeah I know. Well be sure to wish him all the best, from all of us won't cha?"

"Course I will mate. Thanks ever so much. I'll be sure to tell him this afternoon when I see him."

I could not eat more than four chips, a single attempt at the Saveloy and Gherkin combo, one more chip and that was it. I threw the lot in a nearby bin and headed for 'The Bat & Ball' to try and blot out the overwhelming feeling of guilt and selfishness.

He only lived five poxy minutes away from me, literally just around the bloody corner.

But me, rather than take the professional approach and pursue my subject, I had just acted like a spoilt brat and expected him to come crawling back to me with remorse and apologies for bad manners or something. It hadn't occurred to me, or entered my stupid head for one selfish second, that he might have some problem of his own or commitment, preventing him from contacting me. After all, I was in control and anyway after all I had his phone number didn't I? Now I'm starting to repeat myself twice in the same bloody sentence.

The large Gin & Tonic I ordered, did not touch the sides and whilst ordering the second, a familiar voice, behind me said:

"There she is, my beautiful Stephanie, she means the world to me. Byron couldn't say it better, I must be a poet and didn't fuckin' know it. How are you my little darlin'?"

There he was, sitting with another distant but familiar face. Just one glance and I immediately recognised the person I had first clapped eyes on outside the diner a few weeks ago. Totally dishevelled, unshaven, false teeth left in the jar on the bedside table, stains down his shirt, and his hair unkempt and all over the place.

Now I'm no hard nut or softy so to speak, and my feelings are pretty much in control, as a rule. But, when I heard that voice, turned around and saw him like that, I just melted. My knees went slightly weak, my cheeks flushed and I burst into floods of uncontrollable tears, running into his arms as he stood up lovingly, to greet me, as another famous Vinnie would say 'It Was Emotional.'

*

It turns out that his Mum, Violet, had had a fatal heart attack on the Monday morning, while doing her regular cleaning job at the bookies down Islingword Road.

She had led a great life, and had been a staunch supporter of Jumble Sales at the local Churches for years, and basically was one of the characters of the Hanover Area, as it is now known.

She and a couple of friends, Mrs Marshall and Mabel Hussey, who both lived in Grant Street, had shared 12 different cleaning jobs for some 35 years. Just independent small business's, like Bookmaker's, Dentist, Doctor, Accountants and Solicitor's, in the old days it was all like that and they just took their money out of the petty cash.

Of course they always kept an eye on tea, coffee and sugar supplies and made sure there was a fresh pint of milk everyday, keeping the milkman on his toes. That's how everyone got them type of people, in the first place. If you needed a professional person you could bet one of your mates' Mum's did the cleaning at one of their offices and so the introduction was simple.

They were all up and out by 5:30am and also had a system where: if one of them was sick, or unavoidably had to be somewhere else, one of the others would cover and just give them their money. This was done without so much as a second thought.

This was especially handy when in the mid sixties, Mabel said she had been offered the opportunity to go on Holiday with her Son Alan and his wife Val's Family to Pontin's on The Isle of Wight.

For a whole week would you believe?

The other two insisted she went, as prior to this they all refused to go too far because of their job commitments.

Imagine that today, coming back from a week's Holiday and your two mates had done all your work and handed you your wages for it!

George did say, however, that there was an air of mystery about what was going to happen to the property up Scotland Street.

Mum had kept all that sort of business to herself over the years, and no one could make head nor tail of who actually owned the building. Scotland Street was one of those that had 3 storeys one side and 2 storeys the other, why the fuck that made a difference; George could not for the life of him fathom out. It seemed also that Violet, Mrs Marshall (who's son Phil was later to join the ranks of 'Brighton's Knockers') and Mabel had all signed at the same time, with the same Landlord and were trying to find out what the situation was upon death, as his Mum was 'The First To Go' as they put it.

I assured him that I personally knew somebody that would without a shadow of a doubt, be able to clear every tiny little detail out for him, at no cost whatsoever, and would sort out all the deeds and ownership rights so that 'Everyone got sorted out.' What such a bold and forthright statement I was ever to make, live to regret, and find impossible to live up to.

I was officially introduced to Vince at this time, as he was the one consoling George at such an important time. I should have known, who else could it be?

Then we were joined briefly by a younger slimmer looking Vince called Harry, who was extremely polite but just popped in to deliver the news that the Cars and Flowers had all been taken care of for next Tuesday.

When George asked how much he owed him, he just shrugged his shoulders and insisted that you don't talk about money when there are Ladies present, and it had all been taken care of and not to worry about it. Just as he was leaving, after getting fresh drinks, he added:

"We thought 'The Horse & Groom' would be appropriate for the afterwards, does that sound alright Georgie?" George nodded, and added that his Mum used to do the cleaning there and we may as well get pissed with familiar faces in familiar surroundings.

George had livened up a bit, no doubt the few pints and whisky chasers having the desired effect, and undoubtedly very little food in his system, but that's only to be expected under the circumstances, and he suggested a farewell lunch. Vince took charge, and advised it would be a much better idea to go home, get a bit of shut-eye and freshen up for an early dinner somewhere later.

I could see how he had the unspoken authority of years gone by and I automatically agreed. He cordially invited me to join them, which I accepted, and he said I would be picked up with George at 6:30pm prompt, at George's flat, if that was okay.

Vince advised: "The driver will know where to go, and we shall decide on what and where to dine, while having a nice glass of wine." Georgie and I stared at each other and cried: 'He's a poet and don't even fuckin' know it' then burst out laughing, ending in tears, and agreed too see each other later on as planned.

Things were back on track!

I told Grace what had happened, and she was over the moon and wished me well for the evening, but advised me to take it easy on the wine early on, as I had obviously had a few already and not used to drinking at lunchtimes, 'like that uncouth mob'. Duly noted, I brewed up some fresh coffee in my new essential kitchen appliance, the percolator, and had a couple of sandwiches before a long soak in the bath.

*

George was well spruced up when I arrived but I declined the glass of wine and just had a nice refreshing glass of orange juice, in a lovely crystal goblet.

“I bought those for my Mum down in Cannes many years ago,” pointing to the now filled glass cabinet.

“They was quite expensive at the time and I was worried sick they might break. But the girl I was with at the time, was a bit of a stickler for detail and made sure they were wrapped up proper, in some newly invented stuff called ‘Bubble Wrap’. I’m sure they charged a fortune just for wrapping it, but my Mum loved ‘em. Do you know what, I can’t even ever remember when they got used, cos they was only for special occasions.”

There was a toot outside and the Taxi was bang on time. When asking the driver where we were going, he just touched his lips and continued. George shrugged and said:

“Who am I to argue?”

We arrived at The Grand Hotel. George offered the driver a fiver (Poet Know it.) he simply advised that it had already been well taken care of. We were then told to go straight through to the Piano Bar, where we were expected. Very posh.

In we go, and there to meet us was the first large gathering of ‘Brighton’s Knockers’, to which I was to become witness.

I was introduced gradually. Some I had already met: Bingo and his wife Tina; Harry and Pat Nearly; Vince and Trinny Nearly; Ricky Opendaws and his missus Trixie; Long Harry; Bubbles and Beverley; Fizzy and Powders.

These were all work colleagues, who got their nick-names in the simplest of ways.

Fizzy was always drinking cans of coke, when not *actually* drinking that is. Powders surname was Beecham, once the nickname was certified people tended to forget the original name altogether.

Then there was Micky 'Cheatin' Meechin with his luscious platinum blonde girlfriend Wizzy. If I was ever to bat for the other side she would be first in line, she just oozed sex appeal (you can guess where the name came from, she was already going 60 miles an hour).

Then we had Giles Capshaw with wife Delia who turned out to be Tommy Barnes' daughter.

With Georgie and I, this came to 19 people.

Then in comes Paul Desjarlais and his wife Annie. Paul apologised profusely and then proceeded to look at Bubbles and says 'It's your fucking fault anyway you fat fucking runt, you told me the fuckin' Metropole.' Bubbles apologised, then sniggered, indicating he had done it on purpose. The first of many sniggers to be endured that night.

Of all the people I have ever met, Paul was by far the most foul-mouthed fucker (hark at me) you'd ever come across. But it never felt once like he was being rude. It was just how he spoke. I couldn't comprehend how he ever made a living on 'The Knocker'.

We sat there chatting for an hour and I was beginning to wonder if we would ever eat at all, then Vince looks at his watch, and declares:

"Well I am really glad that everyone has turned up, so I suggest we make our way to Eaton Manor, where we have a table booked for eight o'clock if that suits everyone. Or we can just stroll along to Preston Street and have a Chinese where the China Garden has three tables waiting. Who fancies what?"

Everybody was as polite as the next and wasn't bothered one way or the other. Then Harry stands up and says:

"I think Georgie should decide, as this little soiree is after all, in his Mum's honour."

George looked at me, and I just went as red as a beetroot, so he announced:

"Let's keep it informal and go round the Tiddlywinks."

"That's fine," said Vince, "Give me a moment while I just go and call Eaton Manor and change the reservation to Sunday Lunch. Can you just sort out that bar-bill for me Mr Meechin? I'll catch up with you all shortly."

It was only a few minutes walk to The China Garden at the bottom of Preston Street. As we entered, the Lady Manager greeted every single one of them by name.

We had half the Restaurant roped off and our own team of waiters at our beck and call. At no stage whatsoever did anyone show anything less than total respect or courtesy to any of our servers. Nor did we have to wait for more than thirty seconds for another drink or extra portion of the excellent food.

They were all well familiar with the menus, and it was only I that actually looked at it. Realising I might be a little out of my depth, I simply resigned to the fact I would be more than content with whatever was put in front of me and just went with the flow.

It was, without a doubt, a fantastic night and everyone was clearly sympathetic to George's situation. Violet to them also, was

'The First One To Go.' Referring of course to all their Mums. This was clearly an auspicious occasion.

There were an awful lot of stories and escapades talked about that night, but for some reason, I had kind of switched off. Georgie on more than one occasion asked me if I was okay and I assured him everything was fine, but of course it wasn't. I was beginning to doubt my ethics, on the whole scenario, and feeling like some sort of undercover snitch that would eventually let everyone down.

When it was time to depart, all three tables asked for the bill, yet the Bill was presented very discreetly to Vince, who simply turned it over and reached in his inside pocket, like he was going to take out a ballpoint pen.

He placed six hundred pounds in the saucer without any recognisable facial expression whatsoever, (fuck playing him at cards I thought) then beckoned to the headwaiter and said:

"Any chance of a few more of those after dinner mints please Peter? He's a blinding little snooker player that Pete. I won that money down Chick's the other day by laying him against that flash git Dicky Underhand at three to one. It's only a fucking laugh anyway, innit."

When we started to go home, each and every one of them came to our table and shook Georgie's hand, then thanked Vince for inviting them. I noticed they all pressed some money into Vince's palm as they did it. This gave that feeling of solidarity, before they either strolled off or got into their Taxi.

All except Micky Meechin of course. When he shook his hand, Vince stood back indignantly and just started bollocking him, saying quietly:

"Don't be so fucking stupid, you soppy little prat. You got the drinks at the Hotel you sausage. Put your money away, it's no good here, me old mucker." Then hugged him like a scene from fucking Spartacus.

It was quite tearful, where the hell is all this emotion coming from? I thought to myself.

I had enjoyed a fantastic night out, in the true style of 'Brighton's Knockerboys', and could honestly say loved every minute of it. Yet now there was still this little niggling of the morality of it all, but it was just a passing thought, and I was soon to grow out of it.

At a later date both George, most of the boys, and Grace, all just wished me all the best with the writing project, and asked only that I tell the truth, as I saw it, and didn't knowingly shop anyone.

To top it off whilst in the cab home, George started to quietly sob. What the fuck's going on now I thought. After grilling him to tell me what was wrong, he put his hand in his pocket and pulled out a wad of notes that totalled £240. They had all bunged him, (without me, the supposed 'little don't miss a trick merchant' noticing) and he was pretty much emotionally drained. A cuddle ensued.

He insisted on dropping me off first, and promised to call me the next day to meet and finish the rest of the 'Big First Day' story, and then after the funeral we could get back to our project. I agreed and couldn't wait till morning to let Grace know how things had gone.

This was not to be as pleasant as I anticipated. Once I explained how things had gone Grace was no longer my partner in crime, but I'll have tell you about that later

George, called me as promised, by nine on Saturday morning and we arranged for a light lunch and drinks in the 'The Horse &

Groom'. This also meant he could check everything was in place for the funeral on Tuesday, two birds and all that.

He waited at the end of my terrace, outside Alexandra Antiques where he was chatting with Abdul the proprietor, introduced me, and at 11:30am we took the stroll up Islingword Road at a nice steady pace. Just the two stop offs, first at the newsagents for 'The Sporting Life' and then at the Butcher's to buy some nice sausages and make sure Clive knew about the Funeral arrangements on Tuesday. His Mum had only shopped and cleaned there for sixty fucking years plus, he mentioned under his breath.

"Soo," he started, once we had ordered drinks. "We'll have a look at the sarnies in a minute, eh?" I nodded in agreement.

"I have come prepared for this Steph, as I know you have been very patient, but what can you do? Life takes it's prisoners from time to time and there ain't much we can do about that, now is there?" Another agreeable nod.

"Did you enjoy that last night? It was really nice wasn't it?" I'm now feeling like the proverbial nodding dog, but I did not wish to get into any conversation, just the completion of the bloody story, from nine bleedin' days ago.

At this rate I'll be drawing my pension before any literary royalties come my way.

He begins: "That's right, we've copped for all the readies. Charlie is nowhere to be found, probably coz he copped for an unexpected ching and thinks he has got away with the rest of the day."

"So then Vince drives to Hicksies yard and offloads all the crap Barnes'y wasn't interested in. This still comes to eight quid and we split it down the middle."

“Vince just reckoned if his brother was too bloody lazy to even sit in the motor and wait, he could go fuck himself.”

“So, we go looking for Charlie, finds him in the betting office in Southover Street and have a semi barney as to why he hadn’t hung about. ‘Well, you larey little runt, if you think you’re gonna start telling me what to do, like your soppy little lackey here, you got another think coming. I’ve got a good mind to take you outside and smash that fucking great nose of yours right across your boat.’”

“‘Fine, fine, fine.’ says Vince. ‘I now consider you no longer part of the ‘Brighton Knockers’ firm. You do your thing and I’ll do mine, and by the way, here is your share of the day’s work. Don’t ever say you never got paid, coz you just fucking paid yourself all you are worth.’”

“Then he steers him £60, and Charlie is left wondering what he has just done to himself. But of course he was never to admit this.”

“As we walked out, Vince said to me, ‘You know what Georgie Boy? That may well have been the best deal of the whole fucking she-bang. Now, my Charlie ain’t the hardest grafter, but I do trust him I suppose. But I think we’ll be better off without him for the time being.”

“Look it’s four o’clock, let’s park the motor up, find a boozer where we can get a drink and I will tell you what I have in mind.’”

“Never one to shirk a drink I was all for it. So we knock up Ollie Kenny in ‘The Horse & Groom.’ There was a few fella’s playing darts as it happens, so it was no inconvenience. We plotted up in the corner and Vince tells me the plan.”

“‘The fing is Georgie, that Mrs Haggerty, well, she is planning to move to Plymouth. Her daughter’s husband has just got a promotion in the Royal Navy to Captain of a Frigate or something, and that means much more money and away at Sea for longer periods."

"Haggerty's old man is long dead, she has trouble with the stairs, hates living on her own because her son has also just got married and her daughter has asked her to go down there and live wiv them in their nice new big house.'"

"'Her only trouble is, she don't know what to do with all her stuff. As it stands I have told her to contact young Tommy Healey who does house clearances very reasonably, and he is a mate of mine and will give her a good price.'"

"'I have spoken to Tone and told him to give her a nice little quote around thirty quid, but the thing is, now we have got this Tommy Barnes on the firm, and having seen some of the gear he buys, I reckon we can clear her out and make a fucking fortune, just the two of us. I have arranged to introduce Tommy, and while we do that you can finish picking up them flyers we knocked out today.'"

"Well we had certainly made a good start, so I agreed didn't I Steph? So off we goes on the Friday, and it went pretty much the same, loads of the same stuff, plus a few other nick knacks of no particular value. The thing was though, we was now buying all sorts of stuff without having a fucking clue if it was worth anything or not, the motto was: 'If they don't want it, we do; even if, we ain't got a clue. Poet. Know It."

"Vince was quite happy with the Mrs Haggerty situation. Healey offered to clear the house, lock stock and barrel, apart from any sentimental items that would be packed and separated for her in tea chests, and would only charge £35."

"We had lunch, then Vince went for the kill, off he went to number 32, and twenty minutes later came towards me like a two armed fucking bandit (arms in and out, clapping and rubbing his hands together with his eyes spinning with £ signs in 'em like a cartoon character from Looney Tunes, and the thrusting back and forth of the hips)."

"'That's it my son, that's it. We are now officially in the house clearance business. I have just confirmed with Mrs Haggerty, that we will clear everything out of the gaff tomorrow and have paid in full for all the contents, the grand sum of twenty pounds.'"

"I had to scratch my head in puzzlement. I mentioned Tom Healey was gonna charge to take it away, so why was we paying? But Vince was delirious with excitement."

"'Don't worry about that me old cocker, the stuff in that drum is gonna make us very very flush by the end of the weekend.' This obviously inferred that lunchtime in the pub Saturday was out of the frame, and any chance of the bookies or drinking club was highly unlikely."

"Getting back to Barnes's yard was tentative to say the least. For some reason Vinnie had it in his head that it may have been a one off, and was still wary that Jonny 'The Judge' Wadey was getting us at it."

"But as God is my judge it worked out just as profitable, it gets boring quoting exact amounts, but the long and the short of it was, we carved up £140 after X's, and Tommy agreed to lend us his Luton Van, with a driver the next day."

"Once Vince had described to him what was coming his way, he started doing the two armed bandit as well, which I must say was slightly disconcerting coz he had a dodgy eye into the bargain, oh well, you know what they say!"

"So, the next day being Saturday, we sets off for Shoreham again, in all my life I had been there twice and now three times in one bleedin' week."

"Sure as nine pence, Mrs Haggerty was waiting at her doorstep. In we steamed. There was tables and chairs; great big mirrors; long case clocks; mantle clocks; brass beds in all four bedrooms with chests and wardrobes that weighed a fucking ton and half. Card tables; dressing tables with mirrors, well I won't even bother going on about it, but we just kept loading up till the Luton was chocka."

"The driver Sammy made me look like a bloomin amateur when it came to stacking the gear in the motor. But to be fair, we was learning so many different skills now, that it was just second nature and pure instinct to watch someone else do it properly."

"That way we could do it ourselves later on when needed 'A proper education in all things necessary,' as Vince put it."

"One o'clock and Tommy Barnes was waiting in the yard for us and instructed the same thing as before, 'just unload it boys and we'll take it from there.' It was a really nice set up, as once the motor was reversed in the yard, no nosy fucker had a Danny what was going on."

"Vince studied Tommy for five minutes, then declared: 'You know what Mr Barnes, Georgie here and I have been slogging our absolute bollocks off this morning, and I must say Sam there is a credit to himself and you. Coz he has had us earning our money that's for sure.'"

"'Now, if it's okay with you, we are going up those two lanes adjacent to your yard to 'The Cricketers' for some light refreshment and will return in one hour.'"

"'Unless of course you come and find us first. I hold you in high esteem and do not think for one minute that you will try and cheat us out of what we are entitled to. Now how does that sound?'"

"Stephanie, it was pure genius. That Tommy Barnes couldn't believe his ears. Never before had anyone shown such respect and trust, so he just waved his hand and told us to carry on, and for sure he would come over and join us once the new stock was logged."

"While we was having a pint I asked Vince how much he reckoned the load. He thought in the region of £220-240, at which I laughed. So he's gone to me, 'Alright then clever bollocks, what do you reckon?'"

"'Lucky to split hundred quid' I said. 'But before you start trying to get me to take my share now, and buy me out, I will go with your gut instinct, bow down and respect your opinion, now get me anuvver fuckin' drink, ya tight arsed git.'"

"A couple of other likely lads popped in, Perry Bowels and his brother Jimmy. They were always up for a laugh and any little deal they could get involved in. Perry was fine to deal with and would in later years do plenty with us. In fact, he actually ended up with Tommy Barnes yard for a few years."

"Jimmy on the other hand, was granite, and there was always something wrong with anything you tried to sell him: a scratch here; a chip there; not sure of the signature. Anyway, he was always a last resort I suppose. So you was already fed up with looking at the gear at that stage and ended up taking below the odds whatever he offered you, and therefore giving him too good a deal."

"Perry was just telling us about the raw deal he got from the judge when they nicked him for fighting earlier in the year in 'The Mods and Rockers' riots on the Seafront."

"'There we woz', he explained with the proverbial pointy finger, 'Right outside here, just opposite Michael Norman's shop opposite over there. We woz chasing some of them wankers from Tooting, who right fancied themselves.'"

“'Then all of a sudden out of fuckin’ nowhere comes half a dozen chicken-shit coppers who suddenly fink that some order needs to be put in place. I would ’a got out of it wiv my old man who’d told me keep out of trouble, but then, lo and bloody behold, in Wonder-fuckin’-ful Wednesday Night’s Evening orrible Argus there’s only a poxy picture of me running down the road there right out-soppy-side, look right out there, do me a fucking favour. Abso-fuckin-lutely marvellous, it was the paddy wagon for me again, and I never got close to securing the prize from that lovely little Gina that I’ve had me eye on for ages.’”

“‘I thought it was gonna be my lucky weekend didn’t I, fat fucking chance. Still it’s only a fucking laugh anyway in’nit?’”

“They’d kept him banged up for two days and then he got fined a tenner for his trouble, diabolical fuckin’ liberty. The boys made their polite excuses when Tommy Barnes came in, just short on the hour.”

“I asked what he wanted to drink and he said he didn’t drink till after he finished work. ‘So just get me a pint of John Courage Best Bitter for now.’”

“His opening gambit was classically scripted: ‘Well I’m sorry Boys but I’ve got some dodgy news for you.’”

“Here we go, both of us looked at each thinking the same dreaded thought. We are about to get stitched up.”

“‘Look, it’s like this, the Banks are closed as you know, and so I’m not in a position to give you all the money that I reckon the parcel is worth.’ With bated breath, neither of us cracked a note. ‘So, if it’s alright, I’ll give you £400 now and the other £150 on Monday, how’s that?’”

“We both kept our cool, but on this occasion I jumped in and advised that this would suit our purpose, but would it be possible to borrow the Luton again tomorrow to finish the job off. 'Sure' said Tom, 'As long as you look after Sammy for me. He'll probably pick you up. I don't do Sundays. Sorry again about the readies, but if I give it all to you now, I won't have any where near enough to get me through the weekend. You do understand, don't you? Oh yeah, and if you think any of the rest of the stuff, might be any good to me, just leave it on the motor and we'll sort it out Monday, how's does that suit you boys?'"

"Well, as he left us, we both just looked at each other with sheer delight. Vince popped into the yard to arrange the pick up in the morning and slipped Sammy an extra fiver, he had certainly earned it and would get even more tomorrow if things went all to plan."

"Next day, off we go again. We only had the attic to clear and maybe a few bits in the shed. Vince had got his kid brother Harry to come along as Mrs Haggerty had no idea what was up there, so the littl'un would be handy for getting up there. What might be in the shed was a mystery. As we pulled up outside, Vince went ashen. I looked over and there sat a distraught and dishevelled Mrs Haggerty, crying uncontrollably with her neighbour alongside cuddling her trying to console her."

"'What's going on here then?' I said. 'Leave this to me Vince, I'll sort it.' Up I goes and as I get closer, poor old Mrs Haggerty looks up at me, looking an awful lot older than she did yesterday. 'What's up my little darlin'?' I says to her. 'What's going on?'"

"'Well, the thing is, I got so carried away, ordering you all about yesterday, that I forgot to ask you to leave one of the beds. I had to sleep on the floor last night and when I got up this morning I couldn't even find the kettle to make a cup of tea. Oh my God, what have I done?'"

"At this point Vince slides up beside me and says 'Oh come on Mrs Haggerty, don't be silly, we will put you up in a nice Hotel tonight, you're off to your Daughters on Tuesday for a visit, so we will take care of everything for you till then.' She protested that there was no way she could accept such a kind offer, but we insisted. Anyway we had all this gear still to get out, and didn't have time for all this drama."

"Harry was straight up in the loft and all we heard was 'Cor blimey look at that, Cor blimey look at that.'"

"'Come on then Harry, what's up there? Get it down will you, don't hang about, get on with it, come on.' Vince would not let up for one second, poor little sod, he didn't have a chance. Anyway, after about all of two minutes Harry sticks his head out of the hatch and says 'Cor blimey you should see what's up 'ere.'"

"'You silly little git, that's what we fuckin' well brought you for. Now stop prattling on, like a silly little tart and start passing it down,' shouts Vince. First off was a big box of ship's lanterns, then a ship's bell with all the relevant stand and fixings in a sack, then about six Barometers, ten copper bedpans, about ten copper kettles."

"'Do you wanna make a cuppa now Mrs H?' cried Vinnie laughing out loud."

"There must have been twenty paintings. Now as everything came down, I sprinted to the top of the stairs, Vince ran down and along the corridor to the front door and Sam started loading the van. Then came four great big boxes of china, Harry was doing brilliantly (eventually making three full sets of Royal Doulton) a few vases, and five small Bronze statues of Horses."

"Then we had four boxes of train sets, five big boxes of Dinky toy cars and a load of Artists stuff like plain canvases, brushes, oil paint, brushes and easels."

"All four of us did a quick two-armed bandit impression and then it was out to the shed. Vince popped next door for about five minutes, had a word with Mrs Haggerty then joined us in the garden."

"It was very reminiscent of the shed up Kemp Town last week, so it was full steam ahead, and fortunately there was a wheelbarrow to help with loading it all up."

"We had things all under control when Vince, all of a sudden, hit on the idea of taking Mrs Haggerty to Sunday Lunch of all things. I thought it was a waste of valuable time, but Vince knew what he was up to and we certainly hadn't wasted this Sunday morning. Vince asked Mrs Haggerty to call a Taxi and Sammy followed in the Luton with Harry."

"It was along to 'The Amsterdam', and we all had a very pleasant and civilised lunch. Harry absolutely loved it, as he was only just 13 and had never eaten anywhere other than school or indoors. He still claims it was one of the best meals he ever ate to this day, you ask him."

"The departure was the key to this call as far as Vince was concerned. He could make out we had booked somewhere and leave it to her, or just pay wherever she wished to go. The most important thing though, was to not let her see her beloved home of some forty years be stripped of it's soul and resemble a ramshackle hollow shell unfit for habitation."

"In the end there wasn't much we could do about it, we decided, so we just ordered a cab and went back to number 32."

"As we pulled up, Vince announced: 'Do you know what Mrs Haggerty? This house looks like it has had it's day. I think you are making a brave and courageous decision in moving down to Plymouth. I am sure you will be ever so happy with your daughter, and I'm very glad to have helped you take the giant steps you needed to, so as to make it all become a reality.' He then kissed her on the cheek, adding 'Wherever you wish to stay for the next couple of days we will gladly help towards the cost, where would you like to go?'"

"'Oh, thank you Hector and you Horace, it is very kind of you, but I think I will just stay with Mildred and Jack, next door for a couple of nights. She has made up the spare room and then it is all still familiar surroundings for me. I hope you don't mind, do you?'"

"'Of course not sweetheart, whatever makes you happy, bye bye now.' and away we went! Vinnie had sown the seeds when he popped next door of course. What sort of neighbours in those days would not comply with the suggestion that she needed people she knew at these precious times."

"Vintage Vince, and he knew it. He was giggling all the way home. At least till Lancing when all of a sudden there was a bang and Sam had to pull over near Lancing Green car park, exactly where we had stopped the other day."

"It didn't seem a problem to Sammy, he was a driver after all, and it's all part of the game. But once he had the driver's side back wheel off the ground, it was not so simple. We all had a go, but the nuts were rusted to fuck and weren't going anywhere. There was a Setyres place just 50 yards away but it was Sunday, and no-one worked Sundays except men of the cloth and Barmaids."

"'Hold on,' said Vince, 'I wonder...?' and off he goes to the pub at the bottom of the High Road: 'The Three Horseshoes'. Five minutes later out he comes with two blokes. They walk straight up to the motor and start getting to work."

"They both worked at the tyre place, and Vince had bet them £2 they couldn't get the wheel off his motor. They were experienced enough and once they got the first nut off it was plain sailing. They were well happy with a nicker each, and we were all as happy as four pigs in shit."

“As we drove back to the yard, where the van and it’s cargo would be safe, suddenly Vince starts singing:

‘Three wheels on my wagon and I’m still Rollin' along,

them Nearly Boys have captured me,

but I’m still Knockin' them doors,

singin’,

a Higgerty, HAGGERTY, Hoggarty High,

us Nearly Boys never say die,

you can catch us Knockin and singin a song,

stick wiv us and you’ll never go wrong!’”

“What a way to spend a Sunday. I mentioned that maybe we might have Monday off, but the answer was simple, we still had money to pick up, get sorted on this gear with Tommy, then scrap the rest down Hicksies.”

“‘Mind you,’ said Vinnie, ‘I fancy we might have a couple of days off midweek and let the world know we are here,’ and in his familiar Foghorn Leghorn style, cried, ‘Whaddayasay?’”

“The next day, we gets to the yard and waits for Tommy Barnes. Sammy made us tea and thanked us for the Cockle. Barnes’y came in with a bit of a hangover but once he saw the stuff he soon cheered up.”

“‘I think you Boys are going to be quite successful at this game. You don’t ponce about with the prices, which is always good, once they start trying to graft me for every shilling I gets fed up, I don’t need the aggro. You seem quite trustworthy and you ain’t scared of actually doing a bit of graft and working for a living. You'd be surprised how many idiots I have to put up with. They think I am here to give them a living. In fact you are like a breath of fresh air, the pair of ya.'"

"'Right, let's get down to business. You know I can't be arsed with all that brass and copper shit, so that can go in your motor, but you knew that anyway didn't you?' We agreed without uttering a word. 'Now these pictures, I am gonna get someone to look at these for us. What I mean is, I could just offer you a fiver each and call it a day, but I fancy they might be a bit better than that. So if you don't mind leaving them with me for the time being, that's fine with me. But, if you want to take 'em, by all means please yourself.'"

"Well this seemed fair enough, and as he had gone to them first it, made sense to go along with him or he might just say take everything back and we didn't have a Danny about all this stuff."

"'Right', he began, 'I'm not your Dad. But if you do as your told and pay attention, today is gonna be your lucky day. It's not just the gear, it's the people, and I like you two. Most prats would have left little Sam stranded yesterday but you sorted it out and I respect that.'"

"'Now, we've done the pictures. China, Royal Doulton, not very pretty but decent condition, £25 a set. Bronzes, quite nice, a tenner each. Train Sets and Toy Cars, got a buyer for them, so I'll give you £60."

"The artists stuff I'm gonna keep hold of, just in case, as I suspect, it was used to paint some of the pictures. Therefore, if any of em' need restoring: the right age and shade of colours is already here, plus the same brushes make the world of difference."

"Some of the bedpans and a few of the kettles young Sam has pointed out to me can also be kept here, let's say another £45. The Bell has all the right attachments and good nick £50, and £50 the lanterns. That's £320, plus the £150 from Saturday, is £470 lads. Shall we say, don't be dirty at twelve-thirty?'"

"We were certainly not going to argue with that. Straight down to Hicksies and unloaded all what we now referred to as 'the crap'. That still came to £14."

"Then along to the Café, where we proudly presented 'Judge Widdy' with three crispy five pound notes."

"Then bought everyone else that was present, that wanted one mind you, the breakfast special of the day, which was if I remember rightly, two poached eggs and beans on toast with a cup of tea. Me and Vinnie enjoyed ours more than most, on that joyful and memorable occasion."

"Johnny Widdy was well chuffed, and said that if we needed any stuff looking at, we could always ask him. Vince immediately told him: we still had a Lady's Perfumery and Manicure Set in a leather case; a load of pocket watches and a big bag of jewellery that we had forgotten to show Barnes'y."

"The pictures by the way, turned out to be fakes, but very good ones, and Tom put them in the Auction Rooms. They went for an average £14 each so our share was still another £120 after commission."

"I had pretty much lost count of how much we were getting, but Shirley was certainly happy I can tell you. I had been to 'The Pie Shop' up St James's Street a couple of times on me way home for a couple of Beano's and Steak & Kidney Family size pies, along with lovely bunches of flowers on a daily basis, not a bad habit to adopt, so things were going well on the home front."

"I am sure I must have got quite pissed more than once that week, but nothing springs to mind, and that my little darling

Stephanie, completes the real story about how we started the great era of 'Brighton's Knockerboys'."

We had finally got there, it had taken what seemed like absolute months, but with all the drinking, interfering and at first, hesitancy on both our parts, plus the untimely death of his Mum of course. George and I felt we might just have the foundation to continue with this project, now it was up to me to try and put something together for him as best I could.

I wished him farewell and all the best for the Funeral on Tuesday, and he looked a bit fazed.

"What's up?" I asked.

Assertively he replied; "Well you must realise: you are invited to Sunday Lunch at Eaton Manor, after what happened last night. If you don't come to Violet's send off, it's gonna look terrible. Whaddayasay?"

I just nodded of course and agreed to meet him at 'The Montpelier', Upper North Street, for 12:30pm, and would it be okay to bring a pal, as it didn't seem proper for me to never have anyone else with me. George agreed that this was the best way to go, but assured me everything would be taken care of. To this I now made the exception, and told him to be sure to allow me to at least buy one round of drinks, as I did not wish to come across as a ponce. He agreed to this also, but I didn't believe him for a second.

*

Of course there are many other versions of how 'Brighton's Knockers' got started. Coco Collins with Brother Bertie and their little crew, all enjoyed peddling their wares on Brighton Beach. The classic 'Eachy Peachy Sixpence Eachy' was first announced by that little gang, along with 'Choc Ice, Choc Ice,' and get 'Yer Muvver a Mivvi,' were all very popular cries.

The ice-creams were usually pilfered in a professional manner by tempting the shopkeeper to check the out-the-back freezer and they were willing to buy in bulk, the only thing was: to nick everything in the cooler and scarper. Not being dummies, they would cry desperation stakes later and return with the appropriate funds. You can now guess where the saying, 'Yeah I Should Fucking Coco!' comes from.

Of course all the boy's back in those days had a 'Pedlar's License', but even to this day it does not allow anyone in possession of a License to sell perishable goods, so basically they were all flaunting this rule on a regular basis with whatever goods they had purloined for the day.

The other golden rule was that they should be constantly on the move, adhered to on the beach but forgotten when plotted up with a barrow. The License of today stipulates blatantly that the seller is not allowed to just go ten yards up the road when told to move on, and non-perishables only can be sold, no change there then!

Others claim it is down to the fact that the new lightweight sewing machines, by Singer, were to blame. As back in the day all the old ones that weighed a ton, were right good for scrap and henceforth had to be eradicated from every single gaff they could get in.

As it was very rare for the Lady of the house to be helped with any chores in the household they jumped at the chance, usually with the promise of a blinding discount at the nearest department store to have a modern sewing machine in stock. These would have included locally Hanningtons, Hills of Hove and Debenhams in that era, in those times each different Town would have it's own long running Family business which operated stores of 'Grace Brothers, Are You Being Served' stature.

There are of course a few other trailblazers that put their oar in to try and claim their own part in Brighton's Knockerboy folklore but at the end of the day no-one can truly be recognised as the first. So for the time being this piece of literature stands alone.

One things for sure, Stephanie Marchant, was most certainly the first one to write three books about it all !

*

6. Sunday Lunch Wiv 'Brighton's Knockers' & 'Bye Bye Vye'.

I checked in with Grace that evening and we decided to invite one of my more vague, money-minded (nee grabbing, to be more precise) and flighty friends, Louise to accompany me. She was always up for a free lunch, and wouldn't be too interested in why I was associating with such people, as long as she didn't have to part with any cash.

Now, this may seem slightly mercenary, but there are plenty of girls out there who never expect to pay-up or put-out. As long as their hair and make-up are above average, they feel it is their privilege as long as they can hold a sensible conversation.

Grace and I felt this was perfect, as it was a stone bonking certainty, that after at least five minutes, not one soul at the table would be in the slightest bit interested in anything she had to say.

Furthermore, I would be left well alone and unattended to continue gathering more stories and information that flowed freely at such an occasion. Out of their usual comfort zones, these guy's just loved to show off more and more and would be forever topping up the last tale with an even better one.

We all met reasonably promptly and by one o'clock it was nearly all the same people as Friday night. Long Harry was at Ford Market but in his place was a very regal looking Gentleman, Peter Wright, commonly known as the oldest teenager in town, due to his long white ponytail. He was actually referred to as 'Big Sam', he was about 6ft 3in, so no great surprise there. Quite pale in complexion, dressed similarly to Bingo, with smart shirt, tie and Crombie coat, same old shiny shoes as ever, and a pin stripe whistle. Just not quite so well-pressed and a bit on the shabby side. If it weren't for the huge contrast in their size, one could be forgiven for thinking that he wore Bingo's cast-offs.

The Nearly boys were in tow with their wives, as was Pail Desjarlais and Bubbles, (George could not help mention that twice in a week was very rare, and by the time they'd had another day with each other at the funeral: husbands and wives that is; they would all have done enough to last a fucking month.) Fizzy and Powders were also at Ford Market, so came the introduction of Terry Boyle and his wife of the time Georgie. My first encounter with another huge character that I had already heard plenty about

Ricky Opendaws and Trexie were in a celebratory mood, as her daughter Julie, from a previous relationship, had just had a baby boy and so they were now proud Grandparents for the first time. There was sure to be Champagne on the menu this afternoon.

We made our way, after some lively banter, to Eaton Manor, quite a secluded and private venue. One could imagine many a private conversation, or secret rendezvous going on down here. The ambience was very sedate and low-key, so we all simply ordered our chosen roast dinner of the day and chatted away innocently.

We were just finishing the main when into the Restaurant storms three quite burly looking chaps in their late forties, all looking agitated and not exactly delivering Argos catalogues. Pointing at Vince and Harry, the fattest and most red faced of them (Timmy the bully boy Missin) starts sneering:

"You two. Yeah the pair of yah, are both no good pieces of shit. You Nearly's, as soon as I get the chance, I am gonna sort you and your lousy little firm out once and for all, you mark my words. I'm gonna get the pair of you both if it's the last thing I do."

George touched my forearm, and said quietly: "Here we fuckin go, meet the in-laws. Sorry about this Minnie, but when they get a bee in their bonnet, there's no stopping 'em."

My personal take on this, one of privacy invasion and pure ignorance, was nothing compared to the way Harry and Vince immediately reacted.

They jumped up in unison and told the Missin brothers exactly where they could go and what they thought of them. How dare they invade a private, personal function, just because they knew our location, and think they could get away with it, and we'll see you bunch of runts outside right now, don't even fucking worry about it.

The women all made sort of half-hearted shrieks of amazement and fear, but then to his credit Terry Boyle stood up and told the Missin boys in no uncertain terms, that they were out of order. Whatever troubles and bad blood was between them and the Nearly's, if they didn't fuck off right fuckin' sharpish, he and his Brother's would now also wish to join the game, finishing off with;

"And how d'you like them fucking onions? You bullying bunch of prats, go on fuck off back to wherever you came from and don't let me see any of you starting any grief on fuckin' Tuesday, or things are gonna get a bit nasty."

As all bully's act when confronted, I think it may have been Arnie, the reply was easy:

"Oh sorry Tel mate, we didn't know you woz 'ere. We don't wanna upset the girls. You know us. We didn't mean any harm."

Even I could see that this was a load of old bollocks, and an insult to one's intelligence. If there was not someone ready to stand their ground, this would have been a mini-battlefield with the Missin Boys, chalking up another little victory over the Nearly's.

Only fancying the fight when the numbers were in their favour, it turns out that they also had another couple in the motor, ready to come down and help out in the case of resistance. They stayed put obviously, not even prepared to show their boats.

They had probably been somewhere else, got onto the 'Nearly Missin' feud subject, more than likely someone had started winding them up and decided on the spur of the moment to rare up again; it was something in the blood I suppose.

It really and truly was six of one, half-a-dozen of the other. But when you are not familiar with one side, one automatically sides with the people you do know, it's only natural.

Nowadays, an incident such as this would have gone on for ages, people would probably continue to argue outside, trying to resolve the issue without any chance of success, and undoubtedly resulting in the Police being called.

We had all enjoyed the meal, plus the floor show at no extra cost. Coffee and brandy came without so much as a glance and by 4:30 everyone seemed to be getting a bit fidgety. There may have been some slight discrepancy over the Bill but Georgie just put his finger on his lips and advised 'leave it to them'. Some decided to call a cab while others were intent on continuing.

Both Nearly's went home with wives, along with Phil and Bubbles. Leaving an assortment of us heading for either the 'Albany Club', Regency Square or 'The Esquire' down Holland Road. Ricky sent Trexie home, Bingo did the same with his missus, and that left Lee Leechin and Speedy to join the entourage.

Louise was now quite intrigued and so advised she was still up for it. So with George and 'Big Sam' off we go, in a little Taxi convoy.

But where do we go to my lovely?

*

Alan and Sarah Griffiths, our hosts at the Albany Club were only too pleased to see us.

Chris Ellison was there that day with his wife and another nice couple, lovely fellah, does a bit of acting, but without a shadow of a doubt a really nice geezer. He actually won the celebrity 'Come Dine With Me' one time and was and is, always happy to help with local charities in Brighton.

There was also another lively Brighton character, Shane O'Dwyer, a great big Irishman, who had seen better times, on the doors of Brighton's Nightclubs and Bars. These days he was lucky to get in himself, let alone work for them. He had just had a nice little tickle, and was shouting drinks at the Bar like they were going out of fashion. We were not rude people, and so kindly accepted a few shots, along with the complimentary Bottle of Moet provided. Another was promptly ordered, as one was surely not enough for our party.

The main attraction in this little basement club was usually the Pool Table, but nobody else this particular day was interested. So, I suggested the old favourite of 'Killer', where everyone has 3 lives, miss a shot you lose a life, and the last one not to miss a pot was the winner, simple game really, but once you have a few alpha males in the company of women it can get quite a bit competitive. Today was to be no exception.

So there was 10 of us altogether at a pound each. The first game dragged on quite a bit and I was runner up to Chris Ellison, who gallantly decided to share the pot due to my resilience. Next game Terry Boyle was the clear winner, with two spare lives.

Then the fun begins when Shane the Paddy decides he is entitled to two shots, as the last person went in-off. Nobody agreed and so Alan the Club Owner had to tell him to stop fuckin' about or fuck off. Shane, being a bit of a bully, squares up to him.

So Alan just opens his jacket revealing a .38 revolver and saying:

“If you don’t think it’s loaded take a fucking chance Shane. Go ahead, make my day.”

The raising of the eyebrows, as he said this, brought rapturous applause and as we all started clapping we cheered ‘Nice one Al’. Shane was slightly embarrassed and apologised. He then mentioned he was late for an appointment and strutted off in a huff, then as he left the club, Georgie shouted out after him:

“Come back Shane, Shane come back. Shane, Shane come back. Shane.” Everyone just fell about laughing.

We called it a day about a quarter to seven, Louise and I that is, and called for a cab. The rest of them looked like they were in for the long haul, and were in no mood to finish proceedings. I said my goodbyes to all of them and then experienced something for the first time in my life; I felt that nice glowing feeling of belonging, probably because of my own lack of Family when growing up.

I told George I would see him Tuesday and left it at that. It had been another eventful and exciting day, plus of course some more magical moments had materialised and to be getting on with the growing catalogue of stories, concerning of course, ‘Brighton’s Knockers’.

*

Funeral.

What to wear is always a girl's prime concern on such a day. But after due consideration, I chose a knee-length Chanel two-piece suit, white silk blouse with black leather shoelace bow tie. Black Pill-Box hat with veil, black leather gloves, seamed black stockings with Black Patent Leather D&G Brogues. My long black Leather Aquascutum coat was draped over my shoulders and contrasting Hermes scarf, finished the look.

I purposely went with a more pale foundation and face powder, to contrast the dark red lipstick, and overdid the eye-liner a bit to accentuate my false eyelashes. Silver eyelids and with my hair up in a French pleat, courtesy of Grace, I was ready to go.

There were a lot fewer people at the funeral on the Tuesday than I had expected. Grace had agreed to accompany me, so as not to attract too much attention and enable me to blend in with the crowd. I acknowledged quite a few people outside the Down's Crematorium, off of Bear Road, and presumed more familiar faces would be in attendance once the Cars arrived. This shocked me slightly when they did arrive.

Out comes Georgie and his kids, followed by a few older folks I'd never seen. Then to my shock, followed in the third car by all the Missin brothers and partners. The penny dropped, like on a tilt machine on the Pier. Shirley was still one of the Missin family no matter what or who she married. Not a Nearly in sight.

The two previous meals had been private affairs between the Nearly's, close friends and Georgie, and despite their hatred for each other, 'Old School' respect was still the order of the day. The day belonged to the Missin family, despite the fact it was Georgie's Mum. The Nearly boys had no choice but to respect this, and therefore were not really welcome to attend, due to the bad blood between the two families.

These type of funerals were also, still not grand occasions. Violet's generation had withstood the war, rationing and all that went with it. Shirley was her Daughter-in-Law and there was a certain amount of protocol that still needed to be adhered to.

The Minister advised that there would be drinks and refreshments at 'The Ladies Mile' in Patcham for those that wished to attend. Georgie, caught in the middle betwixt family and friends, pulled me to one side and said to just go straight to 'The Horse & Groom', where friendlier faces would be in attendance, but he had to show his face out in Patcham first.

There was to be a distinct note of recognition between him and Grace that I detected, but thought nothing of it for the time being. My instinct took over and I told him that we were more than happy to pop out to Patcham for moral support, and with other things on his mind he just replied we were more than welcome.

A lovely big Pub, the Ladies Mile, and due diligence had been taken care of with half the Pub cordoned off for the 'Private Function'. On their own territory the Missin Family were a complete revelation. No snarls or growls and every single one of them the perfect gentleman. To Grace and I, anyway.

There was also an air of familiarity between Grace and some of the wives but again I took not much notice.

It was here that I heard a little more of the history between Brighton's gang families, it made London or Los Angeles look like nursery school. The Missin's, Bhargie's and associates like Peter Wright and Ernie Price were 'Scoombers'.

Boyles, Mc Cue's and individuals like Jackie Wadman, Trevor Thomas, Powders, Eddie Newland and Bobby Stevens were 'Hawkers'. Whilst the rest were mostly 'Queen's Parkers' or 'Milwood Flats', that being the combo of Kingswood and Milner on John Street.

None of them appreciated what the others called them so this always-ensured immediate tension when in each other's company. Recipe for disaster, whatever way you look at it.

Anyway we stayed for an hour or so, then Bonzo asked us if we needed a lift into town, as he had to meet someone on business. This was the covert invitation to join friendlier faces at 'The Horse & Groom', so we graciously accepted and made a polite yet swift departure. 'Gorgeous' giving us the knowing wink that he would follow shortly.

George had even introduced me to a couple of people as 'Minnie' and a few bade me farewell in a familiar and friendly tone with, 'Take care Min, see you agin'. (How many poets in this fucking town? See even I'm swearing unnecessarily now!)

The greeting at 'The Horse & Groom' verged on embarrassing.

The Nearly's, Boyles, Bubbles, Judge Wadey and his brothers, Charlie Hardwick and his young son Charlie junior, plus a few more increasingly familiar faces, all wanted to know how it was 'Out in the sticks'. But fortunately Bonzo followed us in and took the dairy off the situation.

Now in a much more friendly environment, I was able to mingle a bit. But..... I've gotta tell you, Paul Desjarlais did make me laugh for the first time that day, when he introduced me to his Mum. She used to work at Barnham's butchers in Kemp Town, but had now retired. She was the most glamorous, genteel person I had ever met in Brighton. She had a smooth silver-tongued voice, pristine make-up and was immaculately dressed. Sweetly smiling and saying hello as we touched hands.

I wouldn't go so far as it to say it was like being in the presence of Aristocracy, but it wasn't too far off.

She seemed at first to be out of her depth, but just laughed lovingly when Paul introduced me:

“Yeah this is that tasty little fucking bird, I mentioned Mum, you gonna say fucking hello then Stephanie, or fuckin' what?”

What could one say? We both thought, and simultaneously raised our eyebrows whilst smiling at the same time.

Georgie was not too far behind us, and insisted that we all toasted his Mum for one final time. He then thanked Mrs Marshall and Mabel Hussey for sorting out all the grub, then smiled knowingly to Vince and Harry for the financial back up.

Not much was escaping me these days. But I now felt myself questioning as to Grace’s knowledge of this tight knit community, who seemed also to take her in their midst, without so much as the blink of an eye. Was I getting paranoid or was there more to it? I would see to this later in the week and leave it for now. Today was for Violet, Georgie, and his kids, who didn’t seem that interested in any of the proceedings whatsoever.

Oh well, you can choose your friends but not your family. This had been evident more today than any other time in my life, to my knowledge.

The rest of the afternoon went better than as expected. Nearly everyone I spoke to wanted to tell me about their personal experiences of being ‘On The Knocker.’

One fellow, Melvyn Foster, was particularly memorable. At first it was about his early days as a Boxer, with Tony Brazil. Over in Whitehawk with Billy Boyle, Bobby Bell, Ernie Price and Brian Cordier.

Then how hard it was as a ground worker with the Davies's. Young Ronnie Davies had been Southern Area Champion and would go on to train Chris Eubanks and his son Chris.

He also enjoyed recalling the time Ronnie was introduced to the audience at a Silver Ring Boxing show at The Grand Hotel, as Ronnie 'The Rembrandt' Davies. When asked if this was due to his artistic pugilistic skills, Melvyn burst into laughter and simply explained:

"Naah, it's coz he woz always on the fucking canvas, wasn't he."

Finally, he mentioned the pure joy of dropping a few hundred bills with some of 'Brighton's Knockers' and then waiting to see how much he had 'copped for' once they sold up. He had a few cute little tales to tell, and it was nice to see how people like him, with not too much education, had still managed to get included in the good fortune of his mates and given the opportunity to share in the spoils.

He also enjoyed sharing in the occasion when Trevor Thomas, Jackie Wadman, Terry Boyle and a couple of mates, had got so fed up with young Jimmy Mc Cue on his 18th birthday, a good few years ago now. He'd got a bit too larey for his own good. So they had taken him down to The Broadway, took his trousers down and left him tied to a lamp post. The Mc Cue's were legendary 'Hawkers', and had been the first family, when street lighting was first installed, to run a cable from the nearest street light to their house in Wiston Road. So as not to incur an electric bill worth speaking of, till some jealous git grassed them up of course, 'can't fucking trust anyone' was bandied about!

He went on to tell a few 'parrot' jokes and this was quite refreshing amongst the slightly morbid atmosphere, it was a wake after all I suppose.

Then there was an interesting old 'Scoomber', 'Gaffer Dawes', from another infamous local family. He solved my curiosity about the shiny shoes syndrome. Pullinger's in George Street, Brighton, had been going since 1915, very fashionable in the 50's, and had always kept the best brand of quality British made shoes in stock.

Young Barry had joined the family business in 1979, long greasy haired kid with a giant earring, platform shoes and Lionel Blair strides. Nowadays he had four eyes and was as bald as a badger, but more friendly and helpful than a Good Samaritan (his words, not mine). They regularly, after a 'good earner', bought the best shoes from him and got a discount when it came to re-soling, and from time-to-time, on special occasions, he would gladly shine their shoes for a cuppa, from the next-door hole-in-the wall café.

Mickey Douglas was another revelation. I had heard a couple of people speak about him, in a reserved manner, for fear of being misinterpreted. He was someone to be feared, it seemed, with a reputation for clearing a Bar by just his presence. With an extremely deep voice he was nothing short of princely, not a bad word came from his mouth and was anything but scary.

He had, without a doubt, committed a few acts of violence in his day, but the only thing he mentioned of any consequence, was being proud of 'Borstal Boxing Champion' three times running, I forget the actual years. He also bragged about 1976-7 when he was in charge of one of the wings in Lewes and got the best sun tan of his whole life whilst lazing somewhere whilst his crew carried out their chores with due diligence. Then he remarked about the Accountant he got banged up with:

"This poor little prat had not one vice in his body, so he declared. After six months, he was hooked on heroin, a devout gambler, a chain-smoker and a compulsive liar. Then he started to carry out personal favours for other inmates, on numerous occasions, to clear in-house debts and divorced his wife, what a fuckin' runt!"

There was talk, by the older folks, about how the wives used to take the 'Old Man's' best suit to the Pawnbroker's every Monday, for two bob, then take it back out on Friday for two and tuppence. Nicking the empty bottles from out the back of Pubs, then taking them back to the Off Sales and getting Thruppence each.

What a shame there was no big bonfire night down the Level anymore .

Why don't they have piano's in Pubs these days?

Whatever happened to the Milkman?

Ain't they lucky to have those 'Hoover things' these days, we always made do with a carpet sweeper and all sorts of other old time traditions.

I also encountered Fat Ginger Dennis Mc Carthy, a supposed former London Club Owner. He fancied himself as a bookie, and started laying odds on a game of 'Shut-The-Box', a game I was familiar with. He simply embarrassed himself when refusing to pay out after I thrashed him, claiming it was just a friendly. What an absolute arsehole.

But as soon as Mickey Douglas glanced across and mentioned, half heartedly mind you, and by no means threateningly, he was 'watching proceedings'. Ginger Dennis completely bottled it, apologised and paid up twice as much as he should have. I felt this was only to be expected for trying to take a liberty, and enjoyed drinking a bottle of Veuve Clicquot for Mick, Grace, Georgie and I to enjoy together, at his expense. Blinder!

It's funny how things work out.

Dennis and I became reasonably close friends and did quite a bit of business together in later years. If I were to be put in a corner, there is no other than the obvious that I would rather be with than 'Ginger', he is someone that can be relied upon in times of need.

Unfortunately my one true love was not able to help in one sticky situation, once this was established he told me to get hold of Ginger Dennis, as he was privy to this type of predicament.

Once contacted he did everything he could within his power and the result was very satisfying for all concerned, life can be funny at times, cheers 'Ginger'. Repeating myself again I know.

Another comical, suave and sophisticated chap, was Mickey Blewitt, in Prince of Wales Check suit, shirt and paisley tie with Bally's interwoven leather buckled shoes but no socks, tickled me, when he asked if I fancied a quick line. I declined, so he nonchalantly asked if I would prefer a 'Jubilee', but I was not to be swayed, so declined again. I then mentioned that now was probably not the appropriate time or occasion.

He was well into his fifties but had the posture of a guy just made thirty. I also refused the opportunity to pass on a few dodgy Twenty pound notes, right pucker ones, at just four quid a go. There was not for one moment any insinuation of money changing hands, it was just his way of introduction, this was safe territory, amongst your own.

He was a Londoner made good in Brighton and felt he knew me from somewhere, did I know 'Mick The Meat' or 'Taters Dave'? Now, I know it's only a laugh, but this was just getting bloody ridiculous!

Another nice fellah was Bertie Collins, who talked me through all the good and bad habits of being a great pool player. But once I proceeded to kick his arse, leaving him with 3 red balls on the table, he simply gestured unassumingly with his bad arm, adding that he was suffering from Tennis Elbow. And anyway, anyone that was Georgie fuckin' Balcock's first choice on the table, was certainly worth respecting, 'And I should have known better'.

The rest of his singing is really not worth writing about, honestly, I really mean it, God's honest truth, oh well you know the rest of it. He had his currant, Leon with him, who was to go on and become quite successful at 'The Knocker', but plagued by constant agitation of 'The Old Bill', who made his life quite difficult at times.

Then there was another annoying little prat in the background who seemed to be having a laugh at everyone else's expense. Giving it large on the pool table, he insisted playing with just one arm. Then it was one arm standing on one leg.

Then one-armed, one-legged with one eye closed. Finishing off the game whilst not even looking at the eight ball at all. We all wanted him to miss of course, but the black was sunk and a jubilant cry of 'who's the Guv'nor now then' followed. I chose to ignore these shenanigans. But of course, I just couldn't. So I asked George:

"Who is that flash git?"

"Ah don't worry about him, that's Steve Martin, he's a blinder. Don't you remember him from The Waggon, that day?"

"Oh, of course," I replied. Then the penny dropped, but it was such a transformation, from the person I had met that day. At that point, noticing my interest, Mickey Douglas whispered in my ear:

"I love him myself, but some say he is just like Marmite is Stevie Boy." I simply gave Mick that knowing look of agreement.

At that point the little git cried out:

"Went to the Doctor last Thursday. Told him I'd been constipated for three poxy days. He said 'No shit'." Then proceeded to laugh at his own joke louder than anyone else. Prat.

A familiar song came on the jukebox for the umpteenth time. Rick Astley, ‘Never Gonna Give You Up’ and Georgie insisted on a dance. How could I refuse, but he got a little tearful thinking of his Mum. It was a little embarrassing, but mainly due to the fact nobody knew who I was and I had no idea who they were.

Grace tugged at my elbow at about 8 o’clock, and I had no argument with the fact it was time to go home. Just five minutes and we were home after thanking everyone for such a lovely time and arranging to meet Georgie Thursday lunchtime to show him how the ‘Project’ was progressing.

*

It was only a couple of days, but seemed to fly past, not just because I was eager to show George how things were going, but also because I had been working continuously to get the two separate pieces of work together, and in some sort of consistency.

He seemed more than happy with the progression of things, but then wanted to alter certain things, and the way certain people were portrayed. This had not been mentioned in our initial arrangement. I was taking people as I found them, as agreed, but now all of a sudden Georgie was looking to have ‘Goodies and Baddies’, and this did not allude to the way of telling the story.

So that you, the reader, can make your own mind up and envisage the characters how you prefer, therefore allowing your imagination to develop who is your favourite and who you think are the biggest arseholes. At the end of the day, despite their charisma and fun-loving attitude, they were still a load of tuck-up merchants, willing to go to any lengths of deceit, to get the goods.

It didn’t take long for me to talk him round, but momentarily I was uneasily aware that he may pull the plug at any time. This was the point that Grace just told me to hold the reins in and let things take their natural path.

By now with all the Lunches, Dinners, afternoons in the Pub and the Funeral, I already had a catalogue of tales to get well and truly going, but my loyalty prevailed and I sincerely wanted Georgie to be included on whatever the outcome was to be.

The Lord works in mysterious ways!

*

7. Clear Off Mr Street Cleaner.

I met with George on the Thursday and he was more than happy with the material I had put together. It was one of our shortest meetings and he seemed slightly distant, something was obviously on his mind. But when I asked if there was anything wrong, he advised it was just getting used to his Mum's passing and he was still concerned about the house situation. I tried to reassure him that I could help, but he now wished me to keep out of his affairs and just stick with the job at hand.

Not wishing to offend, I simply agreed not to interfere any longer. This was to prove a wise decision for all concerned. We agreed to meet again, when he returned from his little trip to France, which he did not wish to elaborate upon. Everything was in place for the weekend.

Having arranged with George to meet for Sunday lunch, I was particularly keen, as he had hinted that this was to reveal the finer details on one of their more comical, yet equally profitable excursions. Just down the coast to a little village called East Preston, near Littlehampton, West Sussex.

A couple of likely lads, Fizzy and Cabbage, had come across a kenna that was absolutely polluted with nice gear. Inhabited by a middle-aged couple, who were caked up, but unaware of all the treasures in their possession. They had bought a few things from out of the garden shed and still earnt a decent day's wages, but they were determined to relieve them of all the proper gear by hook or by crook.

By this time now, it was evident that not everyone had the talent or inclination to 'Get In'. On more than one occasion now, our now infamous little crew had been called upon to secure the prizes, on a fair commission basis of course.

The general consensus being, that if you can't get it yourself, put someone else in it and then you have still earned a nice few quid without sticking yourself in the frame, and still copping some readies into the bargain. This also added to the loyal camaraderie amongst the ever-increasing band of chancers, now referred to as the 'Knockerboys of Brighton,' that had been growing at an alarming rate over the last few years. It would continue of course and for years to come, with siblings and second-generation sons, joining the ranks.

We had discussed the venue and settled on The King & Queen, Marlborough Place, as George remarked:

"Dinner was just a dinner, and why waste silly money on the easiest meal in the world to cook."

When we met in The St. James's Tavern, down St. James's Street of all places, we ventured down to the aforementioned establishment. I was able to convince him that I fancied something a bit more substantial, and was not overawed at the prospect of sitting out in the open, with no privacy to speak of, and anyway, I was paying.

Job done, we went round the corner to The Basket-Makers Arms, where one is never disappointed by the food, still to this day the consistently high standards comply. We ordered our Roasts with a bottle of nice Soave for me, and a pint of Harvey's for my companion. As I paid by card, George patted my hand in gratitude. Looking down, I saw a £20 note, accompanied with that magical smile, and took a pleasant intake of breath at this noble gesture.

I should apologise for the drawn out process of these individual tales. But it is essential that you, my captivated reader, also get into the same excited state of anticipation that I was enduring, at each riveting session. This way, I feel that I am sharing something with you, rather than just gossiping, like an e-mail junkie.

"Soo," began George, once we were tucked into a cosy, secluded corner, amiss of any nosey parker's.

"Off we go, well sharply dressed, befitting men of our standing. We'd come up in the world you know? People were starting to take notice and show due accord and attention. With respect mind you. Needless to say our new found wealth and aplomb, had not gone unnoticed by the local Plod. In particular, newly promoted Detective Sergeant 'Nobby' Clark, who had tentatively warned: they were watching and waiting our every move."

"All the while, we was just looking forward to a decent day's work coming our way. I've gotta be fair Min, we also felt a rush of adrenalin many times, in anticipation of things to come. Most especially when we were sent on 'A Clue' as we referred to this kind of call."

"We turn up at the appropriate address. Very respectable area, with most properties two storey detached houses. Parked well up the road of course, around about eleven o'clock, just to suss things out. Lo and behold, only twenty yards away from the target, standing propped up against his bin, is a bloomin' council street cleaner in full regalia. Standard issue dungarees with council logo plastered on the back and front, bass broom, shit shovel and a roll-up on his bottom lip."

"Vince chirps up, 'Well that's fucking marvellous, innit. What are we gonna fucking do about this prick?'"

"Both me and Dick the driver looked at each other, perplexed. We were unwilling to venture a plan of attack, as invariably, Vinnie would discard any input from either of us, like a head teacher giving ashamedly bad Test results to the dimmest pupils in school. Not very encouraging stuff."

“Vinnie's instructions were that we find a Café and take stock over a cup of Rosie and a slice of Holy Ghost. No sooner had we ordered the measly breakfast, than Vinnie pronounced he had the answer to our problem.”

“See the thing is, when you go on a job like this, you invariably know that some kind of stroke or another is most definitely gonna need to be pulled. And the last thing you need is some nosey fucking bastard sticking his trunk in where it’s not bleedin’ well needed. The Jamboree and Holy was pretty much ignored and we bolted back to the plot, via the local Post Office where Vince purchased a clipboard, biro and notepad.”

“'Just wait here. Stick and keep schtum.' was Vince’s instruction, and out the motor he jumps. Well, in he goes, straight up to the Herbert by the bin. We woz keeping a keen eye on proceedings but were just out of earshot. I can, however, tell you, that this is absolutely, exactly, word for word what took place.”

“Up he marches to him, in an extremely authoritative manner, with clipboard projected about two foot from his chest; so engaging his foe in a manner of diss-contempt. ‘My name is Brian Bottomley, newly appointed Customer Services and Complaints Commissioner with the Adur District Council, of whom, I am sure you have now heard of. What is your name? As if I didn’t already know it, you charlatan.'”

“This came along with the all too familiar menacing pointing of the finger and look of disgust on his face. As if in danger of catching some kind of disgraceful disease, by nature of contact.”

“Well, the bloke just looked at him with pure disregard. But in true style and authority, Vince continued with his reprimand: ‘We have had reports that you, yes you. Don’t think I am not aware of your true identity, for one single minute young man. You have just been simply systematically re-distributing the garbage around here, from one place to another, rather than filling the bin, returning to the depot and continuing your work in an orderly fashion as expected of you. But have taken it upon yourself to simply sling said rubbish from one garden to another, causing much distress and genuine disgust to the loyal taxpayers of this parish."

"'I am very close to sacking you right here and now, and then sending you back to the yard with nothing but your cards, you scoundrel you. What have you to say for yourself?'"

"Of course we were not totally aware of what was being said, but all of a sudden, next thing we know, the street cleaner has picked up his bass broom, slung it right up in the air, kicked the fuck out of his bin, given Vince the old Harvey Smith, and marched straight off down the street. Cussing and swearing under his breath, without so much as a backward glance. We couldn't stop fucking laughing for about three minutes, and when Vince described what had happened back in the motor, we was lucky to ever get our thoughts back together at all. Kia-Ora!"

(A little inoffensive expletive from a T.V. ad in the early seventies, about an orange drink, used quite commonly in those days when someone really wanted to curse in a vile manner, but did not wish to offend any female company, or other nosey gits in earshot).

"With said snooper out of the way the coast was now clear to get on with the job in hand, and in such high spirits you can easily imagine what happened next."

*

What did actually happen, was the arrival of our lunch, and it was lovely. George really enjoyed it and had I been posed the question, I would probably have said he was not capable of finishing the lot, but that he did. Barely resisting the urge to lick his plate and proceeded to smile like a Cheshire Cat once completed.

It was difficult not to try and engage Georgie in conversation whilst eating, but I felt myself feeling very connected.

Then I started to analyse: what the hell were they thinking when carrying out these escapades?

Where were they headed? What did they hope to achieve and where did they get the audacious attitude, that they had the God given right, to con anyone and everyone, for their own need. Or was it just greed?

None of the people I had recently met, were what I would refer to as mean. In fact quite the opposite. They certainly had their morals in order amongst one another.

Obviously they didn't all get on with each other, such as the Nearly Missin business, but the pecking order certainly applied. Was my companion one of the Lions in the 'Knockerboys' jungle?

Or just another jackal, picking at the leftovers once the King has had his fill?

Hyena's maybe, they certainly had the laugh for it.

Who were the Monkeys, Crocodiles, Elephants, or Rhinos? As I ran this through my head, I instantly realised that Bubbles would most definitely be the Elephant, not only for his size but also for the formidable memory.

Before I could begin to continue this train of thought, Georgie said something and snapped his fingers, but I was oblivious.

This was not really a jungle where only the strong survive, surely?

If this was the case, it was definitely more a matter of the snidest, sneakiest, most cunning and those without conscience, who would succeed, where others failed.

What had I unearthed here?

I had opened a proper Pandora's Box, for sure.

Back to the case in hand. Georgie enquired as to my health, to which I apologised for not paying him attention.

Then it dawned on me, was this the attraction and main reason for his enthusiasm and attention?

After years of being the sidekick, he was now enjoying star billing and recognition of his talents. So, after ordering another drink, some doe-eyed locals eyed us up, in case we were about to vacate our prime seats.

But George advised we were still awaiting some family members to join us, after some unfortunate delays on the trains, another load of bollocks of course, like a well-seasoned, experienced professional footballer, he was always on the ball and passing it on.

I had to excuse myself for a couple of minutes and went outside for a cigarette, asking George for some privacy as I had a phone call to make.

He was okay with this. Even though one of *my* earlier conditions about our discussions, was no interruptions or 'other business'.

Of course it became obvious, at an early stage, that this was impossible with George, or he would be tarnished as an ignorant twat, if he did not acknowledge the many people he said hello to on a constant basis. Just because I didn't know half the Town it was no reason to penalise him.

I gathered my thoughts quite quickly and realised I had to snap out of my present state of mind, or jeopardise the whole project. Get on with the job in hand, and get what you came for, just like 'Going on a clue' really. I got back to the table and allowed Georgie to pour a much needed refreshing glass of wine.

*

"Well," he continued, with that now all too familiar glint in his eyes, "To not 'Get In' now would have been tragic and would have made us inconsolable."

"So if ever there was a time I wanted to lead the way, this was it. Under the premise that we were just passing through the village, but could not resist complementing on the marvellous front gardens. Was there any chance that the proprietors could advise, where those astounding Georgian Lead Statues of Lions and Great Danes guarding the gates and front door entrance may have come from? As I was interested in commissioning something similar for my Great Aunt up in Hertfordshire."

"The lady of the house said she was not really sure, but if I would like to come in, her husband who was tending the rear garden, would most certainly be only too happy to help with my enquiry. A sly thumbs up behind my back, would have been worthy of a German spy, and given Vince plenty of encouragement for the next phase of our mission."

"The place was absolutely polluted with fine art and furniture, seemingly used on a day-to-day basis. But surely far too much dusting and cleaning needed, to keep the place looking proper. It would be my partner's job to relieve them of all this unnecessary workload."

“After meeting with the husband, Gerald, Annabelle asked if I cared for tea. ‘That would be ever so kind,’ I replied, ‘but maybe my friend Gerald, who is accompanying me could join us?'”

“‘Oh that’s funny, isn’t it? That’s the same as your charming hubby.’ Anne giggled and replied that it would be more than appropriate to invite him in also, and the kettle was going on. Rushing out to the car I quickly gave Vince the S.P. and in we go.”

“It was a joy to behold and without so much as a bye or leave we spent the next two hours, divulging all our worldly knowledge, on all the shitty old things not worthy of a place in their fine home.”

“The first object of ‘Gerald’s’ attention, was a large oil painting over the mantle. Pausing for a few moments, studying the signature, rubbing his chin in contemplation and giving a concerting nod, he then proceeded to remove the picture from it’s position. Not probably having been moved from the picture hook for many years he very delicately rubbed the bottom back left hand corner, as one would caress a sweethearts' tummy, before going for the knicker elastic. Just probing gently, then easing smoothly, yet slowly down, he breathed a sigh of ecstasy, as if laying next to the love of his life for all eternity.”

“It was pure fucking genius. Gerald and Anne were hypnotically transgressed under his spell, and waited with bated breath for his expert disclosure and opinion of their ‘picture on the wall’, which was all it was to them. Until now, that is.”

“'Well,' he declared, in a now authoritative, yet haughty voice, 'If I’m not mistaken, (high pitch) and I very rarely am, (deep pitch) I would put this delightful piece of work in the region of fifteen to twenty thousand pounds.'”

“This was the ‘Top Up’, where it was hinted that a huge sum of money was coming their way. But of course, it was just to get their juices flowing and distract from all the other purchases coming their way, for much smaller amounts."

"Both of them sat down in unison, a look of sheer disbelief on their boats, and yet also trying to look shamelessly unimpressed. Of course they were not in any way qualified to try and hide any emotions from either of us."

"This was our game and we were certainly top of the class in this trait. I suppose a game of poker would be just as entertaining, but when you recollect these times, we held all the cards, with a few extra jokers to boot, and our clients unwittingly divulged their hand from the very first show."

"'Let me make a fresh cuppa.' said Anne, departing to the kitchen. Probably rubbing her hands together all the way to the parlour, whilst Gerald (the master of the house) tried to remain cool, calm and collected."

"'Okay,' stated Vince, 'Now, that pair of card tables, see those, with the old vases on, how long have those peculiar looking things been stuck over there in the corner doing nothing?'"

"'Don't rightly know,' replies Gerald, 'But I do believe they belonged to Anne's Great Aunt, and probably hold too much sentimental value. Nevertheless, what do you make of them?' He has now been infected with the 'Greedy Bug', as we referred to it."

"'Oh I don't know, probably eight hundred quid each, but let's not bother with them today eh? Do not wish to upset the apple cart, do we? Onward Horace.'"

"He proceeds to march straight through to the unused Dining Room, where, to our mutual pleasure and delight, sat two magnificent marquetry cabinets containing an ancient yet unique collection of snuff boxes. Then comes the proverbial light cough, indicating that this is to be the prize, and not to be left behind under any circumstances."

"So, off he goes, circling the two bits of furniture like a leopard in the jungle, whilst it's prey takes a drink from the riverside, unsuspecting of the terrible fate that it is about to fall foul of."

"'Very interesting,' is the opening gambit, 'Do you mind, Gerald?'"

"'Certainly,' replies Gerald, with a courteous gesture of his wrist. Upon opening one of the drawers, Vince looks down and the blood instantly drained from every vein in his face, he went as white as a sheet, staggering back clutching his chest and before collapsing, managed to gain some support on the shoulder of poor Gerald who was now in an instant state of shock."

"'What's wrong? Are you okay young Gerald? Have you a medical condition we should know about? Here take a seat on the Chaise Lounge, do you need a drink of water?'"

"Panic stricken, he was" continued George, "'Oh my Good God!' Exclaimed Vince, nee Gerald, 'I cannot believe my eyes.' With his hand clamped tightly on his cheek, causing an instant blotch on his face like a ripe watermelon or birthmark."

"'It's like the plague; these things are completely infested with the absolutely worst case of woodworm I have ever had the misfortune to witness.'"

"'These have just got to go. Do you realise that if this wicked disease were to spread, it could ruin the skirting, floorboards, roof, joists and every single part of this beautiful house that is supported by wood. Which is of course its complete foundation, not to mention all the rest of your beautiful furniture. This catastrophe could cost you an absolute fortune Gerald.'"

“Then, in a whisper, added, ‘But, I’ll tell you what I am prepared to do. We will take these out of the property for you, dump them at no cost to you, and as there is no longer anywhere for you to put those old snuff boxes, I will give you, now, in cash, now don’t argue please, I am prepared to pay you, in cash mind, two thousand pounds. No, no, no, you don’t have to thank me, you have both been very kind and it is my endearing pleasure to help you out in your hour of need. But of course, time is of the essence, and we must make hay whilst the sun still shines.”

“’Come on Horace, tally ho, let’s get moving while we still have a chance of helping these poor souls.' Poor, being the operative word. Once we had cleared everything out, with assurances of our immediate return the following day with agreed sums to be fully paid in cash. Receipts were duly issued and signed by both parties and we were on our jolly way.”

“As we drove off, the happy couple came to the end of their garden path and joyously waved us off. Like we was on the QE2 departing from Southampton, thanking Vinnie continuously for his kind gesture and behaviour befitting such a true gentleman. What a peach.”

George added: “I did remark, as we pulled away, waving graciously like members of the Royal Family at the Epsom Derby, ‘Well my son, Laurence O’ Fuckin' Livier himself would have been proud of that one.'”

“To wit, in one of his rare moments of self conscious sense of achievement, Vince acknowledged with a raise of his top lip like Cliff Richard and said ‘Thank you very much’ just like the king himself.”

“He had of course, when first examining the cabinets, sprinkled a few worms of his own, slyly into the drawers, and on the carpet behind them.”

"This had been 'A Clue', after all, and so we had come prepared, mentally and physically, to do what was needed, to get what was ours for the taking. Reputations were at stake, and to come back empty handed was not an option."

"Another little sweetener to this particular deal, was the fact that, as purveyors of this sort of lacklustre furniture from days gone by, there may be a few nursing homes that may benefit from our charitable donations, of the pieces that might be saved."

"As we had recently benefited from a modest win on the premium bonds, it would give us great pleasure in doing two good turns in one go, the pair of them smiled contentedly as we took the last few pieces, including the Chaise Lounge, and loaded them on the roof-rack and tied it all down better than a rigger on a North Sea Oil Rig."

"On the way back to Brighton we decided to have a tally up somewhere private before we sell up, not that we doubted everything was kosher, but just in case one or two of our bits was an absolute gem and slipped through our fingers."

"Gay Bunny had pointed out on a previous deal, Hawkins, and Deasy, and Barnes'y, knew a bit more about these things than we did, but as this caper carried on, we were educating ourselves on a daily basis. Sometimes it would be from browsing through a catalogue at the Sale Rooms, or The Miller's Guide when it cropped up."

"Vince had actually pilfered one book from the library and started looking at the pictures alone for some greater knowledge. If only we had been so endearing to our studies at school, things may have been different. A load of bollocks really, as we hardly ever went to school anyway."

"So what the fucking diff, when we did or didn't go? What the heck?"

“Popping by Fizzy’s little yard at the bottom of Gloucester Road upon our return, we had to show him the loot. He tried to buy out a couple of the Snuff boxes, but Vince was having none of it. 'You can fuck right off, my son. You’ve got your drink coming once we sell up, so stop trying to be such a greedy fucking runt.' The point was taken, so he pissed off round to the Eagle whilst we divvied up the spoils, like Pirates of the Caribbean.”

“Would you believe it? When we were going through the little snuffboxes, Vince notices something he remembers seeing somewhere previous. The fact that enamelled boxes are far more 'rare and worthy' than any others and more, to the point, those with erotic scenes were much more desirable (and therefore more expensive to any potential punter). A phrase we would come to love over the next few years, during our many profitable encounters up and down the country.”

“After consulting some readily available textbooks we were in a much stronger position when it came to the selling stakes. Rather than just being happy to turn a quid or two for our efforts, we were now revelling and looking forward to the next jousting part of the battle, to earn a crust from the dealer. Now, far more intent in getting true value and money’s worth for our hard graft and sticking your neck on the line.”

“Let the haggling begin!”

“Tommy Barnes had decided to sell up and retire to Majorca. On his recommendation, our first option was Hawkins' place, on Prince Albert Street. The pure, unadulterated, inexplicable, disgust of his measly offer of £22,500 for the whole parcel, was met with differing reactions from our motley crew. As far as we was concerned we had done our job and so had earnt a ‘decent day’s money.”

“We were well happy with the first offer, but then Vince assured us he was right on the game. These doubtful thoughts were soon dispersed when Vince came back from Italian Tony's gaff with a firm offer of £35,000."

"Margherotti was off to the Bank to sort things out, so we popped into 'The Cricketers' for a quick libation whilst his lackey's unloaded the two motors. During this brief break, Vince ventured back over to Hawkins to politely deliver some clear career advice, and in a loud officious manner instructed: 'You are in the wrong game my old son, you should be running a fucking brothel, you ponce.'"

"As good as his word, Spaghetti returned within half an hour and Vince slipped over to collect the readies. That particular venue is now the home of Food For Friend's (the most successful vegetarian restaurant in the County). But even with its lion's share of the veggie market, it still don't turn over the sort of money that that Italian mother-fucker did in his prime!"

"It seemed there was a slight discrepancy on one or two small items." Georgie looked up into the air, eyebrows raised, at some imaginary ark angel or overbearing family member who had since passed.

"Who gave a fuck? Let's be fair, if it wasn't for Vince, we'd still be grafting tomatoes or peaches down London Road with one eye over our shoulder for a fiver a day. Let alone worrying about the missing six hundred pound from the sell-up."

"For fuck's sake, if we had taken first offer off of Hawkins, we were still Ten Grand better off. You know it makes sense. The thing was, we all probably knew that it was tucked away somewhere else for another little project Vinnie was working on, to be revealed at a later date, to which we would all benefit."

"Dick the driver got a monkey. The couple of ice-creams along the road ended up with £2,600, still waiting with baited breath the speculated price of the lovely picture on the mantle. Jury is still out on that one. Fizzy and Collie copped for £1,200 each, which left me and Vince with £12,000 each."

"I have to be completely, as always, honest. Every time he split it 50-50 with me and I still couldn't quite comprehend it. It was years later when I cottoned on to my unique talent of 'Getting us in' that I realised that if he didn't have me, he didn't have anything. So it was all fair in love and war, and he certainly played the white man did Vincent."

The guy at the Bar gave me a wink, indicating that we were taking up a prime spot at a prime time on a Sunday afternoon. I'm not sure what came over me, but without a second thought, I clicked my fingers and ordered, another bottle of your best white wine and a pint for my associate if you don't mind... with that indignant stare, of, how dare you even dream of interfering with my business, you moron. This attitude was quite obviously contagious. With a little self conscious giggle to myself with glee, at my new found over confidence and belligerence to boot. Very proud indeed!

*

I could no longer contain myself, and finally, with the most sincere look that I could possibly muster. Asked the all important question that had, will be, and will continue to be for all time: "So George, what happened to all the fucking money? Where did it go? What did you do with it?"

*

That, all too familiar, vacant look came across his eyes once again, and the rolling of the mincers, that we have all seen when the prat has been caught out once more.

"Well", he said, with a sad sigh, and surrendering look, "It would have been the Summer of 72' and a pal of ours, Siddy Minter, had a little drinker down Waterloo Street, called The Linden Club."

"Of course, back in those days the Pubs closed by half two and didn't open again till six, so there were plenty of these Clubs operating."

"They were a bit like the American Speakeasies in our eyes, but totally legal. Some had a pool table, the usual one-armed bandit in the corner, but no entertainment to speak of, other than the jukebox."

"They did, however, all have one thing in common, they always had a few faces in 'em. Heavy drinkers and invariably at the weekend full of knockerboys holding court."

"Telling of their latest adventures that week, and how many thousands they had earned. Also, just opposite Sid's, Johnny Poulter had a Bookies and upstairs was the Card Rooms for anything from Poker, Crib, Kalukee or whatever you fancied. On some occasions they would even roll out the Roulette."

"So, anyway, where was I? Oh yeah. Well Sid's kid Alan, was in the Olympics over in Munich, Germany. As we had all seen him fight a few times, I fancied him to do well, so had £3,000 on him to get the Gold. It was a right proper pony decision, believe me, in the semi-final, and we all reckoned he was robbed, but maybe we were a bit biased, so he only got the Bronze, and Poulter got the cash."

He was certainly in a nice flowing mood this afternoon was George. I was actually in awe of him today. He had made a concerted effort for my benefit and did not resemble in the slightest, the forlorn looking old-timer I had first encountered outside the Diner, just a few weeks ago.

I like to think that my interest had perked him up a little bit, he certainly didn't have that 'feeling sorry for yourself' look about him any more. Or was it simply that he now represented a whole new persona, and my earlier, more suspicious thoughts, were in fact the true reality.

"So that kicked the weekend off to a fine start. To follow that up, in the Club, I had a bad run playing Spoof. I'll explain about that another time. A few quid, I gave to my Mum and Shirley. Into the Brighton Tavern nice and early on Saturday morning, about 10 o'clock, after saying hello to a few of the boys who were selling up, the lesser value stuff, direct to the public, along Upper Gardner Street market."

"You should see the shitty gear they sell along there these days. Turkey Hardwick was the only Barrow Boy nowadays with any Fruit & Veg, but it was like a drug habit with him."

"He probably didn't even realise exactly what he was doing and was just going through the motions automatically. But he was still getting a few quid on a Saturday, bless his heart."

"I had the most awful afternoon in the bookies and my only solace was taking a tenner off of Lee O'Donnell, when he said that it was impossible for someone to win 5 Gold Medals at one Olympics. Mark Spitz, proceeded to win 7 and he spat on the Cockle before slamming it into my open palm."

"Mind you things were looking up, when we get a big tip for a Dog running at Corals that night. So a plan was afoot."

"Gets the cab from 'The Kensington' and meet up with a few lads in the Bar. Checking the latest info, and it was still sound and a stone bonking certainty. Number 5 in the 5th race. Anyway, the fucking 5 dog was absolutely pissing it from start to finish, looked unbeatable, and then somehow or other, coming round the last bend manages to get bumped and finishes third."

“I then started chasing my money, didn’t I? As it had been deemed that no bloody favourites were permitted to win that evening, ended up Sunday morning, with that dreaded search through the pockets, to reveal just four poxy quid. Kia-Ora!”

“So then I popped round to see Vince. He was living in Elmore Road at the time. We shared a pot of tea and I proceed to inform him of my tales of woe. It turns out he had done pretty much the same as me. He lent me £500 to get me through Sunday. Couldn’t let people think we were not continuing to be as successful as we claimed.”

“That was the thing in them days. I suppose you have heard it all before. Easy come easy go. One minute you’re caked up, the next minute your skint.”

The proverbial raising of the bushy eye brows ensued and George finished his drink, fondly tapping my thigh he added with that lovely twinkle in his eye:

“Still you can’t take it with you can you? We have to live life to the full, coz tomorrow we may fall. Who said that? I sounded like a bloomin’ General leading his men over the trenches or Colonel Custard himself. Sometimes it was a bit like that.”

“So next thing I know, Vince comes and finds me in ‘The Cobden’, Cobden Road, that night, about 7:30pm. Pubs didn’t open till seven on a Sunday. Vince said he wanted picking up early tomorrow, explaining: 'Peter Widdy has just given me a right cushty sounding call, so we are off to Birmingham. Find Dick and be warned we are also taking Charlie on this one, as I fancy we might have to pull a bit of a stroke.'”

“Those was the days,” reflected George.

“That turned out to be another couple of memorable days. But to be fair darling, I am feeling a bit tired, and I’m sure you have much better things to do this evening, than spend them with an old codger like me."

I did not really wish for things to finish there but I was well aware that it may be wise to call it a day. Go home and spruce myself up and enjoy a few drinks with some of my Girlfriends. The town was quite lively these days on a Sunday night, especially The Papillon Club. It was under The Royal Albion Hotel, opposite The Palace Pier under the guide of Earl Rayner and his glamorous wife, and was rumoured to be buzzing after the Pubs closed.

There would be plenty of other times to hear more about the escapades of the 'Brighton Knockerboys'.

This project had actually become all consuming, so Georgie had made the right call. I called Tracey, who was glad to hear from me, and looking forward to catching up.

She had been with me on that very first occasion, so I thought it would be quite funny to fill her in on the recent events. If only I had known what was coming my way that evening. I am sure I'd have stayed in and watched Songs of Praise and the Hitchcock Film that was on the telly that night.

*

Having asked Georgie where some of the lads hang out, I arranged to meet Tracey and Julliette in the Cricketer's, with a mind to go on to a little pub down Brunswick Street West called The Bow Street Runner.

There we are, perched at the Bar, looking as serene as Flamingos, dressed to the nines, when in strolls a small group of lads that were to add yet another chapter to 'Brighton's Knocker's'.

It was that Steve Martin again, this time accompanied with four shifty looking Herberts. He glanced over to me, acknowledging my presence, but chose not to approach. More important things to hand I guess.

We were just deciding where to go next, when in strolls large as life smarmy Nigel, the stirrer. All we needed. He struts up with a sideways glance and joins the guys at the Bar. Not cracking any interest, we decide to just go along to The Pump House. But before I had risen from the table, Steve sits right down next to me and says apologetically:

"Hello it's Stephanie isn't it?" To wit I reply:

"Yes it is. This is Tracey and Julliette, my friends."

He seemed pleasant enough;

"Look, it's like this. I am with a few friends, with plans to meet others later out in Hove. But for the time being, there's a bloke just joined us that I really cannot bear to be in the company of. He makes me sick and only ever causes me trouble when he's about. Would it be possible to join you girls for twenty minutes or so, let's say, pop round the corner to The Pump House. I'll get us a nice bottle of wine and then I can explain why my behaviour was not what it should have been at Violet's funeral the other day. Whaddayasay?"

Well of course unbeknown to him, he had just reiterated everything we already felt about bloody Nigel. So he had unwittingly endeared himself to all three of us in one foul swoop. The Whaddayasay, just sealed the deal. We did not even need to converse and so the four of us left together, without so much as a by or leave, to the boys at the Bar.

During the three-minute walk to The Pump House, he explained that the guys we left behind had some business to discuss, that had nothing to do with him and he wanted no part in it. 'The less said the better,' he advised.

They were in the ‘Knocker’, game and he was a furrier, cutting making and design of Fur Coats.

“Before anyone gets on their high horse though,” he continued “I do not mistreat animals, it’s a clean industry and I have made plans to leave the country later this year and try my luck in America. Unfortunately the Fur Industry is on its way out due to Public opinion, so it’s across the water for me before Christmas. Tally Ho and away we go.”

The turns of phrase, was obviously a Brighton thing and seemed to flow, like ordinary words, rather than statements, and it now felt that no sentence was complete without a finishing rhyme.

Talk about laying your cards on the table! This bloke certainly left nothing to chance.

Once inside he asked our preference and as we had already had a couple of Wines, stuck with that. Not as worldly as he may have liked, Steve just pointed to the most expensive one and asked me if that was okay. He now came across quite boyish which I found quite sweet and charming, but not my type.

After a few small niceties I then enquired as to the funeral antics.

“Well,” he began, “I didn’t really know Violet that well, but I did know her. My Nan is Mabel Hussey, and I also know Mrs Marshall quite well. The three of them were very close and it was a bit of an eye-opener when Violet done the Tommy Cooper.”

“The thing is, they always make so little of these funerals. But when I turned up with some nice flowers for my Nan, she just sort of had a little breakdown. I’ve never ever seen her cry before, she’s proper 'old school, and stiff upper lip', you know. So I found it a little disturbing, and had to take her home pronto. She's only round the corner in Grant Street. Violet was sort of the 'First to Go' as they say, so it has been quite tough for everyone."

"Of course then I just sort of lost the plot a bit and had a few too many myself, so started being a bit cocky and taking the piss a bit too much on the pool table. Sorry about that."

Finding myself forgiving everything immediately, I asked how well he knew Georgie Balcock.

"Oh George is a lovely fellah. Are you the girl who's writing his memoirs or something? Someone did mention it to me the other day."

The penny dropped for me right at that moment. That was how Georgie was referring to it, to his pals. Grace had warned me that there would be more to our little venture, than Georgie just telling the tales and leaving the rest to me. He wished to be the star of the show as it were, and although there was nothing wrong with that in principle, the way things had gone though; it was Vince who had developed into the main character and not Georgie.

Perhaps there would be a way in the future to change that slightly. It now made sense as to why he desired more input on certain subjects, but this would all get sorted sensibly at the right time. What a lovely chance meeting and fortuitous revelation in total innocence from Stephen. It was a refreshing feeling.

The next part of the evening became a bit of a blur. He suggested a drink at The Bow Street Runner, to which I readily accepted, as I was aware that this was a 'Knockerboy' watering hole, which I had not yet managed to encounter.

Quick cab fare to Brunswick Square and in a flash we were there. It's not a big Pub and there were quite a few people present, but Steve got served immediately and we joined a couple that he knew who were seated at a table.

Wine was poured and he introduced the couple as Tracey and Rob, they were waiting for her Sister and Hubby and were off to a charity auction for some friends.

When the other couple arrived it turned out to be Delia Barnes and Giles Capshaw, so it was nice to be in the loop, so to speak. They told us about the plight of some friends and that a group of them were auctioning off a few bits and pieces to get a farewell holiday for a kid with leukaemia.

They had arranged to have the affair at Woodie's Wine Bar near Hove Town Hall. We were all welcome if we fancied it and Hercules (the Manager and friend) would be sure to lay out a nice spread of snacks to encourage a nice turnout.

This seemed like a nice idea, so we agreed to follow in a cab, but Steve asked them to hold on a couple of minutes whilst he popped out for something round the corner.

Back in about six minutes, he returned and ushered Giles to the Gents with what looked like some dry cleaning in a sheet. When Giles returned he had a broad grin on his face and we all wondered what they were up to?

Picking up on his mates' expression, Giles just said:

"Don't get excited, there's nothing funny going on, I'll tell you about it in the Cab." I was just curious as I knew Stephen didn't even smoke, let alone anything else of a sinister nature. In those days there was not the high volume of drug taking that one witnesses today, or maybe we were just naïve.

I obviously could not resist asking what it was about, once the others left and so he told me that he had donated a Mink Jacket to the Auction, but had to let Giles know it had a reserve of £250, as it was in the showroom for £499. The Girls along with myself agreed it was a nice gesture and were now looking forward to the event with a more animated view.

It was a nice evening weather-wise, so I suggested a nice casual stroll along to Woodie's. It was only about fifteen minutes and would give us all a breath of fresh air. It had been quite smoky in The Bow Street, and even though I had a couple of ciggie's myself, felt this was better than all this sudden rushing around from place to place like a relay race.

People had spilled onto the street by the time we approached, but as usual knowing everyone, Steve just led us straight through to the Bar and joined the hosts at a table.

Delia and Tracey were very excited and chuffed so many friends had turned up. When people are so naturally nice to everyone it rubs off, their Dad Tommy, and Mum Margaret of course, had instilled great qualities in both daughters.

Wine flowed freely that night; the Auction was a great success, with the Mink Jacket, star of the show fetching a princely £425. This meant £175 to the fund and the £250 Steve got to cover the cost was promptly spent. Half behind the bar and then on various items in the Auction, it was a great night and a few more 'Knockerboy' stories were heard along the way.

There were of course a couple of distasteful moments, as invariably there always is at such events. The arrival of the Herberts from earlier met with disapproval of Steve, and he wasn't too shy to express his distaste. He was not alone, and they picked up on the negative welcome pretty sharpish and bolted after one drink.

One of them was a Missin after all and was never going to join in the ambience of the evening. This was a Son of one of the guys I had already encountered, but I didn't wish to get involved in any banter with them, when having such a lovely time.

Obviously Nigel was non-gratis, whilst Tony Desjavus was recognised as a charlatan, gambler and Antique thiever rather than dealer. Just not their night. Gerry McKinnock sat with us for ten minutes then went off home to his wife Poppy. He'd had a row with the others, probably stitched up for readies, and was not in the mood.

Then the most unfortunate part was the Taxi home. For some reason, Steve thought he was coming in for 'Coffee.' It was far too early to consider such an invitation, but ask he did. I felt a little disappointed but it only took one 'No', and after all it did show a bit of interest. But still a 'bloody cheek' all the same.

He was certainly going to have to prove himself a better person, but then again these Brighton people do have a nerve. Although I was telling myself he was not 'One of Them'. Yet he still had that air of confidence, authority and expectation, that I now associated with most of the people I was surrounding myself with.

Maybe even I had developed a few subtle changes to my own behaviour. My language had certainly fallen foul on a couple of occasions that evening as Tracey and Julliette had pointed out. They of course came in for coffee and just started to teasingly giggle at my expense, about the pathetic 'Surely I can come in for a coffee' request.

We laughed. Recounting the evening they both had the same question, 'Is it always like that when you go out with these people'. To which I happily replied, 'Oh yeah, but sometimes it gets a bit lively'. We laughed a lot more.

Steve called everyday and left messages on my answer phone at 10:30am, morning tea break. 1:00pm lunchtime, and again between 5:30 – 6:00pm when he had finished work, but I was not to be swayed and did not return his calls. He would have to suffer for his indiscretion. No two ways about it.

Then of course the weekend came and went without a word and of course I longed for the call. Even if I had misjudged things, there was no way I was going to chase him. So see how things would pan out.

Grace tugged at my conscience slightly when she enquired as to his whereabouts and mentioned that in passing my Dad had enquired after him.

She also mentioned that there had been a couple of bunches of flowers delivered whilst I was out and she had placed them in water for me in my favourite vase.

The one that Georgie had given to me under severe protest. It belonged to his treasured collection of crystal left by his Mum, but he had been extremely insistent, stating that there was no way he was about to start putting flowers out and so it's best use was in the home of someone that would put it to good use.

They did look nice and I was tempted to call him, but decided to get back to the job in hand and keep up with the pre-arranged appointments with George for the time being.

Then of course, fate took a hand once more and whilst having a chat and couple of casual drinks with Georgie, he mentioned that Steve had called him to make sure I was okay and offer apologies for any misunderstanding at the weekend.

George insisted that he was a genuine chap and that I should certainly consider giving him a second chance.

There was of course no fate involved in this really, just whatever you choose to believe and I simply chose to think about it for the time being.

8. 'Let The Tales Begin'.

Thursday had been allotted once more, for an afternoon at George's for tea. Mainly to go over what I had now put together and to discuss what the next steps were, who to show the material to, and how to go about it. This took all of five minutes because George was bored and just wanted to see what information had been gathered.

These will be set out in sub-chapters for easy reading.

The Coffin Tale

Working down in Hastings one week, they had decided to try one of the more renowned impoverished areas, a council estate no better or worse than in Brighton. But not being local, always meant there was the possibility of an aggressive reception. Referred to by most of them as the 'Russian Roulette Knock.' In such sensitive and potentially explosive areas, it was generally felt that the 'Straight Knock' was the best way to go. No flyers or Bills to be dropped, just the immediate approach with no prior warning as to what was coming their way.

Why show the enemy your plan of attack? Only a mug would do it.

Having been at the game for a few years now: George; Charlie Hardwick; Vinnie and new boy on the firm; young Harry, were only too happy to start 'Knockin' Doors' earlier than usual.

Vince thought nothing of it when a stout lady resembling 'Norah Batty', answered in her Housecoat, slippers with stockings rolled over her ankles and hair in rollers. She was mid-fifties, but hadn't even bothered putting her teeth in yet. There was no sign of remorse in her appearance. It was her very own well-polished front doorstep after all, so why should she?

She certainly didn’t mess about and asked immediately what his game was and what did he bloody well want, at 'half-past fucking eight in the fuckin’ morning, you cheeky little sod.'

Totally at ease with the greeting, Vince went into his patter, but whilst peering over her shoulder, noticed that there was a coffin in the front parlour room. Apologising for troubling her at such an inconvenient time, he then slipped in a very professional piece of advice at no charge:

“I must apologise once more. But before I leave you, may I advise you to be ever so careful when removing your dearly departed, from that lovely fine table, as it is quite a very valuable piece of furniture.”

This woman, whose name was Winifred, was clearly not often thrown off the scent easily, but enquired as to just how valuable it might be. Vince now with the upper hand, advised that if not scratched, when the coffin was moved, could well be worth anything up to thirty pounds. The woman was quite shocked and he could now see he had her full attention:

“Well, I think you’d better come in young man,” she said “and if you bring your mate over there in with you, (pointing at the lurking Harry) maybe you can tell me if we can sort something out. My Husband is still in that box, and the costs of all this palaver is going through the roof, and thirty quid will certainly help pay for things.”

Harry was called over and they promptly moved the Coffin onto a couple of trestles, from the cupboard under the stairs. The Funeral Directors had left these, but Winnie thought he looked better on the table, but was by now quite sure he didn’t mind being moved for a good cause:

"Not much he can do about it anyway, is there?" she distastefully murmured, under her breath, as the Table was being carefully inspected. The thirty pounds was counted out, five pounds at a time, in a well practised method that seemed to make it seem so much more. (Dickinson's Real Deal and all those other Antique shows only copy the craft of the 'old knockerboys.')

These tried and tested methods only caused the client to look around at their other unwanted or even everyday used possessions, to see what else may be of interest, to these seemingly frivolous, stupid idiots, with more money than sense. The six matching chairs were soon located, Vince purposely broke one of the legs whilst examining them, so could only offer ten pounds.

The matching dresser now had nothing to match so may as well go for another tenner. Winifred was now up to Fifty pounds and delirious with joy, the funeral costs had now been fully covered, plus a nice round of drinks down The Red Lion. So everyone was happy. The boys were especially happy when the whole lot was snapped up by Tommy Barnes, the first dealer to look at it for £850. Right Result!

*

Softly Softly Georgie Porgy.

It was on more than one occasion that the Amateur dramatics were taken to the most extreme and deceitful level, even for these rascals. Still, you have to take your hat off to them, for the inventiveness and sheer determination, to go to any lengths, to secure the prize.

Such an occurrence was when Bingo, Fizzy, Powders and Perry Bowels were in Bournemouth early one summer. Bingo had got very ambitious and driven right up outside a huge detached property, in it's own grounds, with a purely 'Devil May Care' attitude.

It had not been a very profitable week so far and this little team were not skimping on the expenses (X's), so something had to occur.

Having been greeted at the door by Georgie (my friends call me Porgy), one of the most outrageously camp men he had ever come across, (and they certainly come across a few in Brighton), Bingo then had one of his greatest inspirations, examining Georgie a little closer, he devised his plan. There he was: Georgie in all his glory, silk dressing gown with cravat tucked in his open necked shirt, quite tubby, three chins, pink cheeks and small bags under the eyes, piggy little snout of a nose, and wispy blonde hair, on a high brow. Tiny square specs were on the bridge of his nose, Irish linen trousers with expensive silken house slippers and a sickly sweet smell of too much 'Old Spice' aftershave.

This geezer has just got to get it, thought Bingo, and had proceeded to examine some of the fine things on show. Bought a few bits of Staffordshire that were tucked away in a cupboard, then advised his business partner would accompany him later for a second opinion on a rosewood table clock. It appertained that an ancient faceless Aunt had left it to Georgie when she passed, but he really wasn't that fond of it, or the little table it rested on either.

Bingo explained that he and his business partner Lawrence, were in dire straits, they were looking for as much fresh stock as possible to replenish their Antique shop in Brighton (oooh! headquarters remarked Georgie) as they were trying to sell up. He also made an offer of £350 for a Cheese Cover, but this was not for sale under any circumstances advised Georgie.

Perry was to play the part of business partner Lawrence, Bingo, whose name was Reginald by the way, was to make an excuse of needing the Lavatory and whilst out of the room he would tell Georgie the state of affairs.

Introductions were made and Tea was served, Bingo announced he was feeling very stressed and would Georgie please excuse him for two minutes whilst he put some water on his face, no worries.

“Oh Georgie,” began Perry, “Poor old Reggie. It’s all gone so very wrong for him this year, has he told you?”

“No,” says Georgie. “Pray tell.”

Perry begins to reveal all, but swears Georgie to secrecy:

“For Heaven’s sake please don’t let Reginald know that I have told you this, but I feel you can be trusted and it’s breaking my heart to see him in such a terrible state. The thing is, Reggie and his wife have been having a hard time of it, what with her finding out about the affair with Him and Alan. He told you he had other, you know, interests, didn’t he Georgie?”

“Oh we all have our ‘Gaydar’ you know,” lied George.

Perry continued to explain that they were in the process of selling the shop and he would be keen on some of the things Georgie had to offer.

The rosewood clock and table were well worth a thousand pounds if he was interested, and even a few of the porcelain figurines in the old display case could be worth looking at a bit closer, but, hold on, here comes Reg...

When Reginald appeared he seemed slightly more at ease, and sat with legs crossed opposite Georgie and began to play with the forelock on his forehead and suddenly seemed so much more desirable to Georgie.

Perry made an excuse to pop out to the Car and Reginald had his meltdown right there and then:

“Oh, Georgie, what am I to do? I must get out of this country, I am at my wits end, as soon as we sell the shop I have to get away.”

“Ah, don’t worry Reggie,” Georgie consoled, sitting next to him and putting his arm around his shoulders. Bingo still swears to this day that old Georgie got physically aroused immediately.

“Now you listen to me, I have a little place down in the South of France, they call it a Château, but I don’t know. Ooh, I must be a poet and didn’t know it. Anyway, as soon as things have settled down a bit for you, you are more than welcome to come down there and spend the summer with me. It is by the Marina and we also have a nice little Yacht to take us out for a spot of fishing. Now what do you say? Aren’t things looking better already?”

Reggie was overcome with gratitude and couldn’t thank him enough.

Georgie was now in control of everything and accepted a cheque from Lawrence for the table and the clock, the display case was no good without the figurines so that was to be loaded on the motor as well.

The total was then rounded up to the grand sum of £2,000, and hands were shaken all round, albeit Reggie did get a slightly greasy and overeager sweaty palm when bidding farewell.

Georgie expressed an interest in one final word with Lawrence, and asked him to join him in the kitchen. Here he wrapped up the Cheese Cover and gave strict instructions not to let Reggie see what was inside the box till they got safely home, it was just a little present. He waved them off, blowing kisses, and shouted after them that he looked forward to July when he and Reggie would meet again.

They nearly decided to cancel the Cheque, which was often the case in such deals, but this time it would have been far too greedy, even for them, considering.

Considering!

The rosewood clock was by Charles Frodsham, 19th Cent, made £14,000 at auction. The little table was George III Pembroke, inlaid with chequered boxwood lines £1,500. The empty worthless marquetry display cabinet was Edwardian satinwood with a couple of drawers with neo-classical inlay, slipped in at £4,500. The figurines totalled in the end to £3,750, the 'Surprise' cheese cover made £800.

The other bits and pieces Bingo had at first bought, still made another grand. This came to just over £25,000, less expenses and the two grand they actually paid. As far as anyone knows, Georgie Porgy is still fuckin' waiting for the imminent return of poor old broken-hearted 'Reggie.' Still, it's only a laugh any way innit?

*

Every Cloud.

George had enjoyed remembering one particular 'Clue', that Banjo and Billy Green had taken them on, down in Torquay, back in 1968. An elderly couple had a lovely Bungalow that was loaded with porcelain from their time living out in Asia. Evidently they met as teenage sweethearts, and both came from Armed Forces families, stationed in Hong Kong, just after the War.

This may sound strange, but even that long ago some staunch military personnel still believed in trying to keep the 'Family' together, despite recommendations to the contrary.

With both sets of Parents being of the same view, their relationship blossomed with everyone's blessing. When the news of the patter of tiny feet was imminent, shotgun wedding was arranged and no-one was any the wiser. No-one was bothered to check calendars for dates, with what everyone had just experienced (what with the war and everything) it was the last thing to worry about. This information may seem irrelevant, but having former knowledge of the family history, before meeting their prey, could sometimes be extremely advantageous and beneficial to the final outcome.

All four had gone down for the trip and were all too familiar with the surroundings and B&B arrangements available, also Pubs, Clubs, Restaurants and other social benefits.

A few flyers were dropped in Paignton, for the sake of something to do, more than anything else, and to justify the expenses. Georgie had no problem, 'Getting In' and casually advised that his Partner Hector was better qualified to value the porcelain. Well, after only twenty minutes Vince announces to Horace that they have a 'Haggerty' on the cards. George and Mildred were intending to retire to South Africa, and join their only Son and heir, on his Farm, just outside Cape Town.

As worldly traveller types, their son had the same free spirit and had met and fallen in love with a Diamond Miner's daughter when travelling in Australia. They did not think it was worth carting all their worldly goods and belongings to the other side of the world, and it was hardly likely to fit in with the surroundings or décor.

They enjoyed mentioning that they had their memories and nothing could ever erase them. So they could now go and enjoy the Sun and still have plenty of time watching their grandchildren grow up. Apartheid certainly didn't bother them, that was for sure.

With the assurance, that everything they had, was for sale, at the right price, and that it had all been purchased in Asia, from China, Japan and surrounding countries, including Thailand,

Malaysia and Taiwan. A right good result for all concerned, was on the cards.

They had come prepared, and as the anticipation was contagious, all the boys had been speaking of for days was how much they could make if things went well. Vinnie and George had both been reading up on the products to be at their mercy.

A 'Haggerty' most certainly occurred, and they parted with, £6,700 for practically the whole contents of the Bungalow. The beds were not much use, so left for convenience as they had not yet signed for the Sale of their home, and the 'Bill of Sale', for all the contents, was signed by all relevant parties.

The trip back to Brighton was spent analysing the booty. They had to hire a Transit Van to load-up, and Banjo had agreed to take it back early next week, work with Bill for a couple of days, then get the train home.

Easy peasy lemon squeezy.

Everyone reckoned the 5ft tall pair of immaculate jardinière were the prize, whilst Vince thought the little Ivory carvings called Minsky's would fetch a nice few bob. Back home in good time, they just went straight to the Auction rooms in Lewes to offload the booty, thus avoiding all the fuss with the local dealer's trying to outbid one another.

They were glad they chose this ploy, as it saved a most embarrassing chain of events emerging in front of the Brighton mob. The first disappointment was the collection of bowls, all mass-produced in China in the sixties, the jardinière pair were fakes and the same applied to nearly every piece that they off loaded on that fateful miserable drizzly afternoon.

Even the weather was against them, and a few potentially rare Chinese rugs got dropped in a big puddle right outside the auction rooms, but were discarded as bedroom rags by the Auctioneer anyway. To say they were a bit sick was an understatement.

It was like a dark cloud had descended upon them and entered into the room. Billy Green was the most upset as he had promised to take his Daughter and Grand-kids on a nice little camping Holiday down to Bracklesham Bay. Her husband had just got a three stretch and she was finding things difficult. Bill started muttering to himself and said he would take the motor back himself and ram it straight into their fucking Bungalow, the cheating old bastards.

He got the bang needle and threw a shoebox of shitty little statue bases on the specialist oriental valuer's desk, spilling a couple as he did.

James the valuer went as white as a sheet, and froze, as if he'd seen a poltergeist or something, then began to choke and asked his assistant to fetch him a glass of water.

Once he had calmed down, he explained that if he was not mistaken the three small statue bases, plinths, looked like they were from some ancient dynasty or something of that nature, and could possibly run into the tens of thousands. Talk about light at the end of the tunnel. He takes their instructions and off they go to Sotheby's in London.

When they got the news that one went for £10,200, the next for £11,600 and the last and most rare made £15,900 you could say we were made up. Some of the furniture made up for the 'X's, which included Banjo's trip back to Torquay, but sadly he had to make the trip alone. They were all too busy enjoying themselves and planning their individual trips. But a deal is a deal and he had agreed to do it. That sure was one cloud that had a silver lining.

That gave them £7,750 each. Billy Green, bought a new motor, forgot about Bracklesham Bay and took his daughter and her kids to Disneyland California instead. He then went on to visit The Grand Canyon and lost the rest of his money at The Circus Circus Hotel & Casino in Las Vegas, he said it was the greatest time of his life, and after all: 'It's only a laugh anyway, innit!'

This was perfect timing for George as he had hooked up with a girl he felt strongly for and planned to take her to St. Tropez, the real hot spot of the time, reserved only for the rich and famous.

When someone mentioned years later that Jeffrey Archer had a similar tale in one of his books of short stories, Bill Green remarked:

"Well, where the fucking hell do you think he got the idea in the first place? You Muppet."

*

Pork Pie Pranks.

Georgie always loved to tell this tale.

"Once, of course, the reputation of the new 'Brighton Knockerboys' was established, the 'All Night Café,' had become the 'All Day Café' also. Where tales of the latest victims, of what seemed like the modern day 'Jessie James Gang' were revealed. Vince automatically took lead speaker at early doors and then the rest of 'em would just continue with revelations of how they had earnt a months money in two hours by following in our footsteps."

"We was legends in our own lunchtime Minnie." George proudly announced one afternoon.

"Anyway, we didn't blank the geezers that had now been put out to graze: the likes of Benny Weakes and Spider Mitchell. When we was at the graft on the barrows, they was always there to help out wiv' the collar. Now there seemed no need for their services."

"It wasn't like you could take 'em on a clue or anyfin', coz they stank to high heaven and were totally unpresentable. Even dropping bills was a non-starter by association alone."

"We had to keep up appearances of course and these days we had our suits regularly made to measure and sorted out at the dry cleaners. Mum's and Missuses all quite proud how we was all doing in our new found ventures, not that they paid much attention to what we were up to, as long as the readies were on the table, they didn't really give a toss."

George added: "Before I go much further, I must make an attempt to describe Benny. He made Albert Steptoe look like James Bond. Always in wellies wiv his strides tucked in the top. Two or three shirts under a waistcoat, two belts and braces, and shaved every leap year."

"He usually had some kind of donkey jacket or overcoat on, summer or winter, and was never without a filthy cheese cutter cap on his bonce. To mention that his hands and nails were filthy, under the fingerless gloves, seems unnecessary, but he was probably Brighton's answer to a coal-miner."

"So, this particular morning I was feeling a little under the weather due to an extended session in The Cobden, and it turned out that Vince fancied a rare day off for his own reasons.

Found out later it was a dental appointment to sort his roast beef out, but he never made it anyway."

"Vince has a sly word with me and Charlie Hardwick, about laying an outrageous bet with 'The Judge Wadey' and 'Bubbles' who was a new kid on the block, but seemed okay and game for a little wager."

"He starts off with 'I bet, old boy Benny Weakes 'ere can eat three standard Pork Pies, in just three fucking minutes without taking a drink. Any takers to beat the Bakers. Whaddayasay Judge or howaboutchou fat boy, do you fancy yer chances?'"

"Bubbles rose to the bait immediately and enquired to 'The Judge' what he fancied the chances. The comeback was expected, 'Well, what sort of financial commitment are we looking at, and what odds are you giving for such a ridiculous commitment? For a feat that you are not even prepared to attempt yourself, yet expect a poor fellah who hasn't got any teeth to speak of, or a fucking shilling to his name to do it for yah. Come on moneybags make it worth our while and we will definitely have a go. Whaddayasay Bubbles?'"

"'I'm in Judge,' Bubbles agreed. Vinnie stuck Charlie up to offer the odds. 'We propose,' began Char, 'This feat of daring do, three standard Pork Pies in three standard minutes with no liquid benefits once the clock has started at 3/1. Minimum bet of 10/- a man."

"Plus if any of you have got any bottle whatsoever, we will inject a slither of 'House Hot Mustard' onto the top of each Pie for extra interest and offer 9/2 at the same stake.'"

"At this stage Benny winced, but Vince gave him a sly wink and slipped him 10/-, the deal was done and there was no way Benny would let us down."

Georgie got all excited again whilst telling how many people jumped on the band wagon and how even some of the market traders got involved in the action.

"The sweetest bet of all, £2 coming from the owner of the Café who said if he could pull this off, Benny could have free Tea for the rest of the week, into the bargain. Typically it was a Thursday, so it was not exactly the gift of gifts."

"As Benny bit into his first Pie, his eyes watered as the mustard hit his tongue, but with the promise of another ten bob, nothing was never gonna stop him being the hero this day."

"Four minutes passed and Benny swallows his last morsel, and right on the nose Vince cries: 'That's it, he's only fuckin' gone and done it right on three fucking minutes. Well done my son, come on lads pay up. Actually don't worry about it right now we all know who we are, let's pop round The Basket-Makers, have a couple of drinks and settle up there.'"

"It was always handy to get an early drink there, John The Wad ran the Pub back then, and everyone agreed."

"Min, I'll tell you what, it was the only time I ever fucking saw Benny Weakes buy a drink, bloody marvellous. There we woz having a nice shant when in walks Joyce Pool. Now she was the best hoister in town and usually only stole to order, but on this occasion she had just pilfered a few sets of the latest thing from Bellman's in London Road. Made to measure curtains."

"Not one of us had a fucking clue what size we would need so she was a bit pissed off. Always ready for a party she grabs hold of Benny and starts dancing about and shoves his face right in between her great big Eartha's. Poor sod, what with the Pies and the recent four pints of Guinness he scarpered straight into the karzee and the sound was none to pleasant."

"The Landlord feared the worst and ventured into the Gents. Next thing we hear his 'You dirty filthy dirty rotten old bastard get the fuck out of 'ere now. What the fuck have you been eating?"

"Cor it fucking stinks. Oh my good God what the fuck have you done to yourself now?' As he marched Benny out at arms length he held his thumb and forefinger over his own nose to eradicate the disgusting smell that was coming from Benny's now filled up trousers."

"He had not only spewed up over the toilet, he had also deposited in his own pants. Although it was common knowledge that he never wore pants anyway, so the chances were his wellies were now quite full to the brim with his own shit as well."

"Sadly the party was over for Benny and his day ended there." George couldn't help but snigger.

"The first time he ever buys a fucking drink and gets sent home by half past fucking ten. Oh well, it's only a laugh anyway innit? But Steph, that's how it was in them days."

*

The Epsom Derby 1974.

Of course not every money making escapade was now exclusive to just knockin' doors, and this was a particular incident that became legendary and very nearly exclusive to the characters in these tales.

It was still in the era of 'The Big Race' being held on the first Wednesday in June. Traditionally on the same day since it's first conception and only changed in what would be termed as recent History, did it move to the weekend at the bequest of advertisers, and T.V.

Someone, possibly Judge Jonny Wadey, mentioned that the joint favourites Non-Alcho and Giacometti were absolute stone bonking certainties. The only things worth backing, and it was probably the first Derby for years that was literally a two horse race.

Rising to the bait, Vince announced that he fancied a rank outsider could upset the apple-cart. When he mentioned Snow Knight, he was to suffer a severe barracking from everyone in The Cobden that rainy Monday lunchtime. As always, he was unperturbed, and later that day advised his little crew to keep an eye on the weather, and that it may well be necessary to go up to Epsom that week, and stage a coup.

Georgie was getting quite excited when explaining this story and I could sense the sheer admiration he felt for his pal, and the pride of being a major player in the forthcoming events of that week. Therefore I will pretty much quote his version of events word for word, as by this stage I was able to write down his oratory quite efficiently.

"So, we were all slightly inquisitive as to why Vinnie had stuck his neck on the chopping board, and leave himself open to ridicule by the rest of 'em. Should he be proven to come out with such an outrageous prediction that came to nothing."

"The next morning in the café, it was still pissin' down locally and none of us fancied trudging up and down sodden streets, and so the mood was bleak to say the least. When Vince arrived wiv Harry about 8:00am, the mood instantly changed, and when he asked me and Charlie Hardwick to join him at the table there was definitely a conspiratorial feeling in the air."

"Something was afoot and the adrenalin started pumping when he began in that slow hushed tone, which he reserved for all cunning plans about to be revealed."

"Vince began, 'Right then lads, now I know you think I made a bit of a prat of myself last night in the Pub, but if I'm right about this and we have a bit of luck, everyone of them knob-heads in the boozer who took the piss yesterday are gonna be kicking themselves for years to come.'"

“'That Snow Knight has actually got some terrific breeding, it is very well bred from Derby and cost just over five bags at auction by a knowledgeable lady. Neither of them two fancied nags like the heavy going, this one don’t give a shit what the ground is like, and the odds as they are, are extremely favourable.'”

“'This is my plan. We have got, from my reckoning, £12,000 in the kitty, and if you fancy having a bit of faith in me, and I never wanna let any of you down do I? We are going to go up to Epsom tomorrow and pitch up on Tattanhum Corner and lay a book of our own.'”

George continued: “The thing is Minnie in them days, anyone with a few quid in their bin could go to a meeting like that and chance their arm. We were to pitch up next to a couple of local bookies from the Dogs, Sydney Starr and Davy Ki-Ki. They knew us all and were happy to let some locals have a go.”

“Not like these days, it’s well over-policed and no one really wants to give anyone a piece of the action. But in them days it was different. It’s not like that pair of Jew Boys hadn’t taken a nice few quid off of us in the past out at Corals, the Dog Stadium”.

“So, Vinnie continued to explain about the weather still being good to us, as far as he was concerned, and if we wanted ‘in’ then all well and good. He had already asked brother Charlie, who had dismissed the whole idea as ‘Dipsticks in Dreamland, once again.’ Harry was up for it, I was to bring the good luck as always, so didn’t really have much choice. Whatkoudissay?”

“Charlie Hardwick was prepared to give it a go, as long as things didn’t get too out of hand, and we were probably going to meet up with a few other local faces once we woz pitched up.”

“The final piece of the puzzle, was just to hope that the rain kept coming and keep our fingers and toes crossed. So then Vince decided there and then that we would go for it, and gave us our instructions for the afternoon. We sat around for a while and then Vince gave us our compiled lists for the afternoons graft. "

"We had each selected an area in the Town where we would go and place our each-way bets at Bookmakers for the next day. We all agreed that it was not worth having a big bet at the course, as if we copped well, there was a fair chance the Bookie would do a runner, and we were only laying out a couple of hundred quid any way."

"Vince declared that nothing was set in stone just yet, but if things went well, we were not to go boozing tonight and meet at the Diner same time tomorrow. 'Smart, sharp and ready to go.'"

Once again this euphoric feeling was descending on Georgie, and it was like he was going off into a trance. No harm meant, but it was like Vince was playing a Fagin-like part to keep them all under his spell. With the promise of rich rewards, as long as they all played their particular role, in a military type fashion.

"It rained all fuckin' night long in Surrey," said Georgie. "When we all met promptly at 8:00am on that Wednesday morning, well, we could hardly contain ourselves could we? We woz like excited school kids going on a trip to the fucking Zoo for the first time! Anyway, Vince told us to keep cool and reminded us that we still had to have that bit of luck."

"The journey was uneventful, just discussing what had happened to Patti Hearst, the daughter of some American Newspaper magnate. We all had our own opinions, but none of us predicted the true outcome of her turning up and help robbing a Bank. That certainly gave Old Randolph Hearst something to write about, we jested."

"Vince had just had his latest toy installed in his Rover motor. A Radio Cassette Player. State of the art. 'I was fed up wiv that Eight

Track Cartridge player,' he told us, but of course he only had one tape at this stage."

"Mind you it was a corker: Elvis Live in Las Vegas. The first track was the intro to the show, instrumental track from the Stanley Kubrick Film, 2001 A Space Odyssey and it really added to the excitement on the journey when he blasted it out at full volume."

"Well fed up at one stage I insisted on the radio and of course the number one at the time was Sugar Baby Love by The Rubettes and we all chimed in to that one, cushty"

"So, we were there nice and early, and although the weather was miserable, none of us were. When we greeted the Brighton Bookies with Cheshire cat grins, they just looked puzzled and bemused, like we had finally lost the plot. The final piece of the puzzle that Vince had concocted, was quite simple, but equally daring and potentially life threatening."

Georgie now looked totally animated and about to reveal the whereabouts of Lord Lucan or something equally as mysterious. Continuing in that annoying low-key tone of voice, that gave me a headache and forced me to lean closer. With hunched shoulders and that conspicuous stare through the top of his eyebrows he carried on:

"We kept a low profile most of the day, we were solely there for the main event. A few faces said hello, but we were on strict instructions to keep schtum. The two well fancied horses had great form and had beaten the rest of the field at one time or another, Non-Alcho was 6-4 and the other one Giacometti was 7-4. We were about to start taking bets, and as planned, with Harry and Vince on the podium, they opened up offering 9-4 and 100-30 respectively."

"Well of course they got plenty of punters straight away, grabbing the ridiculous odds. As expected there were a few doubting

Thomas's ready to start spreading the word that they were charlatans and would disappear as soon as the race started."

"This is where Charlie and me stepped in. Waving wads of money with ten minutes to go, Charlie steps up and has £500 on the nose Giacometti. Then, three minutes later, I steams in wiv £800 Non-Alcho."

"This had the desired effect, as when these bets were placed, both Harry and Vinnie took the wagers with the aplomb of multi-millionaires without a care in the world."

"I remarked to a couple of Geordies, that I had already taken a Grand off of these two, and Charlie had made a big fuss on the last race when he got paid out £900 for backing the winner."

"At these type of races a lot of the big bets come in late and there was a sudden surge of punters slinging money at the pair of them from all angles. The exercise was complete."

"When the race was about to get under way, every single one of us needed to use one of them inhospitable smelly portable toilets on offer, and the blood had drained from all of our faces. We were all in this together now, so we all shrugged our shoulders and simply waited to see how our fate was to pan out."

Now came another bit of classic Georgie. He's done no less, would you fucking believe, than got up out of his seat and walked into his kitchen, remarking over his shoulder:

"Would you care for another glass of wine then Min? I think I'll put the kettle on and make a cup of tea."

My curt reply was to be expected:

"Get your arse in here Georgie or things are gonna get nasty, whether this is your place or not."

He comes flying back in the living room with the biggest grin I have ever sin, shouting at the top of his voice:

"It fucking well pissed it diddun it? Fuckin' well pissed it, it did. It came flying right round Tattanhum fucking corner right where we woz, took up the lead, right there, right there in front of where we woz."

"Right there on Tattanhum Corner, and Vinnie just screamed: 'We've done it boys, we've fuckin' well dunnit. Go on my son, go on my son. Home you go, there's Snow fuckin' problem 'ere, go on my suun.' And that was it!"

"Steph I tell you, it was abso-fucking-lutely brilliant. If anyone ever tells you that there ain't nuffin better than sex, I can assure you that there is. Because at that moment, I can honestly say, I was right up there in heaven. Nothing got close to it after that and it won by two lengths easy."

"Of course, forever the perfect strategist, Vince did not show quite the same elation as me, Harry and Charlie. He took it in his stride, gave me the wink and calmed Harry down as quick as possible."

"A few punters still needed to be paid out on various bets, so this was taken care of in the usual professional manner. Like when you leave a gaff with all the goods and the victims are still unaware of what has actually taken place."

I, myself, felt like I had actually been there myself, and could not contain myself, so questioned the takings and winnings.

"Well," began Georgie, in a more constrained tone, and back to his normal state, "We took off as soon as things were sorted with the winning bets and casually packed up the book, with a defeatist look on our boats as if we had lost readies on the race and could no longer honour anymore bets."

“We had parked in quite an optimistic spot, that would guarantee a quick departure if things had not gone to plan, so had no trouble with any unnecessary traffic blocking our exit.”

“Do not avoid the question please George, or I’m going to get the hump,” came my reply.

“Sorry darlin', I couldn’t help it.” I then of course experienced that charming schoolboy grin, that kept me coming back for more every time.

“We stopped at The Bolney Grange on the way home to have a rough recky on the days events, asking for a secluded spot. We knew the Guv'nor there, from previous excursions, so he guided us to a private room with assurance of no interruptions.”

“All four of us, had every single pocket crammed full of cash. The boys had amassed a total of £6,460 on the book. There had been plenty of small bets and the highest denomination of note was only £20 at the time, so they had siphoned off plenty of money to Charlie and me during the race, just in case any little gang might see them as a mugging opportunity.”

“Then Vince asks if we have our betting slips on us, to see what we have to collect from the bookies, later this afternoon and tomorrow. Harry was first up, and the look on Vince’s face was incredulous. He cried out, ‘You soppy fuckin’ prat, you didn’t take the 40-1 you fuckin' idiot. What the fucking hell is wrong wiv you?’”

“I jumped in at this stage and advised Vince, that I had also not taken the price. Vince then countered with: ‘What the fuckin' hell am I working with here? What about you Charlie? What have you got to say for your fuckin' self?’ Charlie advised that he had followed Vince’s instructions to the letter and taken the advice of 40-1 as acceptable.”

“Here was Harry’s moment of triumph. So he says to Vince: ‘I s’pose you took the 40-1, then did ya?’”

“‘Course I did,’ says Vince.”

“Harry then reveals the best news of the day: ‘Well, you know-it-all, it fuckin' well finished at 50-1, you fuckin' lemon. You were so up yer own arse with your master plan you didn’t even read The Sporting Life or any of the morning papers, and not one of ‘em gave that horse a fuckin’ cat in hell’s chance.’”

“Then changing his tone to one of love and affection, continued: ‘But, on this particular occasion, I am prepared not to make too much of your oversight on that particular detail, and despite the two of you costing us a considerable amount of money, forgive you unreservedly, whaddayasay Georgie?’”

“I concurred, and at this stage, of course, we all just fell about laughing for ages, then we had a couple of very pleasant drinks and drove back to Brighton like the Four Musketeers having just saved the King of France. Job done! The funniest thing was that the following week the new number one single was ‘They Call It The Streak’, By Ray Stevens, and Vinnie drove every fucker crazy by screaming ‘Lookadat Lookadat’ every time it came on the Radio, fuckin brilliant.”

Epsom Derby 1974

1st	Snow Knight	50 - 1
2nd	Imperial Prince	20 - 1
3rd	Giacometti	5 – 2
4th	Bustino	8 - 1

The winning trainer was Peter Nelson and was ridden by Brian Taylor. The winning time was 2mins 35.04 seconds. Not quick, not slow. But since that day, there has never been a winner at such a big price. The closest was a few years later at 20-1, but this is no History lesson, it is just a declaration of faith between friends and family.

I did ask George what the total tally was but he could not remember as he advised he was quite drunk for about four days!

We decided to work it out together, once and for all.

Once the original stakes were deducted + minimal expenses,

Harry 5 x £20 E/W @ 50-1,

Georgie 5 x £20 E/W @ 50-1,

Vince 5 x £20 E/W @ 40-1,

Charlie 5 x £20 E/W @ 40-1.

The total collected from all the bookies was £22,500 winnings, with £800 stake back, less £80 tax paid in advance, netted the quartet £23,220.

Then the day itself added another £5,800, bringing the day's earnings to one shy of thirty grand: £29,020.

This was £7,255 each, which in 1974 was not a bad day's work by any means. But what a way to earn it!

Of course it could all have gone incredibly wrong, and there are many occasions when things did not go to plan, but as Georgie, Vinnie, Harry and Charlie always say: 'It's only a laugh anyway, innit!'

*

My Personal Opinion.

Here was an historical event that cannot be questioned, but it did of course, once again bring up the question of integrity and self-belief. Here it was, a fantastic coup, with nobody getting hurt or conned. Admittedly they were not licensed, but then again neither were plenty of others. Yet it seemed that this was clearly a one off, straight job, and they would soon revert back to their wicked ways, back on the 'Knocker'.

It was obviously the only thing that was really challenging, allowing them to get truly excited, so maybe it was the con that was at the root of all ambition and sense of success. Only when someone had been subjected to some kind of inadvertent and costly experience, at their mercy, was it truly worthwhile.

Who knows? I have stopped trying to fathom it out, but still find the company of 'Brighton's Knockerboys' exhilarating and posthumously proud to regard them as friends, for all their faults and fancy-free attitude to life.

Maybe this is where the allure and fascination lies. The whole lifestyle aspect. Most of them have at one time or another been banged up for both short or long term periods, yet have not considered taking on a new career.

This actually, is not particularly fair, as many have taken a different road at one time or another, but always with the 'Stitch up' in the back of their minds.

When the Hurricane of October 1987 hit Brighton, they reckon no doors were knocked, regarding any interest in Antiques anyway, not for ages. They had all bought ladders and were suddenly Insurance Loss Adjusters, giving helpful advice and able to get the roof repaired at a discounted price.

As long as they got a share of the Insurance claim. Any D.I.Y. enthusiast that fancied having a look for themselves, couldn’t get hold of a ladder for love nor money.

Then there was a Government Scheme to help the elderly get free loft fibreglass insulation, on The Isle of Wight; the project was completed in record time. Due to the extremely enthusiastic influx of Brighton Knockerboys, knocking every single door to advise how they could help.

This also of course meant that they had to gain access to the property, so who knows if any of them were able to give valuable advice to any of the home-owners about any old items of no intrinsic value, ‘up there in the attic doing nothing.’ At the very least, the loft had to be emptied of all contents just to get the job done. Who knows what was up there?

There are unfortunately many cases, in the wintertime, of elderly folk starving or freezing to death due to poverty, and afraid of running up fuel bills. What’s the point of having 3 tea chests full of China, porcelain and old candlesticks, if you can’t afford to eat? An oil painting sandwich is just not functional, as Arnie Missin once remarked. The painting in question of course, had fed a lot of people that particular week.

There was one instance on The Isle of Wight, where the couple were living in one room. Once the loft was cleared out, they had brand new insulation installed for free. Then with the money received for the old crap that needed to go, they were able to have fitted carpets throughout the whole Bungalow and central heating into the bargain, everyone a winner.

So, there is no doubt they could all turn their hands to something new when the situation arose. Fitting a few layers of that itchy yellow stuff between the joists in the roof was a small price to pay, if it enabled easy access to a potentially lucrative property.

As some of the boy's have said, half the time in an old gaff, the people may have bought the house before the War and never even been up in the attic. This meant that anything of value wasn't even theirs to sell really, by definition of ownership. They should try and contact the previous owner or heirs, to pass on the funds received, fat chance.

So, if they discovered an old painting and got paid an honest £500 cos they thought it might fetch a few bob, and it turned out to be worth a few grand, who's cheating who? All of a sudden someone is offered a couple of hundred pounds for some rubbish they never even knew existed. If never investigated, when they passed away, any benefactors may well just empty everything out and throw it all in a skip.

There are many interesting stories of someone finding valuables in skips, but they don't have a, 'you're guilty', finger pointed at them.

You can't say they are not inventive, and by no means scared of a bit of collar, so they must be entitled to the rewards for ingenuity. Who's to say otherwise? Not me that's for sure.

One of the main causes for their notoriety should be left at the door of the Police, who continuously falsely accuse 'Knockerboys' of not being 'Qualified' to ply their trade.

On numerous occasions the 'Men in Blue' blame unsolved crimes on one group of people without any substantial evidence, as it is the easy way out. This of course only adds fuel to the fire, instilling bad public opinion of a bunch of unskilled hard working guys from Brighton who are just trying to earn a crust, relying on their skills of wile and cunning.

Some unfortunate ‘Brighton Knocker's’ are continuously bombarded with unsubstantiated accusations of fraudulent behaviour.

When one of the dealer's on Dickinson's Real Deal offers £20 for a Gold bracelet, you don't suddenly have a Policeman come out of the crowd and slap 'em in handcuffs, and bang them up in the cells for 24 hours.

I myself, now have a slightly biased opinion on this argument, as I have come to know the object of the debate personally, but sod it, I think I am in a position to voice this side of the story. Maybe I'm too involved, or have I been got at?

I did say at the beginning, in The Preface, that you may detect a change in myself, by just simply turning the pages and this is evident in both my attitude towards the subject in hand and also towards life itself. The Devil May Care attitude towards life that ‘The Knockerboys’ have is not exactly original.

These stories, and all the characters that are in them, could potentially come from anywhere in the Country, it just so happens to be Brighton. The weird thing, and questioning thought is though, that are such characters, and so many of them, to be found in every small City or Town in England?

I think not, and therefore Brighton is, and remains to be, a major part of the equation and makes it a most fascinating place to live in or visit. So many visit or come to study at Uni and never bloody leave.

Also of course, is that natural mischievous talent, to just want and desire to wind people up, another glorious Brightonian trait?

*

9. ' The Stitch Up's'
'To have you in stitches'

This chapter I should tell you, is in a slightly different style to all the rest, yet again another twist in the tale, as it covers many different events both on the job and in social situations.

Now we know, after quite a few years, that nearly all of 'Brighton's Knockers,' still treated the whole lifestyle as a bit of a game. None of them thought it would last very long, and of course it was just a laugh anyway, wannitt!

However, the piss taking was not reserved just for the Pub, but quite a few opportunities arose when working with new partners. As after a few years, despite earning good money together, there would be some 'Scream Ups', and certain groups would go their separate ways.

When this occurred, of course, there would be a huge backlog of different calls to amalgamate together. Where they had tried their best to 'Get In' with no luck, and not willing to share the 'Clue' with anyone else, they would then share with their newly formed partners. Bearing in mind that now having worked 'The Door' for a good few years now, not one single one of them trusted each other as far as they could throw them.

Now, however, they would be happy to take a chance that their new 'Best Buddy' could 'Get In,' where the last useless, lazy, good for nothin' runt could not.

This was such an occurrence when Old Charlie Hardwick teamed up with Paul Lambert and Georgie to go and work down Littlehampton way for a few days. The Bills had all been dropped and after lunch they were in a little village called East Preston.

George mentioned to Charlie that him and Vince had a blinding deal here many years ago.

He could not quite remember the gaff, but possibly it was that one there which now had a 'Stable Style Front Door', so he should give it a go, whilst Georgie observed. Up goes Charlie bold as brass and knocks the door. A big strapping young lad about 28, with cap sleeved T-Shirt and tattoos all up his Arnie Schwarzenegger biceps, opens the top-half of the door and enquires to the purpose of his visit.

Unperturbed, Charlie explains that they were in the area for a short time, and interested in purchasing any of the goods advertised on the flyers that they may have enjoyed reading about yesterday or this morning, for their consideration.

The kid tells him to hold on for two minutes as he may have something of interest; Charlie glances in Georgie's direction, indicating that something was afoot. The next thing, there is a bright flash of light from inside the hallway, and young 'Desperate Dan,' comes flying towards Charlie ranting and raving that his Auntie Anne and Uncle Gerald had been severely ripped off by 'robbing bloody bastards, just like you a few years ago.'

He now had his picture on a Polaroid that would be shown to his poor relatives now in a rest home, and also the local police, now his card was marked, finishing off with: 'And if you or any of your scummy money grabbing conning little gits comes near my house again, I'm gonna smash you to kingdom come.' Point taken!

Back at the motor and young Lambert declares no joy, Georgie also, and Charlie needs a cup of jamboree.

At this stage, in the Rosy Rooms, Charlie winks at George and begins to let the youngster in on a little clue he may have found and felt there was sure to be a nice few bits of gear in a particular house, but he had had no joy. Maybe, just maybe, he might have a bit more luck seeing as he was a nice good-looking young chap, who was on the ‘up-n-up’.

‘Titchie’ rose to the bait and declared that now was the time for the ‘New Breed’ to show the ‘Old Timers’ how it was done, and ‘Come on then, show me, where is this place then, let me get to work, and I’ll show you how it’s done.’

Paulie goes marching up to the Stable Door as large as life, then goes and knocks the gaff as directed, looks over his shoulder in a cocky kind of way and waits for the answer.

Both Georgie and Charlie are peeking from behind a nearby fence within earshot, so as not to get any later reports, which would be subject to discrepancy.

So the door opens and larey bollocks Lambert begins his introduction. All but ten words have come out of his gob, when there is a sudden eerie sound of a crunching, bone on bone kind of sound, indicating that the disgruntled dealer on the door has copped for a blinding right-hander straight in the boat.

The next thing heard was ‘Desperate Dan’ shouting, at the top of his voice: ‘And if I ever see you, you horrible little shit, or any of you thieving runts again, I’ll chase you out of town myself. Now fuck off.'

Catching it in the eyeball was a lucky escape for Lambie as otherwise he may well have had his jaw or nose severely broken, and before he even reached the motor his eye was the size of a tennis ball, by all accounts.

Both Charlie and George complained that they could now no longer work in this village again, and had wasted at least 75 flyers, and why the fuck did he not ‘Get In’, what with all his charm and charisma?

They didn't stop sniggering, all the way home or for years to come for that matter.

It was years before 'Titchie' cottoned on that he had been stitched up. More to the point, only a couple of days earlier, Paul Lambert had been caught, sauntering out in a drunken stupor, out of the knocking shop outside 'The Conquerors', Brunswick Street East, with his trousers half way down his legs. With the Tom shouting at him that his two-inch dick only made him a bigger prick, than he already was.

Hence the nickname 'Titchie.' Nothing to do with his height at all. He was having a terrific few days. All the way home he moaned and moaned, but they just told him to shut the fuck up. You're goonered anyway you prat, go back and work with your soppy little brother, you just ain't in our league son.

*

Another new development 'On The Knocker' was money lending. As always the 'Easy Money' was 'Easy Spent', and invariably the stock money went the same way. Readies were desperately needed to go to work, petrol had gone up, Hotels now required a credit card or deposit, so the graft started before even leaving Brighton on a Monday morning.

So one particular week young Stephen Boyle had managed to persuade big brother Terry, to part with the stock money, so that he and the youngest of the Boyles Richard, could go on a clue in West London. This arrangement suited the dealers, never mind if they were related or not, this had nothing to do with family, it was all strictly business.

It meant when they stuck up the stock money, the borrower, relative or not, would come back to them with the gear, sell-up at a bargain rate and they could deduct the loan from the total. Of course they had now developed an extremely competitive nature within the 'Knockerboy' community.

And of course 'New Blood' was breathing down their necks all the time, some of these new entrepreneurs were even showing signs of actually being genuine and honest-to-goodness businessmen, perish the thought!

So anyway, this time Steve and Richie went off on the 'Clue', hoping for a decent day's work. They had previously negotiated a very nice deal with a young fellah whose Mum had passed away, but the family couldn't sell the house, or at least exchange contracts, till it was cleared, a classic 'Haggerty.'

Steve was no mug, he had been well educated by both older brothers, so rented a Luton van and loaded up all the best gear first and sought out a different avenue for the booty, sod letting Perry get the Golden Goose. He had already noted a large Antique come second-hand furniture business in Battersea, called 'Harvey's', and he had found out that it was a Father-Son affair.

So he sets about his plan. Introducing himself to young Jonathan, he explained they had some fantastic items of interest plus a very lucrative proposition, and would Dad Jon be prepared to let the youngster join them for the day, after looking at the stuff already available.

Jonathan was up for it and had a good gander at the gear on board, then advised they would purchase everything on the Luton straight away. That meaning in two hours time, after unloading, doing a stock take and visiting the Bank.

It was no secret that his old man was absolutely granite and wouldn't part with a shilling till the gear was on their premises. This was taken care of at a tidy profit, but then to be fair, Jonathan had not exactly paid over the odds.

He knew his local clientèle only too well and was certain to make a decent profit out of this lot.

On the way back to the gaff in Barnes with Jonathan on board, Steve explained his situation. He wanted to unload all the Cream gear in London but still get back to Brighton with enough to cover the Loan from his brother plus a bit on top.

A great relationship was formed and continued for a few years and only naused up when Jon and Jonathan Harvey moved to Brighton themselves and therefore could no longer provide 'outsider' funds.

The upshot of course was that Steve was able to sell nearly all the good money earning items in London, then return to Brighton in a well depressed state and pull up with young Rich outside Terry's place in the Lanes.

The Luton was full of moderate pieces, plus a few interesting bits that might make a profit 'if they were lucky'. Steve tells Terry that it was a complete waste of time and if he hadn't borrowed the money off his own Brother he wouldn't have even fucking bothered. Whatkanyadoo?

Steve and young Richie had stopped off at Bolney Grange on the A23 and carved up £17,000, this was £8,000 each and a generous £1,000 for Paul Lambert who had given them the clue.

The haul on the motor came to £5,400, which Terry gave them, and then of course he deducted £2,000 for the stock money. There was £400 expenses to cover the day, young Jonathan was certainly worth the expensive lunch.

He was still probably finishing the 'Haggerty' as agreed. Fucked if they was gonna be bothered with all the other shit, left in that big old house. Anyway he was local to the area, it was his Manor and was bound to make a nice few quid on the rest of the stuff left behind. Everyone was happy.

It would have been a great little coup, but as young Rich walked into 'The Dover Castle' that night, he was unaware that Stephen was in the back bar playing cards. When someone asked how he had done on that clue in London, he replied that it was a waste of time and that his brother couldn't pick a winner of a fuckin' boxing match after the fucking result was announced and a fighter's hand raised in the fucking air. He had cost him five hundred poxy quid in 'X's and he was never gonna work with him again, the tosser, even if he is my bruvver.

The whole bar erupted into laughter when Stephen Boyle got up and confronted him, but Richard, not being the bravest of the Boyles just scarpered and wasn't seen again for a fortnight.

Rumour had it, that he had bolted off to Kent and slept in one of the makeshift huts built for the Hop picking season, no gas, no electric and not much else. Oh well, it's only a laugh, innit? They made up of course and no harm was done, just don't tell Terry!

*

Harry Nearly always enjoyed telling about the time he and Vince had been taken on a call by Eric Prince up to Sheffield. Neither of them reckoned him for a second, he was always more aligned to the Missin brothers, and was not to be trusted.

If, however, they thought they had a chance of nicking a few quid that they should have got, it was like double yer fucking money, and Hughie Green wasn't in the divvy up!

So, up they go, and did their best to 'Get In' but had no joy, at least that's what they told Eric, no way they were gonna put him in it, whatever happened. Things had started to get a bit more spiteful in this game, and even though he gave them the clue, he was still not to be trusted or treated with due respect, the muggy runt.

Anyway, they had checked into a reasonable Hotel, and for some reason snaky Eric had to go off on another 'Call.' This was totally unacceptable as a rule, if you were working together everything was shared, but sod him. Let him have a go, and if he buys anything, once it's on the motor it's ours anyway they reckoned.

It turns out, innocently enough, that he was only after a local bird from a few weeks ago. He met them both back at the Hotel and advised that there were three birds coming to the Hotel later, for a nice evening Dinner and Dance, which was a regular weekly feature at the Hotel.

At this point Harry pointed out that now he had tumbled why they had all booked separate rooms instead of the usual Doubles or Triples, to save on the 'X's. Things were now clear, not only could slippery bollocks Eric not 'Get In' 'The Clue,' he was determined to 'Get In' some bird's knickers, and was using the Nearly's for all purposes. He was in for a rude awakening and sound educating.

Once the penny had dropped with Harry, he was none too happy and so devised a slippery plan of his own. He was well aware that his Brother never entertained such propositions when working away, and he himself was well happy with his missus.

They were also both well aware that a slimy little shit like Princey would always have one over them, if they 'Played Away' while they was away, but it just wasn't their style, the pair of them.

One of the few things they both agreed on, 100%.

Harry agreed to have Dinner with them, but Vinnie unfortunately cried off with a terrible migraine at the last minute. Vince crept into Eric's room whilst they were dining and lifted the four-poster bed onto four breeze blocks that Harry had located and nicked at a nearby building site earlier.

The evening went quite well, then Harry simply told the two Girls that he was gay and had to join 'A Friend' on the other side of town, 'Thanks for the evening, and Eric will take care of the bill, bye bye girls,' waved and sauntered off. Sniggering all the way back to his room.

NEARLY.

He was no Nearly boy for nothing, he had noticed that all the punters left their shoes outside the rooms for shining, and just couldn't help himself by swapping loads of pairs from outside one room to another, it took ten minutes but what can you get for nothing?

Two hours later, and there was an almighty crash from one of the rooms on the floor above and cries of 'You Bastard, You Lousy Fucking Bastard, You Done It On Fucking Purpose You Lousy Fucking Bastard', then pathetic claims of 'Sorry love I had nothing to do with it honest, please believe me.'

Then there was the almighty cry from the Richard, in true Dusty Springfield style: 'I don't love you any more, let me go. Fuck off, let me go, let me go. I don't want you anymore!'

The door was then slammed in no uncertain terms.

Alone in their rooms both Vince and Harry smiled smugly together at exactly the same time.

The next morning was equally as remarkable.

The stewards were knocking on all the doors to enquire who, and who did not have the correct footwear, as the early risers had nothing to wear. Not only had Harry swapped all the shoes, he had also put them at different starter positions, it was panic stations all round.

They met for breakfast in the Dining Room and no-one cracked a note, till Vince mentioned a couple of chances on the way home he and Harry might call on, and if he was up to it, maybe Eric could do a few 'Cold Calls.' This inferred that he was not 'In On' the calls they had, but if he, was to get lucky, they were all in on it, not Prince's best day's work.

Not being without a 'Clue', they steamed into a couple by eleven o'clock and managed to get a week's money, sheep faced Eric had not much to say for himself. As they were just hitting the final leg of the A23 Vince started humming a familiar tune, Harry picked up on it immediately and began to hum alongside, then when the moment was right they both burst into the chorus in sync:

Please Believe Me,
Let Me Go.
Coz I Don't Love You Anymore.
Please Believe Me,
Let Me Go.
Go on Eric
Fuckin' Let Me Go.
I Just Don't Want You
Any fuckin' more.
Please Please...

At that point Eric went ballistic and insisted that they stop taking the piss out of him. They absolutely pissed themselves, and had to pull over on the hard shoulder to relieve their bladders, laughing at each other, whilst slippery bollocks Eric sat in the motor at the back on his jack.

Go on. Say it yourself!

*

There were of course, a few Weddings along the way. Gaffer Dawes himself had about five, with kids coming out of his ear holes, to this day he can't always recall who belongs to who. But he loves every last one of them, dearly.

Unfortunately this type of behaviour doesn't always render the best behaved kids, and at most times at least a couple of his offspring are under Her Majesty's Pleasure for one thing or another. Oh well, that's life.

On one such occasion Gaffer had decided to keep things 'Low Key' and had just the bare minimum catering, and had the reception above one of his large warehouse style showrooms. There was a fair wad stuck behind the Bar and most people were just interested in having a drink anyway.

There were a few shenanigans that lovely sunny day. At one stage Kevin Douglas and a couple of his pals got fed up with one of the other guests, who was considered to be behaving too boisterously, and decided to strap him to the roof-rack of their Volvo Estate. But being good-hearted chaps untied him after twenty minutes, poor sod.

The same guy was at the Bar a while later and was ordering a round of drinks, knowing full well that the 'Free Bar' was no longer available. A few of the Knockerboys ordered large ones, and mentioned not to leave out the girls, purposely, just to stitch him up, but he wasn't worried, and was fully aware of what was going on. When informed that the round came to £37.50 he was not in the slightest bit perturbed, and the onlookers were all disappointed at his disdainful attitude and cool reaction when informed of the bill, and paid it without batting an eyelid.

He simply placed forty quid on the counter and advised the barmaid to keep the change. Considering a pint cost less than two quid at the time, this was merely polite but not flash, not yet anyway.

He then announced, for all and sundry to witness, “You lot have already had a good laugh at my expense once today, so you’re not gonna get another fucking one.”

Then he turned back to the barmaid, “If any of these ponces want another drink, send 'em over to me luv!”

With that he strutted off, leaving most of them with their mouths agape, amazed at his cocky and resonant confidence and attitude.

The same fellow, allegedly threw Gaffer’s Son Eddie out of a window a little later in the day, due to some bullying issues perpetrated by the Dawes boy, who was trying to build a reputation of his own, didn’t get too far with that one.

His identity will be revealed later.

*

A keyboard player who did the rounds and was familiar with what was required provided the entertainment. The problem was one of the guests had a right cob on, about Percy on the piano, and was sure to let him have it once a couple of large Vera & Philharmonics had set in.

Sure enough, when Percy started to play his favourite old tune of Cool Cool Water, it was too much for Arnie Missin, and he proceeded to aim an ice bucket straight over his crust. It was half ice half water by this stage so was not harmful, and it was only a laugh anyway, wan'nitt?

Percy, however, did not take too kindly and began creating a fuss. This was the most memorable moment of course, as some comedian, (Georgie) shouted out:

"Hold on Percy, you're only paid to play the keyboard, now we're all getting a song and dance for the same price."

Percy was red-faced and then suffered more humiliation when Arnie's mate Powders added:

"You should count yer'self fucking lucky mate, if you was playing Any Old Fuckin' Iron sunshine, then you would have a terrible headache an' all."

Of course everyone started to laugh, and even though it was not his best moment, they all chipped in for Percy to buy a new keyboard set, and every single one of them knew he was at the 'Top-Up' when he declared how much it would cost to get a decent replacement.

*

Another of Harry Nearly's favourite escapades was 'The Great Cardiff Conspiracy.' This was an accidental foray that was totally misguided from beginning to end. The gang had decided to give 'The Welsh' another try.

No pun intended, they were just good at Rugby and sod all else.

Vince travelled up with Harry and had arranged to hook up with Paul Desjarlais and Bubbles. They got to Cardiff but the Hotel they fancied was fully booked due to an International Rugby match. Nothing any of them had the slightest bit of interest in.

Bubbles and Paul had got there a day earlier and discovered the problem, booked themselves in but no room at The Inn for the other two Herberts. So they had to suffer and consequently booked themselves into a smaller Guest House a little further out of town, but right on the coast.

They were in fact in Barry, but not even aware of the exact location. It's only about the same distance between Brighton and Worthing and having travelled all that way it was immaterial.

On the way to the better Hotel, to meet up with their worldly co-conspirators, sauntering just behind Cardiff Arms Park, they came across a derelict demolition site. Now, still being on a coastal location Vince was at the wind-up.

A fellah was examining a large pothole on-site and upon seeing this Vince chirped up, 'Oy what the fuck do you think you are doing young man?' He looked across with a puzzled look on his boat and said, 'Nothing, boyo, and what's it got to do with you anyway?'

Vince was straight on him;

'Well let me tell you this, you startling little upstart. If you have found any Doubloons be sure to put them back exactly where you found them or you are in serious trouble my son. NOW, I am in charge of this Historical excavation site, and am authorised to arrest and charge anyone trespassing here between these barricades that I deem fit. You may not be aware of the crime you are committing and therefore I am prepared to take no further steps, at this particular stage of proceedings. Get the fuck out of there now!'

Then looking at Harry, remarked:

'The local constabulary are supposed to be guarding this site. We will have to arrange our own security first thing in the morning, make a note.'

So, the Herbert comes towards them and asks what the hell is going on. It turns out he is a local reporter and was just taking a peak as there was no official notification from the Council as to what was going on. A local resident had phoned the paper to find out more information and his Editor had asked him to investigate.

'Well,' said Vinnie, 'You may well have a little scoop on your hands, me old cocker. My name is Jeremy Archibald Nelson. I know, I know, heard it all before, and yes, I am a direct descendant of the great man himself. I am here representing The Natural History Museum, The Royal British Naval Academy and H.M.R. Customs & Excise. Now if that is not enough to impress you, I suggest you take a good look in a mirror, before you end up in her majesty's custody on a charge of High Treason.'

The Welsh accent made it so much more comical, but the chap didn't know this. 'Oooh, bloody hell,' he went, 'what the heck have I stumbled on my good sir. I am so sorry. I really had no idea. About what actually?'

Here Vince gave him the 'Top Up'. 'Well you my little Welsh treacle tart, have just been fiddling around in what we believe to be the long lost burial ground of Captain James T. Morgan's long lost treasure. (The mention of long lost twice in the same sentence is priceless.)

'Now you listen to me, it has only just been confirmed that this is the very site that that famous pirate, held up for some twelve years, between his feats of daring do, skulduggery and absolute terrible acts of tyranny. We are at this very moment awaiting the arrival of one Dr Sydney Wells and Professor Miles Newington from The University of Sussex to come and verify our fantastic discovery.'

'They are world-renowned experts in their field and we are just so excited. Do you think it would be possible for you to keep this a secret? At least for a day or two, and then I think I could arrange for your paper to get the exclusive. Whaddayasay?'

Harry said: “The kid was made up and promised he would not tell a living soul until we contacted him on the number he gave us.”

Harry found it hard not to keep giggling whilst conveying the details. They advised the kid of their temporary address, but also said that the experts had V.I.P. clearance to stay at that nice big hotel round the corner where they were hoping to greet them shortly. 'Just give us a chance to clear things up with the Government,' were Vinnie’s last words to the avid reporter.

“Well.” said Harry. “We gets into this nice posh hotel and finds out where the other two are staying. Pops down to the Bar and having a nobble, when one of the Bus boys comes over and asks if we are the Historians or maybe even the Archaeologists from Sussex University. Vince gives the wink, and then we are all at it. I claimed to be Professor Newington and Bubbles is Doc Wells. So then we are informed that the Editor of the local rag wishes to speak with at least one of us on the phone as a matter of extreme urgency.”

“Now the thing is Steph, we have only been in Wales for about two hours and all of a sudden the world wants to know what we are up to, we don’t even want anyone to know we exist.”

Harry usually took a backstage position in these matters but in Wales for some reason he seemed to come out of his shell a bit and got proper involved.

I will let him take it from here:

“I goes to the Phone and tells the bloke that I cannot possibly under any circumstances discuss our presence in Public. But if he called back in five minutes, I would make my way back to my suite in the hotel. To be fair I just could not resist it."

"As good as his word, the Editor phones just as I enter the room. Things just escalated from there really, and by the time I had finished the call it seemed that Captain Morgan's Long Lost Treasure, was a stone bonking certainty."

"The next morning papers were delivered to both Bubbles room in Cardiff, and our little bolt-hole in Barry. Headline news in every one of them it was. 'Brighton Boys Bring Home The Bacon' was our favourite."

"But the trouble was it had caused a kind of hysteria all over the City. Everywhere you went there was only one topic of conversation, the accent again made it all the more comical."

'Ave you 'erd? Captain Morgan, under our noses fer all those bloomin' years, would you beleeve it.'

'Wunder how much loot they've discovered?'

'Are there any old bones with the jewels, I wunder?'

'Ave you 'erd, they've discovered old Captain Morgan's Long Lost Treasure? How much d'you reckon it's werth?'

Harry tried to contain himself but found it difficult.

"But then the crunch came," he added.

"We had been out most of the day and had no joy whatsoever. All anyone wanted to talk about was Captain Fucking Morgan's Long Lost Fuckin' Treasure. Could not for the life of me get any single one of 'em's attention for a single bloomin' second."

“We gets back to the Hotel as arranged and there’s ten fuckin police cars lined up all along the road searching and questioning every single person.”

“Unable to avoid them, we get questioned and are immediately identified as the perpetrators of the scandalous unfounded rumours that have encapsulated the City. Carted off to the Manager’s Office, Vince declares his total innocence in the mayhem that had ensued, since his little wind up. We woz only having a laugh, was his only defence.”

“The Chief Constable who supervised the interview was not impressed. He advised that we Fuck Off immediately and do not return to my City ever again, or 'I will have you fitted up like a Saville Row Tailor before you know what’s hit you.'”

“Of course he also could not help smiling and grinning whilst he gave this reprimand and we knew he had actually seen the funny side of it.”

“Of course we had to have the ‘Top Up’, and as we left the border Vince cried out, out of the car window, ‘Cast off me hearties. Ship ahoy lads; it’s off to pastures new. Tally ho and away we go!’”

*

It has to be said that these lads, and many others like them, did do well for themselves and their families when travelling all over the country seeking their fortune. But as per some of the exploits I have shared with you, they certainly had a bit of a laugh doing it!

But of course it wouldn't last forever, it was only a laugh any way, and surely, someone would write a book about it one day!

10. New Kid On the Block.

It would have been about 1970 when a fresh face hit the Brighton Antique Dealers scene, with a too good to be true attitude and work ethic; his name was of course Micky Dawes.

Tommy Barnes had had enough of all the day to day haggling, and dealing with all the shenanigans that now accompanied every deal.

He was already planning his early retirement to Majorca, this would come to fruition a couple of years later.

Micky had the unique gift of foresight and recognised a niche in the market. Get the stuff out of the country and realise top dollar for all the goods being bought 'On The Door', by this now formidable and mercenary army of Brighton Knockerboys doing their best to earn a living. Top Dollar of course comes from only one place, America.

So he put into place an export business module that would never be equalled, let alone bettered. The container loads of gear that began to cross the Atlantic at his bequest has only been equalled by the similar copycat activities of the Chinese today. The difference being of course, Micky was sending quality hand-made furniture, porcelain and numerous items of high value and top craftsmanship for the benefit of those able to afford it, out of the Country.

Of course sometimes these otherwise never to be inherited, traditional goods would go towards enhancing Hotels, Inns or establishments prepared to pay for something unattainable on their own shores.

The tiddley winks on the other hand, manufacture bargain bucket, sub-standard goods that have been copied and re-produced for mass market flooding, in low-paid sweatshop factories.

Usually the 'latest crazes', and then sold to those in the low-income and even poverty-stricken status people in our society.

It was, and still is, all a false sense of saving as half the time the electrical goods work for about ten minutes, then never again. The continuously worst products are the cheap AA or AAA batteries, after a couple of days the purchaser returns to tell you,

"Them batteries we bought the other day, they leaked and ruined the remote control, what are you gonna do about it?"

No comment on how this situation is resolved, but the people trying to save a few bob are always left out of pocket. It's all just 'Swag' really.

Another nail in the coffin comes from the Pound shop scenario. It is no longer left to the hardworking entrepreneurs that are willing to get up at some godforsaken time of day and trek off to Market. Instead it is down to minimum wage status and load the shelves with all the sub-standard stuff. Still that's progress for you.

A predicament that should not really be acceptable by any of us, in today's modern Western World. Still, hey-ho, let's leave that at the door of our Politicians who allow such behaviour. Those that go to China on all expenses paid trips, get 5* treatment and can't fit the backhanders in their luggage once they have crookedly negotiated the latest 'Trade Deal' with our Asian allies.

They then pat themselves on the back before they return to their second home or residence somewhere out in the countryside. Those same silver spoon Herberts that smarmily ignore the Telephone, whilst swilling their complimentary Brandy or

Champagne whilst their constituents call for help, facing the latest predicament or plight they are in.

But I don't take myself too seriously so there's no reason why you should. Let's get back to the fun side of life!

*

11. 'What's It All About, Georgie?

On one of our more sobering meetings, and once again, trying to figure out how to proceed, I broached the subject of how home life had worked out for Georgie and Shirley back in the 'old days', but this was clearly a subject to be skirted around.

He briefly mentioned about not wanting to move over to 'Scoombeland' as he referred to it, and in them days it was not unusual for the Wife to stay home with Mum as long as the old man brought home the bacon and put money on the table to make sure the kids were sufficiently taken care of.

Theirs was not the only marriage like this, but unlike the weekend Fathers of today, when the Sunday came around, the whole family would go out together in a most natural way. It was quite acceptable for families of the time, that did actually live together, a man might work on a building site for instance, to work six and a half days a week and then spend Saturday afternoon in the bookies and hardly see the kids anyway.

Then, when the big day out arrived, whether it be a Sunday of Strawberry picking, a visit to Drusilla's or Chessington Zoo, maybe even 'The Changing of The Guards' at 'Buckingham Palace' came around, it made the event so much more memorable.

It was a vague recollection for Georgie, but he said at some stage Shirley asked to move in with George and Violet with the kids in Scotland Street and it just happened. No big fuss, it just happened.

*

Things continued to go well in the 'Knocker Game' despite everyone selling-up on a Friday and saying to each other, 'Better do well next week,' and 'This can't last forever.'

Then they had a blindin' great deal down in Torquay and decided to go up to London and get tickets for the World Cup Final: 'Us against the Germans' could not be missed Not if they could bloody well help it anyway.

Five of them got the rattler on that memorable and momentous occasion, yet fateful day. But despite having more than enough readies to get hold of the best tickets on 'The Black Market', they just couldn't quite find the right 'Ticket Tout.' Surprise, sur-fuckin-prise.

Vince announced however, at this stage, in an optimistic tone that, "All was not lost, and we should make our way over to the East End where he hoped to locate someone with regards to some other business interests, which would benefit all of us."

"The atmosphere was great up in Wembley but none of us were great Football fans anyway, and once we knew there was no chance of 'Getting In', we may as well find some better things to do anyway, just like on the knocker, all in a days work."

Destination, 'The Blind Beggar' down Mile End Road, 'George Cornell' had been shot by one of 'The Kray Twins' back in March so it seemed completely appropriate to all concerned. Triffick!

On the way in a Black Cab, Vince explained that he had heard of a little team up this way that could prove very helpful with regards to those impregnable gaffs that no-one could 'Get In.' He began:

"So, just coz they won't sell the gear at any price whatsoever, to any of us, and then proceed to treat us like second class citizens unworthy of breathing the same air, I propose to relieve them of these goods in another fashion. I have it on good authority that there is a fellah' up here that has got the best team of screwers in London."

"Now, they have heard all about how us lot down in Brighton are getting a good living just walking out the door wiv' the stuff. The thing is of course, we've all got a nice few drums where we know there is tons of Silver or Tom that we have no fucking chance of, ever, in a million lousy years, of laying our bloody hands on. It's gonna be a bit cloak and dagger, but I wouldn'a come up 'ere in the first place if I didn't reckon it was worth a go. I can't fuckin' stand football anyway."

"What do you boys think? After all, if we can't walk out the door wiv the gear let's let someone else take it out the fucking window. I'm sure we can do a decent deal on the spoils, and I'd love to see the look on the boat's of some of them snidey bastards once they realise the insurance money don't come to the same money that we had offered to buy it for in the first place. Come on whaddayasay?"

George explains: "We was already on our way so what was we gonna say? Typical Vinnie, always at the graft. There was me and Vince, Banjo, Bonzo and young Stevie Boyle, all ready and ripe for the turning. Billy Green was saving himself for his trip to the U.S.A. so had decided not to bother coming."

"Of course not every single place was impregnable to the charms of 'Brighton's Knockers,' but if it was never going to be possible for even the best to 'Get In' there was now always going to be a plan 'B', to be put into operation. 'No Brainer,' really."

"This was Vinnie's pitch, it seemed we were all happy, and also aware that this was about to be another landmark in the 'Knocker Game.' It was, all of a sudden, quite exciting, and therefore we had all completely forgotten about the football by now. So, when we, all five of us, waltzed into the most infamous Boozer in English

History, not one single solitary one of us could give a flyin' fuck that Geoff Hurst had just made football history by scoring the first ever hat trick in a world cup final, about seven miles away, seven fuckin' minutes ago!"

"It was a couple of hours before Vince mentioned that there had been a 'Connection.' The information was all above board and a few faces were willing to meet with a couple of us, but not the whole crew mind you."

"He reckoned it would be best for him and Bonzo to go, 'On the Meet', and the rest of us would catch up later, at another venue. Everything was sorted, the Kray's had just recently managed to take over the running of a new Club in Soho, called the 'El Morocco', in Gerrard Street."

"Us three could go to a nice little Restaurant in Chinatown on the way first, have a little bit of scran and then join them at half-seven for more fun, drinks, dancing and entertainment. What's not to like? There was a car waiting, at our beck and call, so off we all jolly well went."

Funnily enough, this very same day, The Twins arch rivals, The Richardson's were raided by the old bill. Charlie was arrested for torture, brother Eddie got put away for five years for affray, and the 'Torture Trials' began early April 67'. The gang were subsequently found guilty on counts of fraud, extortion, assault and GBH.

Charlie got 25 years, Eddie an extra ten to the five years he was already serving, and various other terms for the rest of the gang. This included 'Mad' Frankie Fraser who in his defence, declared the torture and mock trials carried out by the gang were grossly exaggerated. Charlie was released July 1984 after 18 years.

This obviously left the coast clear for the Kray brothers and despite a couple of short jail terms, for what they would consider minor indiscretions, the world (or at least London) was their oyster and they enjoyed a fair crack of the whip with regards to the underworld of the City for a good few years.

*

There was this fellah, 'Barney', who was to be the spokesman for a gang of tea-leaves known as the 'Bethnal Green Berets'. His commander-in-chief, was known only as 'Bob The Burglar', and it was highly unlikely that any of us, or our colleagues, would ever meet him or know his true identity."

"It was explained that this was for our own good and that he, Barney that is, would be the go-between for all and any operations that were to be accepted and completed, or for any reason, at their discretion only, aborted. If of course everything went well and relevant information was 'spot-on', once the goods had been secured and sold, we would get a 'Very nice drink'."

"In London circles this usually meant about 33% of the booty, so if it was worth £30,000, £10,000 could be expected, they never ever welshed, and also would never ever 'Grass' where the info had come from."

"Whenever Barney showed his face in Brighton, we always knew a nice few quid was due, and usually had a new 'Job' to add to the list at the ready. Bearing in mind some jobs were worth an awful lot more."

"It could be said that sometimes we were slightly lazy or even greedy. If a right nice parcel looked a bit expensive, the thought of just sending 'The Bethnal Green Berets' in, seemed easier and more profitable, also much safer than trying to pull a stroke and getting nicked yer'self."

"Now Barney, he was a strapping geezer, 6ft 4in and stocky with it, dark rhino-like skin, jet black bushy eyebrows overshadowing his bright glistening brown eyes, high chiselled cheekbones and an almost feminine looking mouth, with a professionally styled pencil moustache, attached too dangerously close to non-existent lips."

"His slicked back, jet-black hair stuck to his skull like a second skin, yet still presented a very formidable adversary. His previous job must have been beating the drum in the lower deck of a galleon for the galley slaves."

"If one was ever to be on his wrong side, his fists resembled a great big bunch of fucking bananas that would probably put even Lennox Lewis in a panic, and if you searched for a weak point to initiate an attack, well, good fuckin' luck with that one!"

"Yet there was a menacing look about him that made one feel that if you took the slightest, tiny little liberty, it would never ever be taken in good faith and any sense of humour was extinct, therefore negating any form of negotiation once you had been discovered in any form of indiscretion."

"Otherwise known as 'Having Yer Balls Chopped Off', no questions need to be asked, none to be answered, things were already settled, so just accept what's coming your way, accept gracefully, and then, just hope it ends quick!"

"There's no need for all the intricate details, cos it get's very bloody boring. So, the upshot was, once we met back up in the Club, Vince looked well pleased with himself, and Bingo gave the thumbs up, with facial expressions only, of course."

*

George then took to a slightly different attitude when recalling the events of that day and for a brief moment seemed even reluctant to continue.

He did however carry on, but in a secretive and pensive mood:

“Everything was going seemingly well, AND THEN, BOSH!”

“Like a bolt of bloody lightening out of the fucking blue, comes this stunning young blonde bird, that just absolutely blew my mind. I was still relatively sober, but this Girl was just absolutely stunning and made for me, and from the very first moment we laid eyes on each other, we knew we were meant to be.”

“We danced for twenty-five minutes before we even exchanged names, and when I asked her what she wanted to drink, she just made a crude remark, that stays with me till this day, and I will never ever forget, or tell a single solitary fucking soul.”

“We were both married, neither of us, ‘In Love’. My marriage was boring, Hers was distant, and they never shared a single thing together.”

“I was happy, she was miserable. Until now, that is.”

“I was on the Sunny South Coast, and she was stuck in miserable misty foggy London. Baa humbug.”

“We both decided to meet the following weekend in Margate. I had a call there and she had a sister there, perfect.”

“It went on for a few weeks, but then became slightly intense, and so I gave her a bit of an ultimatum, biggest mistake of me life. I said I could not keep skulking around and wanted things out in the open.”

“So we broke it off and that was it, three weeks on the ‘Feeling sorry for yourself’, piss, and then back to the old drawing board.”

“Such is life.”

*

“I have to say Min, you do so seem to remind me of her from time to time. It’s just the way you have that sideways glance about you, I dunno.”

*

“Then, me and the boys were at Brighton races in the summer of 1968, and Vince has a meeting with Barney to discuss one of our latest ‘Operations’. I was in the Silver Ring, you know, for Owner’s and Trainer’s.”

“And there she is.”

“Looking as gorgeous as ever, in a shimmering flowing and flowery gypsy type dress, off the shoulder and over the knee, made exactly just for me. Poetry don’t come into it.”

“She also had a more assuming ‘Confident’ and ‘Blossoming’ manner about her, that I had never witnessed before. This was down to the fact that she was now a Mother. I don’t know what I’d been taking, but as soon as our eyes made contact there was no holding us back, and we just ran into each other’s arms, like star-crossed lovers or war-torn prats or whatever. I don’t fucking know.”

"Anyway it was bleedin' incredible. I told her I was in love with her, and she was the only girl I would ever love and all that old bollocks, but I meant it, I really did, and I was gonna take her to St. Tropez, next week, for a fantastic fortnight to remember, or never forget, I dunno."

"I said to her, 'You make up some excuse, or, just fucking lie and leave the bastard, and I'll do the same.' I meant every word of it, and that same night ended any, and every possible affection between Shirley and me forever."

"There was no doubt in either of our minds, and we met six days later in Brighton to have a sensuous night at 'The Grand' before we got the 'Golden Arrow' train to Paris, then down to the South of France for the best six days of my life."

"Anyway, I've said enough about that for now, the long and the short of it is, things did not work out!"

Anger came over George then: "You can keep trying, wishing, pissing and shitting, but if it ain't meant to be, then it ain't meant to be. So, if I can't be with her, then she can't be with me. What's the fucking problem? That's just the way it is, and the way it will be!"

Georgie then sort of disintegrated, in a wishy washy way, right before my very eyes, so I left him to it whilst I went to get a glass of wine.

This really and truly was the last he wished to speak of it, so I took it on board and left it like that.

*

George continued:

“Well after all that, the whole town knew I had sort of been unfaithful. The Missin Boys, left nobody in the dark about what they thought, and so I was pretty much given no choice but to join the Nearly Family and associates.”

“As I said, Shirley had moved in with me and Mum by then to Scotland Street, but it was best for me to get a drum of me own, or it would have caused too many arguments and bad feeling. The worst thing was about the kids really. But would could I do?”

Georgie then poured himself a whisky, downed it in one then poured another. Hence the language and bitter attitude escalates slightly, over the next couple of paragraphs!

“There was this song in the charts at the time by Love Affair called Everlasting Love that haunted me. Then there was another by Gary Puckett and the Union Gap.”

He then went right into one, singing:

“Fun Girl, get out’ta my life,
my love for you, is way out of line.
Better run girl.
You're much too fun girl.”

George then explained: “That always made my girl laugh. But still, Whatkanyadoo?”

“We all carried on. On the knocker that is, and then all our prophecies came true. ‘The end was nigh’.”

“That fucking horrible two-faced wrinkly old bastard ‘Arthur fuckin Negus’ started a programme on the telly called ‘Going for a fucking Song’. That really cattled things, and all of a sudden the world and his uncle was a bloody expert on all and sundry.”

"Then, to top it up, no pun intended, they come out wiv' this uvver' load of shit called 'The Antique's fucking Road show.'"

"Well to be fair Minnie, that really and truly was the beginning of the end for 'Brighton's Knocker's'. Not only was the general public being educated, there were also wicked and spiteful rumours that any persons from the Brighton area pertaining to be dealer's in Fine Art & Antiquities were also liable to be of questionable character. Fucking charming, I'm sure. Kia-Ora!"

"Now, not only did everyone think that any piece of unwanted rubbish up in the attic was worth a mint, but also, anyone from Brighton was a fuckin' toe rag or one of 'The Great fucking Train Robber's', wiv nothing else to do wiv themselves, other than rip-off all the poor old souls of 'Good Old England'."

"Charmed, I'm fucking sure!"

*

"So nowadays, I have resolved myself to looking up the occasional 'Clue', or doing the 'Backy' run from Newhaven to Dieppe once a fortnight. I can always make a few bob on the few bottles of spirits, that we offload to various boozers."

"I usually take a couple of the scousers with me who can do a nice bit of thieving in the Duty Free on the boat, and pick up a couple of things from them Hypermarkets. Then it's just a case of trying me best to get a couple of quid wherever I can or can't. Whatkanyasaay?"

"I do Boot Markets on Bank Holidays but it usually ends in tears and petty arguments. Every prat finks they can buy everything for tuppence, and the haggling usually ends badly."

“Last time I just smashed a tea set to pieces right in front of the bird who was trying to knock me down to £10, it was worth £40 and I only wanted £15. Just pissed me off. Of course everyone else said I was being petty, but twenty years ago we wouldn’a’ took less than £50. Oh well, that’s life.”

*

Another swig of his drink and then Georgie turned things on me all of a sudden. He enquired as to how things were going with Steve Martin.

I told him things were fine, but he had that instinctive look in his eye that indicated that this would not suffice.

“Well,” I began, “Grace thinks he is all right and he seems to get on okay with my Dad.”

“Don’t give me all that old bollocks,” interrupted George.

“What do *you* think of him I asked.”

“Oh I really don’t know Georgie. What can I say? He told me when we first met, that he was going off to America to start a new life. So how can I start saying there is any future between us when he’s already made plans to be elsewhere?”

“Would you believe this? He said the other day that since he’s going off in November, he has to do certain things before he goes, so as not to look like a nobody when he is in the States.”

“I said like what?”

“So he says: 'Well, I’ve never actually been to Paris, do you fancy coming with me next week?' What sort of a bloke is he?”

George just shrugged his shoulders.

Fat lot of good he was.

*

Steph and Steve Take A Trip.

This had all came about fairly slowly, after Steve had introduced me to South Lodge, a 5 Star, Luxury Country House Hotel in Lower Beeding. It really was a bit out of his league, but the world loves a trier. The service was impeccable, the food Michelin Star standard and by then, the company incorrigible.

By this time also he had secured a Credit Card and took great pleasure in producing it, albeit I had to show him where to sign, and how to include a tip!

Still a bit of a prat, but now he was my prat!

*

We were having a few drinks one evening in The Bow Street Runner and he suggested I view his showroom round the corner. Keys in the door, Security code used and ‘We Were In’, just like on the knocker.

He laid ten mink coats on the luscious carpet floor and we consummated our relationship. It felt sensuous, special and naughty.

That's all I have to say on the matter.

It was after this liaison, that I agreed to join him for the trip to Paris, the following weekend and it was divine.

I had allowed myself to be whisked off my feet.

It felt at times that he didn't have a clue what was supposed to be happening next, and he seemed to be winging it at every stage.

Still, I found it all quite entertaining and amusing, and things seemed to be panning out okay.

We found ourselves staying in some unexpectedly luxurious accommodation at Le Meridian. Checking-in was quite funny, as when they asked for a credit card, he just put his hand in his pocket and chucked a wad of notes in front of the pretty prim and proper receptionist.

Immediately after signing the register, he asked where the nearest bank was. I wasn't sure if he noticed my wry smile

I didn't wish to steal his thunder so allowed him to take the lead wherever we went. Most of the time.

We did the Eiffel Tower bit and had lovely meal in a Kosher Restaurant, completely by chance.

Whilst strolling aimlessly around Paris, we climbed a huge set of steps at one stage and were both in need of a rest. It was a busy little area and so we stopped to have our portraits done by a street artist. This was quite comical as Steve wore his Trilby and had just insisted on buying me a cute Air-Hostess style pillbox hat.

Secretly, I treasured this artwork and despite continuous requests as to it's whereabouts, never let-on to Steve what happened to it.

The highlight was popping into The Ritz where Steve could not resist ordering Champagne in 'Le Lounge'. The lady at the piano looked familiar and it turned out to be Nina Simone. She was staying at the Hotel and was just tinkering at the Baby Grand Piano for her own pleasure.

Steve could not help himself and told her we were on our honeymoon and requested she play that famous song.

We danced and sang harmoniously together. Who cares what the other guests thought? But we did get polite applause. Ever since that night, I like to think of 'My Baby Just Cares For Me', when I think of him.

He had avoided my enquiry as to how long the trip would take, and so I was pleasantly surprised when he suggested the next morning that we should remain in our suite and take breakfast in bed, it was of course much more comfortable at the small dining table provided, so we dined in our gowns.

TV was a no-no so we found Radio Luxembourg and relaxed in each others company, and proceeded to get to know one another more intimately.

Upon my strategic questioning, Steve began to reveal some of the more mysterious ways of the world and the fascinating characters to which I had recently become acquainted.

I can just hear him saying, like it was only yesterday;

"Well it's no big secret, if someone comes out with a one-liner, off–the-cuff remark like, that everyone starts laughing at it, they tend to carry on repeating it, till it becomes their own line so-to-speak.”

“Some of these phrases get into ‘The General Population’ and soon enough everyone is using it. Take for instance ‘Kia-Ora’, my Dad was well known for using that one. Well that is from that orange drink TV ad, but is commonly used when one would much rather say ‘Would you fucking believe it!’ but there may be women and children present, whose old man reckons they might be offended. Most of us Brightonians are quite polite when it comes to Women and kids y’know”

“Years ago there was another TV AD only on Southern Television, about Unigate Milk. Somehow or other they had Red and White Stripes on great big straws, the jingle on this went something like, ‘Watch Out, Watch Out, Watch Out, There’s a Humphrey About,’ now that doesn’t sound too funny the way I’ve just said it but when someone hasn’t got a clue what you are talking about, anyone else present, who is in the know, finds it hysterical.”

“Mind you I personally came unstuck on that particular one. One year when we were on a family Holiday at Pontins on the Isle of Wight, my Dad had decided to make me an outfit for the Fancy Dress Competition. A great big red and white striped cone that made me look just like a giant ‘Humphrey.”

“The trouble was, we realised after the event, the judges in these contests would be made up of members from the audience, and of course everyone on Holiday at the Camp were from all over the country. None of ’em had a fucking clue who the bloody hell ‘Humphrey’ was because they had never seen the poxy Advert had they.”

“Still Whatkanyadoo? Whatkanyasaay?”

*

“After I boxed in New York I was a bit cheesed off at losing, but this geezer comes up to me and wants to talk.”

“I was none too happy but decided not to be inhospitable. Then I realised it was actually one of the main celebrity guests of the evening, only Rocky Graziano. He’d been a World Middleweight Champion many years before, from a rough part of New York and looked on course to spend most of his life behind bars.”

“But with a chance meeting in a famous New York Gym, he had given a highly rated fighter a right pasting in sparring. They went on to make an Oscar Winning Film starring Paul Newman on his life story.”

“'Come on kid let me getch’ya a Bud at the Bar.' How could I refuse? He did at first assure me that the kid I had just fought, was one of the best guys he had seen fight recently and that I had nothing to worry about.”

“I asked him accordingly what he actually did with himself these days; ‘Aah I dunno,' he goes, 'I stick my name on a couple of Pizza joints, do a few toothpaste commercials, and stick my ugly mug at fancy charity do’s like wot weez are here at tonight. Still, Whatkanyadoo? Whatkanyasaay?'”

“And that Steph, is why so many people in Brighton use that saying when they have just stitched someone up and don’t have a reasonable excuse, valid reason or much else to say. I can’t resist using it when I’m out and about and I suppose it has kind of resonated with plenty of other people.”

Steve also, could at times use the perfect vocabulary to explain something sometimes. I can only suppose that he benefited from Brighton’s School’s system which deserves the credit for providing an above average standard of education for all it’s pupils.

"The other one that comes up quite a bit about 'Only being a laugh,' is down to the fact that Brighton people are always taking the piss out of each other, and also, we are very unsympathetic types."

"It is true to say that an awful lot of 'em are also quite untrustworthy, and that old chestnut, 'My word is my bond,' ain't worth the paper it's not written on."

"If someone does a deal up the market at five o'clock in the morning, loads of deals are done before daylight I can assure you. They think they're buying something hookie for well below the market price, then when they get a better look at it later, they find it's not what they thought it was."

"It's no good having a scream up after the event, coz they themselves thought they woz mister clever-bollocks, pulling a stroke in the first place."

"So then the perpetrator of the con just says: 'It's only a laugh anyway in'nit?' Then comes the proverbial Whatkanyadoo? Whatkanyasaay?"

"That's my Brighton KnockerBoy Education fully disclosed, and even though I'm not in that business, many of their traits can be used in all other walks of life. I only hope that what I've learnt from them up till now learnt helps me out in the future."

That's enough of the pillow talk.

If it can be regarded as such.

The rest of that morning is personal.

The travel arrangements had all been very haphazard, to say the least, but I suppose we managed to get there and back in one piece. As he kissed me sweetly in the Taxi when dropping me off at my place, he whispered in my ear in a truly corny but sincere fashion,

“Well at the very least, we’ll always have Paris!”

*

12. The Great Gatehouse Caper.

One story had eluded me up till now. On three separate occasions the 'Gatehouse' subject had arisen and yet each time someone had advised it was best 'left well alone'.

Of course by now my insatiable appetite for yet another truly hilarious escapade, that everyone swore blind was completely true, was such, that I took the extraordinary measure of actually organising a private party, at which all relevant parties concerned were invited, plus a couple of new faces.

Obviously the antics that these Herberts had got up to over the years, to seize their prey, had rubbed off on me, so there was no compunction or shred of guilt on my part in reversing roles and doing the same to them. Elementary!

I concocted an old family tradition, celebrating The International Day of Peace, 21st September. This would be in jeopardy, unless a dinner party was organised and attended. Just to make sure they would all arrive on time, I suggested that nobody was to go to the Pub first and to arrive by 8pm. With of course the full knowledge that not one of them would heed my instructions, except Steve of course.

The upstairs facility at Michael's Mediterranean restaurant Il Bistro, in Market Street, The Lanes, was appropriately reserved for 9:00. With perfunctory arrangements in place for Joe the waiter being available till the early hours, on the understanding of a generous tip of course.

All the relevant scoundrels promptly showed their boats by 9:15, all present and correct and all to plan. Quite proud of myself really.

Head of table was Vince, flagged by Charlie and a new face to me, Jimmy Mc Cue, a bright pink face in fact, with rosy cheeks.

The hairstyle reminiscent of a balding Teddy Boy, sticky out ears, boxer's nose, bright glazed eyes and overshadowed by bushy eyebrows, that should have been trimmed years ago. The lips seemed pursed, but they were just chapped from the weather and the total lack of any alcohol for some 15 minutes now.

Georgie took a chair next to me, after offering me my seat opposite Vinnie, for full theatrical effect. Dick the driver sat alongside Steve and Charlie.

After selecting our drinks, plus a bottle of House Red and White wine, we made a little small talk. I had asked Georgie if it was okay for Steve to join us as we had been seeing quite a bit of each other lately. This was no problem. Steve was familiar with everyone present, but would not probably have much to offer on the topic at hand. The fact that he was aware of my ruse, did add a touch of amusement.

A favourite at Doncaster Races had ballsed up a Yankee for Vince that day and unsurprisingly, George had backed the winner in the same race, much to the chagrin of our main attraction. All the while, I was feeling that nervous tingly glowing feeling down below, in anticipation of the tale to be told.

Unaware, that this particular evening, was about to become folklore legend, all of it's own.

"Well" said Vince, "George has been chirping on at us all for ages now, to let you in on one of the best little earners of the lot, but I'll tell you this young lady. (pointing his finger menacingly, directly between my eyes, yet with that cheeky, boyish twinkle in his eyes at the same time.) What we are about to tell you is 100%, 24 carat, God be my judge, absolutely fucking true!"

How could you possibly doubt the man?

"It all started off, Charlie will tell you, (completely discarding Charlie's existence of course.) We had a lovely deal with some old dear at a gatehouse in Kent, sweet little thing she was, but as sharp as a tack. I still say to this day she had a bit of Gipsy in her."

"Anyway, the attic, as it turned out, was absolutely chock-a-block with gear. There was copper kettles, coal buckets, the most beautiful fire-guard you have ever seen, a few prints and loads of other stuff. I'll tell you about all that in a minute."

A slight pause to take a few glugs of his best bitter and it was back to the case in hand. He certainly enjoyed being the centre of attention, but this was Vince's stage all the time and the audience were transfixed, as always, especially myself.

"There were a few of those writing desks, you know the type, they unfold like an ordinary box, then go on a table top. These ones all had the silver ink wells, with dark blue glass still inside and were in great nick. They were making £80 each at the time, so £40 for all 6 of 'em was only fair."

"Covered the petrol money, dinnit?"

Bearing in mind it was less than 50p a gallon at the time, I would regard this as the first of many exaggerations coming my way this delightful evening.

It never ceased to amaze me how, when one of them made such an outrageous claim, the others would all nod in agreement, like those nodding dogs in the back of a car that you won at the fair, yet would never actually dream of buying, unless of course you get insured by Churchill that is.

"Quite fortunately there was also an old stainless steel cutlery set, Sheffield of course, as the lady pointed out, well worth a fiver that quite fortuitously turned out to be Sterling Silver and fetched £870 at auction. Very pleasant. Of course I knew it was silver anyway, but there was no need to get the old girl's hopes up, that just leads to disappointment, would you not agree?" More nodding ensued.

Our starters arrived, but Vince was now well into full flow, and when he giggled and spluttered at the pair of damaged Oil Paintings at £4 each, going for £1,350 at Sotheby's in London, poor old Georgie suffered a flying prawn, launched through the air from Vinnie's mouth directly into his left eye, with Marie Rose sauce all over the adjacent cheek!

'Oops sorry Georgie', was the only remark,

"Now where was I?" he continued, "Oh yeah, a scruffy looking little old rocking-horse fetched the princely sum of £1,650. That was the one that you said to throw in a skip coz it wasn't worth two bob, wasn't it Dick? You prick!"

Dick did an impression of Dopey the dwarf and slid slightly lower down in his seat, then held his head in hands and declared, through his muffled face, "Ain't you ever gonna let me forget the one fucking time I made a poxy mistake?"

Everybody then just began to tut-tut at the same time, and when Vince began to shake his head from side to side and give him the old turned-up bottom lip treatment I thought Dick was going to leave us early.

Then Georgie jumped in and declared, "Aaah well, Whatkanyadoo? Whatkanyasaay? It's only a laugh anyway innit?"

We all laughed together, at that moment and would continue to do so for the rest of the night.

A few other items were described as our plates were taken away; the haul netted the gang a tidy profit of some £7,800. Once the X's were sorted, Dick the driver realised his £450 was the best week's money he had ever earned, maths not being his strong subject, despite his ricket on the rocking-horse.

Sitting there like an excited 7 year-old on Christmas morning waiting to open my presents, I egged Vince on to continue the story. He nodded to Georgie, expressing permission for him to take over.

"Well," George began, "We obviously knew the Gatehouse was just the entrance to something much more grand, so Vince gave me the nod to try and find out what treasures might be at the top of the drive. "

"Of course Emily, our most recent benefactor, who was well chuffed with our most generous valuations of the stuff up in the loft, was only too happy to oblige over a cup of tea and some garibaldi biscuits."

"'Oooh,' she cooed, 'That's Lady Hughes you know. She is such a lovely person and has kindly allowed me to live in this Gatehouse rent-free for as long as I wish, due to the lifelong service of my husband Rowland, who sadly passed away last year. Funnily enough, that was all his old junk up in the attic that you so kindly relieved me of.'"

"So I said: do you think she may have a few odds and ends, or bits and pieces that we may purchase for our next period film, what do you think Emms?"

"'I honestly don't know. The thing is though, I don't see her too often. But I must tell you, she is extremely religious and unless in some way the Church were to benefit, I doubt she would even entertain a visitor.'"

Nobody even acknowledged the delivery of the main course, as we were all spellbound and intrigued by the forthcoming events. They were all at it, weren't they? They all knew exactly what was coming next, but were revelling in my obvious delight at being let in on another of their adventures, as the story unfolded, incredulous!

"Soo, we had what they call these days a brainstorming session, the next day, in 'The Horse & Groom', down Islingword Road, and decided that the best course of action was through the local Parish."

"Of all people, it was Dick the driver who suggested bringing in another player, and that Jimmy here would make the perfect priest to 'Get In.' Arrangements were made and we strolled down to 'The Basket-Makers', Gloucester Road, to finalise plans and fill Jimmy in on the plan of attack."

"He had a bit more barnet in those days of course, but nevertheless he doesn't really look much different now. So then off we go to Derek's barbershop down Edward Street, and the makeover began, trim round the ears and a lovely comb-over effect like Bobby Charlton used to have, commonly known as 'The Walnut Whip'."

"Vince had already secured a right nice Dog Collar from Brother John and then we go next door to Jack Balls, the pawnshop for a nice, nearly new, black suit, with just the right wear and tear to look pauperish enough, befitting a man of the cloth."

"Jimmy tapped us up for a nice little pair of Brogues and a Trilby hat as I recall. I'm sure they never came out of his cut when we had a divvy-up."

"Don't you fockin start all that bollocks again Balcock," shouted Jimmy, across the table. Still a bit fiery after a couple of Scotches.

But immediately Vincent raised his arms in mock surrender and just said in a lovely soothing tone:

"Calm down, calm down, we are all friends here, he's only getting you at it. Aren't you Georgie?"

"Yeah, course I am. Don't be silly, Jimmy."

Vince now took centre stage once more:

"Soo, off we go, back up to Kent. It was a lovely sunny day as I recall, but to be quite fair, and don't take this the wrong way Jim, the chosen one, Father James, as he was now known, had a distinctly strong odour of Johnnie Walker about him."

"It was, however, agreed by all, that this was not detrimental to our cause and a few Trebor mints, En Route to our destination would suffice to eliminate any problems 'Getting In'."

"We checked into a cosy little Hotel just a few miles away from The Gatehouse, and enjoyed a late Breakfast, prepared by the lovely widow Doreen, who had had her eyes on me from day one from a few months earlier."

"This was never going to happen, as I always made it a golden rule, not to mix business with pleasure. I was getting plenty with me bird Trinny, anyway."

"However, I was never one to shirk a bit of innocent flirting if it led to a considerable discount when settling the bill. Invariably we forgot to mention the ghastly exaggerated Bar Bill, which most certainly could not possibly be as much as that in just two nights, Doreen would just raise her eyebrows and shrug it off. Job done."

"We left it till about twelvish as planned," continued Vince,

"And on the short journey, constantly drummed into Jimmy about the reasons for his unannounced visit. He was the new Parish Priest and wanted to acquaint himself with the Lady of the house about whom he had heard very nice things."

"He also wished to run a fundraising idea past her for the church roof, which was in disrepair. Having had some great response at his last position, he had gained a little knowledge, but his retired brother Archibald lived locally and was available to give his humble opinion on any articles that may be available."

"All proceeds were to be given directly to Father James and should there be any items of potentially higher value maybe we could find a private buyer or collector, so avoiding any silly auction house fees or commissions."

"Well, when we got near the House, none of us could actually speak for two whole minutes."

George jumped in: "It was so funny, this place was like Downton fucking Abbey, we was perplexed to say the least. Vincie got all serious and said to Jimmy, 'You'd better not fuck this up Jim. D'you know what? I've got a semi on. I'd rather get in that gaff, than Joan Collins's knickers. Come on my son, get in there, and be sure to let her know we are waiting. But only to help and advise.'"

Back to Vince: "Father James walked straight up to the front door and after only 30 seconds was let in by what looked like a maid, but we couldn't be sure, still at least he was in."

"For 25 minutes we sat there, imagining the treasures that might be coming our way. George was to be the furniture expert, whilst I was more inclined towards the Art, any available Sculptures, Jewellery Clocks, Watches and Objay D'art."

“There was a brief discussion of Holiday destinations if things went well, when all of a sudden the front door burst open and Jimmy was hurtling towards the motor screaming at the top of his voice: 'Start the fockin motor! Start the fockin motor, for Christ’s sake! Start the fockin motor!'”

“I said, he’s taking this religion lark quite seriously isn’t he. George laughed and Dick turned the key in the ignition, took the handbrake off, and started to turn round, just in time for Jimmy to jump into a moving vehicle and fly down the drive.”

“So what the fuck happened Jim?” I enquired.

It was now Jimmy’s turn to explain the events, and he talked directly to me in a very soft accent that you would only usually hear on the other side of a confessional box.

“Well, in I goes, as right as rain. The place was like a museum. Huge pictures on the walls, everywhere you looked, floor to ceiling mirrors, huge vases all over the place.”

“The lovely maid kindly led me into the drawing room and advised that Lady Hughes was actually with someone at the moment, but had left strict instructions not to be disturbed. However, should any unannounced callers visit, to let them in then notify her when taking in tea and refreshments.”

“It turned out that the maid had only just started that day from an agency, as the permanent woman had taken a leave of absence for a family funeral in Ireland.”

“So, I’m sitting there running through all the things we had talked about. It seemed like an eternity and they had already said that if I was in there for more than ten minutes it was a good sign. So I was really up for it and looking forward to it.”

“There I was, looking at all the gear in the place. Now I’m no fockin’ expert, but the gear in the bloody hallway alone, looked like it was worth £3,000, and that’s without all the other shite our Vince could undoubtedly wangle out of the gaff.”

“The maid came in and said it was now convenient to meet the mistress. Nice one. So she opens the door to the Library and invites me to enter. In I go.”

“Well, would you fockin’ believe it? The Lady is sitting in a nice comfy armchair, a little table in-between and sitting opposite her: it’s only the Arch Bishop of fockin’ Canterbury!”

“Whats-his-face, you know the one on Songs of fockin’ Praise.”

“I couldn’t fockin believe it.”

“So, I had it on my fockin’ toes straight away. You should have seen their fockin’ faces (pointing at Vince, George and Dick the driver) when I came running out. I thought for a minute they was gonna leave me behind. Talk about getting caught with yer pants down. Jeezus!”

“The thing was,” piped up George, “When we were on the way home, we discussed, who’s stupid fucking idea it was to bring in another face, on a clue we had found ourselves?”

“Lo and behold we all stared at Dick at the same time and in unison declared ‘Don’t fuckin' bovver, ever again. Stick to the driving and the poxy fuckin' flyers.'”

“Then, as we were just coming past Pyecombe, Jimmy mentioned the possibility of a little call in the village by the Golf Course. Not to let the day go amiss, Vince gave the go ahead and I was sent up the garden path once more to see if I could ‘Get in.’”

"Absolute cinch. The old boy Rupert, was in a very jovial mood and invited me in. He had a few medals, some pocket watches and possibly a few other odds and ends. Then he said anything in the garden shed was mine for nothing, as he was expecting delivery of a new shed at the weekend, from the local garden centre."

"This was the cue to introduce my associate Nigel, to negotiate prices, whilst I have a nose around in the Garden. Introductions sorted, Vince nicely Nigelled up, was in his element and was about to check the upstairs while 'Rupe' put the kettle on."

"The shed was a revelation, couple of jug and basins £40 minimum, big bag of tools, rusty but good sellers at Sunday markets, some nice little prints and an old oil painting."

"The thing was though, I really fancied the frame for at least a couple of hundred and we did know someone who had a contact with the auctioneers who reckoned his mate was one of the best restorers there was, this would certainly test his skill."

"Vince ended up with a suitcase full of Tom. Rupert's missus had died two year's previous and he hadn't even touched her stuff, except let the Sally Army take her clobber. Right result."

"The fucking picture, only turned out to be by some famous artist from the Royal Academy, circa 1875, Sir Christopher such and such, don't rightly remember, anyway it only cost £150 to restore, fetched three fucking grand. Oh what a life."

It was clear the alcohol was having its effect on all of us, but I was really still in a state of shock, from the main story being such an anti-climax.

I sat there totally stunned, and they all just went into rapturous laughter.

My obvious disappointment must have made me look transparent, and then of course the penny dropped. It had been a harmless prank in their eyes. A nosey young bird sniffing around, asking loads of questions, spending valuable social hours with old George instead of going down the town with her mates.

It had been weeks in the making, but they then proceeded to explain, that the whole thing had brought them all back together again, plotting and scheming.

Setting me up in 'The Cricketers' down the Lanes, that was the first mention of 'The Gatehouse Caper' and they had all rekindled fond memories of one another.

The next time was in 'Hove Place' whilst having lunch in the lovely garden, someone had popped over to say hello to George, a jeweller I think: David Le Bloom. George explained I was doing a little story on the notoriety of Brighton's Knockerboys and Dave immediately mentioned 'The Great Gatehouse Caper,' to wit,

Georgie swept it under the table. Discarding it matter of factly.

Next time it had been brought up by the master himself. Vinnie, who had also added that it might make for a night's entertainment, if any special occasion was to crop up, and others could also contribute with other amusing anecdotes or stories of daring do. 'Upon the road of fortune and fame,' as he put it.

And I had thought it was all my fucking idea. What a plonker. They had played me, from the very beginning and I fell for it, hook line and sinker, and don't regret it for a single bloody second either.

Georgie, of course, had instigated the whole thing. But he assured me it was out of the fondness of his heart, that he had developed for me over the past few weeks.

That by dangling the carrot of the 'Big Job,' he knew I would keep coming back for more.

These guys certainly knew how to read people and of course, although I had been 'The Mark,' there was no animosity and there was no 'ripping me off' clause in place.

The thing was, of course, the story was absolutely true, and Vince explained that not always, did they get their man and sometimes they would go on a call expecting a 'nice little earner' and the door never even got answered, let alone that they 'Got In'.

*

My only consolation was that Steve had no idea either and was not in on it. He had become quite dear to me and I trusted him 100%. We had gone up to London a couple of days before, to meet Dad and although I thought it went well, when the bill arrived they had gotten into an argument over who was paying.

Steve had told me his own Dad always had to pay and that this made him self-conscious when with others.

My Dad also tried to stand his ground.

Afterwards we laughed about it, whilst having a drink in The Savoy, and Steve did make the 'Old Man' laugh by insisting he let Dad pay for the Champagne, it was only fair.

We had a great evening and then went on to Ronnie Scott's where Eta James was performing. I danced with my Father and Steve and had a lovely time. The highlights were: 'I'd Rather Go Blind' and 'At Last', the night seemed to go on forever.

At one stage, whilst Steve visited the gents, Dad suggested I might really like this guy. ‘I suppose he’s okay,’ I replied. He then pointed out that he had never been on a date with any boyfriend, and myself ever before. The point was made.

Years later, when a V.I.P. guest at The Roundhouse in Camden Town, for a B.B.C. Special: Paul Weller and Amy Winehouse did a fantastic duet called ‘Don’t Go To Strangers’, and it reminded of that memorable night. Anyway, back to the situation at heart.

*

Dessert was served. Of course George and Jimmy both went for the Liqueur coffee option, but the night was far from over. Having observed the reception of the house wine, Vince whispered something into Joe’s ear and within moments a bottle of Château Neuf Du Pappe and a well chilled Chablis were opened in front of Steve and I.

Vince didn’t touch the stuff himself but he recognised others needs, without exception. They had their moments these boys.

I wish sometimes, that I had had the foresight, to record that night, because it just seemed to go on forever, with one story after another and all taking time out for each other and, as always, behaving like true gentlemen.

It was quite comical how each recollection began the same 'Do you remember when?'; 'How about when so and so...' or 'What about when...' They all knew the same stories, but all slightly different versions. The one discerning factor though was: 'Now this is a true story, you won’t believe it but...'

I then enquired about the time when Paddy Wadey had 'The Clue' up in Birmingham, that Georgie half-mentioned a couple of weeks ago.

"Aah, now that was a fucking beauty, that was," jumped in Vince.

"Patrick Wadey, Jonny 'The Judge' Wadey's brother, was a blinding grafter. But he often went in for the kill, a bit too quick. Patience was not his strongest point."

"So, we was having a nice sociable Sunday lunch drink, in The Bush, down Arundel Road, and he tells me about a gaff up in Birmingham that he and Powders got in."

"He reckoned the old dear wanted rid of everything, so she could move to a nice little flat in Skegness. So she could join her pals and enjoy her latter days of life by the seaside. The family holidays there, brought back many pleasant memories and all that old bollocks."

"Anyway they were cracking on with relieving her of all the decent stuff, China, tasty couple of bits of furniture, Silverware and just getting to the Jewellery when in struts the fucking daughter who lives next door."

"'What the fookin' 'ell is going on 'ere?' she's gone. 'Who the fooking 'ell are you?' and all that crap. A right bloody nuisance. Absolute nause."

"At first they have tried to reason with the muddy, but it only went from bad to worse, so to speak, and ended up wiv her threatening to call the local plod. The pair of them had already had a couple of tugs and complaints from unhappy previous punters in the area, so could not afford to hang about."

"The one thing Paddy recalled, was that the muddy-water had remarked that it was a 'good fookin' job she had come home early from work that day', that day being a Tuesday."

Vince continued, quite animated and excited himself in telling the tale, and revealing the intricate details that were about to unfold:

"So I had it in mind, the way to play, before we goes up the road and I go and find Georgie, that night in 'The Cobden'. Then I let's Charlie know we needed him on 'A Clue' and I would tell him what to do."

"Soo, up we goes bright and breezy the next day, straight to Leicester, about 30 miles from Birmingham. Now I don't know if you've noticed Minnie, but me and Charlie do look very much alike, well anyway back in the day we woz often mistaken for one another. This was to be the occasion, we would make it pay."

"We select a fine substantial Hotel, The Grand Melton, and Charlie books in and pays for three days, B & B. We then have a little scout around for a Chemist, and there's one just around the corner."

"The strictest instructions were given. Now whatever happens, at 11am tomorrow, you go down to reception and tell them that you have a terrible toothache and where is the nearest Chemist."

"Then you make a great old fuss round there and insist that you must have more than just the lousy Paracetamol or any other over-the-counter shit or whatever else they have to offer you."

"You know the score Char, it must be a grand performance and is essential to the operation. Charlie was quite happy with this, as he is actually a bit of a lazy git and thought his part in the proceedings was a doddle."

Charlie piped in, “Hold on a fucking minute, who said I was lazy, I always pulled my weight. Don’tchoo start......”

“Aaah shuddup Charlie, I’m trying to talk to Stephanie mate. Give us a chance, will ya?”

“Yeah, shut up Char,” said Georgie, “Can’t you see he’s talking?”

I had to snigger inwardly to myself at this point, as they were all trying to get in on the act. Everyone of them wanted to be part of the story, but didn’t like it when they were portrayed as a bit-part. But of course there was always only one starring role, and in those days it was always Vinnie.

“Anyway, as I was saying before I was so rudely interrupted,” continued Vince, “He can do what he likes in Leicester and might even have a bit of luck straight knocking if he fancied, or he can just go to the bookies with the expenses provided and chill out with a drink or two.”

“BUT, under no circumstances, could he let the crew down by not carrying out his instructions. It was a bit like planning one of them Mission Impossible episodes, what wiv all the timing and strategic planning involved.”

“They were orders really and truly, but my older Brother got a bit narked and touchy from time to time about being told what to do.”

“Mind you Min, you’ve probably heard about that sort of stuff before.” I nodded.

More drinks flowed, but Vince was in his element and continued vigorously.

"Soo, me Dick and Georgie continue up to Brummy, with the first part of the 'oppo' in place. We drops a few bills, then books into The Grove Hotel on the Hagley Road at lunchtime. About three o'clock, Powders and Paddy Wadey turn up and book in with the Luton Van."

"We go out in my motor, so they can show me where the gaff is. I know they could have just given us the address, but we always liked to do these things together in them days, and be properly prepared. Not like now when everyone's at the tuck up."

"We have a lovely meal that night, in what Birmingham would regard as a Fine Dining Restaurant. The drinks were a little bit over the top, but we were all feeling enthusiastic as to the exploits of the day to come. The thing is Min, also when knowing you are gonna pull a stroke, it may well be the last decent bit of scran you have for a while, if things were to come on top."

"A hearty breakfast in the morning, gave us all a fresh outlook and Charlie called bang on time, 10:15, to let me know everything was cushty at his end."

"Off we go, me and Georgie, wiv Dick, Powders and Paddy following at a safe distance in the Luton Van."

"Give me a little break," says Vince and George takes up the story. George begins:

"Well there we woz, 10:45 and up I goes and knocks the door. A little sweetheart she was. I gave the usual patter as previously discussed and after about two minutes Muriel invited me in. 'Funnily enough,' she remarked, 'a couple of weeks ago I met another nice young chap, who showed a similar interest into the same things you mentioned.'"

"'Yeah, funny that,' I replied."

"Once we got down to the graft, I let Muriel know that my colleague, Albert, was also available to give some sound advice as to the value of her goods. So 'why don't we let him come in and we can get the whole lot sorted in double quick time, whilst I go to the Bank and get her all that lovely cash I had promised her.'"

"Also into the bargain, once we had sorted it all out we had our own removal vehicle available to do the job promptly so as not to keep her hanging about.'"

"'Oh this is all going swimmingly,' she replied, 'I'm so glad you came around. I have been wanting to take these steps for ages, but my Daughter keeps telling me I am better off where I am."

"Really and truly, I think she just wants all this stuff for herself and that prick of a Husband of hers. Oh do excuse me, but they make my life a living hell you know."

"Since my Bert died all I've seemed to do, is bail them out one time after another. Ah, that looks like your friend coming up the path. Shall I let him in?'"

"Let him in, I thought to myself, you try fuckin' stopping the bastard."

Vince took over once more, "Soo, in I go. Georgie is sitting there perched in a chair, like Little Lord Fuckin' Fauntleroy, he was. With a lovely delightful looking china cup and saucer of tea in his mitts. I reckoned the full set would make a few quid, so thought to myself, he can fuckin' well wash that up a bit lively."

"It was like walking into a showroom. Paddy Wadey had certainly found one here and today was going to be a big day. In an authoritative tone, I took out my pad and paper and instructed the lady of the house, that everything would be logged by my assistant and that today is the first day of the rest of your life. She was chuffed to bits."

“Dick was called in to help and he flagged Paddy and Powders to pull the Luton up outside, The Wadey boy was to stay in the back of the motor and load up just in case he got recognised.”

“Two and a half hours later, we were done. Not exactly lock stock and barrel, but it was only fair to leave Muriel a few bits and pieces of sentimental value. Photographs weren’t exactly worth sod all anyway we joked; still she had plenty of readies to help kick start her new life on the East Coast.”

“We actually gave her £4,500, which was a lot of money in them days, but not a smidgeon of what we were about to get for the booty.”

“Going ahead as planned, we headed back to The Grove. It had a nice private car park at the back, which was why it had been selected, and to our joy, sitting in Vince’s motor was Charlie. 'Everything alright boys?' he asked. 'Cushty,' we advised. He immediately jumps into the Luton with Dick and Powders and bolts straight back to Brighton, leaving Me, Peter and George to stay one more night. A very pleasant evening too, was spent by one and all, as I recall.”

“I did of course, check with Charlie how things had gone in Leicester. He said he had gone down to reception at exactly 11am and asked where the nearest Chemist was as he had an absolute blinding toothache. Once instructed he had gone round and danced a merry hell how he was in so much incredible pain. The guy there was sympathetic but could not prescribe anything stronger than what was available on the shelf.”

“Charlie had gone the extra mile this time. He had done no less than grab the poor fellah by the tie and dragged him over the counter with the threat of knocking all of his teeth out and this would pass on a similar sensation as to the pain like the one in Charlie’s poor fucking head.”

"'Please, please please help me out. I don't care, I really don't care. I will sign anything just so long as you can help me out, I won't tell a single living soul, please.'"

"At the mercy of a Nearly boy giving it their all, most people do crumble, and crumble the chemist did, especially when put under such pressure at 11 o'poxy clock in the morning. Charlie then returned to The Mowbray Towers, as we liked to call it, and informed the receptionist he was not to be disturbed under any circumstances, even though he was expecting a call."

"The aforementioned call was made at 11:45 promptly when Powders assured Char that 'They Were In'. At midday precisely, clutching his jaw and extremely uncomfortable, Charlie checked out and said he couldn't care less he'd paid for 3 nights, they could sort it out another week. He just had to get home and see a dentist before he jumped out of a fucking window."

"He then proceeded round to the Chemist at 12:15 and thanked him graciously for his kind gesture with those prescription painkillers, he certainly had saved the day. 'Thanks matey.'"

"Then bunged him a brand new crispy fiver. He then took the half-hour drive to Birmingham, with a big wide grin across his boat, all the way."

"The next day, was to be both exhilarating, tense, and one of them you never forget," said George. "We had already discussed the night before, that we were well aware there would be a 'Scream Up' and we all had to be on top-form, no shirking."

"Me and Vince were well aware there would be a tug before Brighton, but this was the first 'Proper Stroke' we had done with Widdy and so were just a tad precarious. It's all very well giving it the large in the Pub or Club, but this one was definitely gonna come on top."

“Soo, just as we were pulling onto the M40, the sirens have all gone off and we are pulled up by three Old Bill. So Vince in the passenger side enquires ‘To what do we owe the honour Gentlemen. What is it you require from us. Whatever you wish to discuss, I am sure can be resolved in a civilised manner.’”

“Well the Brummy copper starts off with the old: ‘You Sothon twats. You think you can cum up ‘ere and rip off poor old ladies and fook back down to fookin’ Brighton and think youse can gerraway wiv it. Well my little beach boy bums, t’day is not yer locky day.'”

Vince now continued: “Soo, I says to him: 'Well if that’s the way ya wanna play it, fucking well get on with it and explain yer fuckin’ self. Do not think for one minute you Brummy runts can just pull us over wivout any poxy excuse, rhyme or reason, coz you fuckin’ well can’t. What the fuck is all this about you wanker?'”

“The copper carried on, ‘Well, where were you yesterday morning at 11am Sir? As I have reason to believe you were at a certain address in Birmingham where a disgraceful act of deceit and misrepresentation was conveyed.’”

“So I just rubbed my chin and said, ‘Well let me think about that for a moment matey.’”

“Took a slight pause and then informed the officer, that as I recall, I was actually in Leicester.”

“‘Ooh yeah,’ he came back with, ‘And how do you intend to back that story op, then sonshine?’”

“This is where it gets good, my little Minnie.”

At that point I realised the sheer brilliance of these boys, and Vince was in his element.

"I goes through me pockets and pulls out a small plastic container, that pills are packed in. 'Oh yeah, here we go,' I says, 'I got these yesterday for a toothache, which I was suffering from, at a Chemist in Leicester. There look at that, there is the address, oh, and would you believe it? It actually has the time and date printed on the front label as it was a special prescription."

"They was having none of it, but could not manage to get a direct line to the Chemist, things were not so technical and immediate in them days. So the upshot was, we had to follow one of the Police Cars into Leicester to verify the alibi. The two other Panda Cars, had decided to be no longer involved in this folly, no matter how much, or what, was supposedly missing from the complainants house."

"It was definitely the Daughter who had called the filth. We still reminisce, to this day, what her face would have looked like when she walked into her old dear's house that night. Keeping an evil eye on her inheritance on a daily basis, with not a care in the world for her own Mum's well being. Well we had seen to that, I bet her old man was in a right old pickle an' all."

"Soo, we get's to Leicester and arrive at the Chemist's. Out I get and follow the little runt, at his beckoning, into the shop. As we enter, the Pharmacist takes one look at me and cowers behind the counter, saying, 'It's not my fault, he made me do it, look I have a signed disclaimer here for those prescribed painkillers.'"

"The coppers were well pissed off, as they hadn't even asked the poor bugger yet if he recognised Vince. With the shock of the uniformed Police and that complete and utter nutter from yesterday, all walking in at the same time the Chemist, who was not necessarily accustomed to such high drama, didn't look as closely as the Old Bill may have assumed. After all, this was the plan in the first place and it had been executed to perfection."

"The tally for this particular venture, was quite astronomical. Paintings found in the attic alone fetched £12,000." Georgie enjoyed reeling off what they got for the haul.

"Tommy Barnes snatched our arms off, for a collection of what they call Cow Creamers. Some were Whieldon and are distinguished by their rich tortoiseshell lead glaze coloured by the inclusion of different metallic oxides."

"He was well chuffed as he had a proper Norman for these and paid more than what we were expecting. Mind you, we now had a terrific relationship with Tom and everything was done with due respect and diligence. After all it was only a laugh, wouldn't last forever and all that old crap. Still the £11,000 was a great kick-starter in Brighton's Lanes that next day."

"Paddy Wadey and Powders had decided that they were happy to take whatever we felt they were worth, in the spoils. Very wise move, as it was well known nowadays that Vinnie despised greediness in the split. He always offered what he thought was fair, and on this occasion he was more than fair and agreed to share equally, after X's. We both knew of course that the Tom was not included."

"That was the part of the deal, that went into our pension fund as he liked to call it, but the subject never arose. Especially when they did get their cut. Best bit of money they ever earned and we took all the flack and aggro that went with it. But then, hey ho, we woz the guvnor's at this game."

"There were half a dozen Tapestry's shoved into a £900 Ottoman marquetry wood casket. They were from Brussels, woven to a design by Teniers, coloured in wools and silks. Nearly overlooked: but we are dealing with the 'Nearly Boys' 'ere. They came to eighty fucking thousand pounds. Even we could not believe it, but did not refuse the Auction House cheque."

Vince joined in again, recalling the spoils of their venture:

"A nice pair of Venetian painted plaster Blackamoor figures on waisted pedestals with some sort of foliage, quite big at about 70 inches. Made ten grand. She had a lovely collection of Silver Tea Sets, and dessert suite, but they was all stuck up in the loft, so 'not much value there. They would take an awful lot of work and elbow grease to get back to their true glory, but we'd give 'em a go anyway.' Over twenty fucking grand, in a job lot at Christie's."

Vince now came up for breath: "Need I go on, my delightful Minnie?"

"I think not Vince." said I, "but can you vaguely remember how much you earnt on that shambolic deal?"

Looking indignant, Vince came back with: "It's all very well for people to say we were, let's say, not completely honest. But the thing is, if that horrible greedy little bitch of a daughter of Her's had had her way: poor little Muriel would never have got fuck all."

"She'd have spent the rest of her life, miserably, next door, to two ungrateful bastards, and never got to decorate her lovely little two bedroom flat in 'Skeg Fuckin Ness', now would she boys."

They all concurred, simultaneously. Accompanied by clapping and a rousing 'Here, here', and a distant, even if in a slightly sarcastic manner, 'jolly good show old boy, jolly good show'

"Do you know what Steph, Howsabout this then. Would you Adam and Eve it? We bumped into Muriel a few years later in Skeggy, and she was as happy as Larry."

"She had even met a nice old geezer called Cyril and was, as she referred to it 'living in sin, and loving it', and she couldn't give a toss what her daughter and greedy git of an husband were doing."

"She told us there woz murders when her daughter found out about the sale of all the stuff. She had tried not to let on who had purchased everything, but when the Police got involved, she was backed into a corner."

"We of course understood, it was not down to her, it was all the grubby little muddy water's fault."

"Then we met them the next day and insisted on buying them both afternoon tea on the front. During which of course we discovered Cyril had a few items no longer of any use and proceeded to take that stupid Coin Collection off his hands, that was taking up all that drawer space. It still made three grand though!"

"All in all, we carved up two hundred and ten thousand pounds. As there was six of us, that was £35,000 each, and although there was a cunning plan and a few expenses involved, it wasn't bad for two and a half hours work."

"The Jewellery that got slipped under the carpet, was worth another £40,000 but that was needed at a later date when one of us might be in a bit of Hubble-bubble."

"And that, young lady, is how you have a proper toothache, cause a heartache, and when laughing about it, end up wiv a fuckin' bellyache!"

*

And so it would go on.

Until George, in full flow, was trying his best to catch his breath. He basically couldn't stop laughing, whilst talking.

It was about one night in 'The Eagle', Gloucester Road, and something to do with a pianist. Suddenly he went as red as a beetroot clutched his chest and fell off his chair.

Being George a couple of us thought he was joking, but Vince knew immediately and called out to Joe to phone 999. It was to be to no avail as once he passed out George was never to regain consciousness, and was pronounced D.O.A. at the hospital.

This was a very sad ending, but to be fair, even though it left us all a bit numb, the usual humour was still prevalent. Jimmy said it was typical of George to do it before the bill had to be paid, and Charlie remarked that Georgie Balcock was the first person he knew that he could genuinely say 'Died Laughing'.

Vince settled the bill in a quiet, pensive mood and remarked solemnly and sincerely:

"There goes one of the best. They don't make em' like him any more."

"That's right" agreed Dick the Driver, "They broke the mould when they made Georgie."

The funeral, just a week to the day later, was another story altogether, for more than one bloody reason or another. They say it was one of the biggest send off's in Brighton history. The service had to be held in St Peter's church, so as to get everyone in, and then just across the road to 'The King & Queen' for the wake.

I was so very grateful, that I had had the chance to meet what they referred to as 'A right proper fella,' 'One of your own,' and also 'A true character.' If I heard the term 'Diamond Geezer' once more I think I would have screamed.

The guys I had met over the past few months were all really genuinely sad that day, but still took the time and managed to introduce me to George's son, even though he was clearly shell shocked. It was nice and very kind that they showed me due respect, in honour of George's memory, despite my relatively short lived part in his life.

"It's what Georgie would have wished for." Vince whispered in my ear, the hairs on the back of my stood up at this point.

Of course another major denominator on this occasion was that now George had passed on, our original agreement of any personal financial benefits or beneficiaries on his behalf, was now invalid.

There had been no legal documents signed on either part, or regulatory agreement to say or not to say. Business is business as they say, and therefore I was no longer obligated to adhere to any alleged hearsay pre-arranged confidences.

I will state at this stage that, I have not, under any circumstances, reported or divulged any information that was not willingly volunteered, for financial gain, to any individual or coerced anyone to say anything that they did not wish to confide.

His legacy of course, amongst other things, is this book. He said time and time again that nearly everyone 'On the knocker,' always said that their daring do's would make a great book.

If only it was written in a way that people actually believed, these incredible stories were true and not fictitious tales dreamt up by a bunch of Walter Mitty's, and mentally inept, corrupt characters with no morality.

I met so many new people that day, some I had heard in passing like Banjo, Monkey, Squirrel, Badger and John The Wad.

Yet the main common denominator was the fondness they all held for 'Gorgeous Georgie Balcock.'

Steve was with me all the way. I'd thought George was well known, but this prat knew everyone, but never blanked a person even if he didn't have a clue who they were. It wasn't till I was speaking with Gerry McKinnock one day, that he revealed Steve was locally quite famous, due to his boxing days, but totally oblivious to the fact.

It was, though, unfortunately, to become one of the most traumatic days of my entire life. Getting a bit above himself, one fellow, Gordon Bostock, started going on about the time Georgie pulled off the coup of his life. Bringing up the subject of 'Bob The Burglar' and how Georgie had charmed the knickers off of his missus when she visited Brighton one day with her lovely baby daughter.

There were a few raised eyebrows, as he began to chirp on, but he didn't really give a toss, and when someone tried to intervene, he just told them to piss off and mind their own business.

'Minnie here was a friend of Georgie's, so, keep yer' bleedin' nose out!'

I was later to learn the true story of these events, and Joker was nowhere near the real truth, but he hadn't meant anything maliciously. He said that she was probably the love of Georgie's life and that he had never recovered from that terrible tragedy and had transformed into a shell of the man he was before.

Then it appertained that this bird had left her old man 'Bob The Burglar' and buggered off to the French Riviera in the summer of 1968 with George, who had just had a lovely little tickle on one of his trips down in Torquay, with £1,250 burning a hole in his pocket.

Bearing in mind you could have bought a couple of houses in Grant Street for that amount, at the time.

Anyway, they had rented a Yacht from the Marina, that had a speedboat attached, and so had a bash at water skiing. All being hunky-dory they were up to having a go at anything at the time, things did not go so well and there was a tragic accident and the Girl died.

Georgie did his best to save her and nearly karked it himself, in his attempts to save her from a burning boat. It had crashed against the protective walls of the Marina. There was nothing sinister about it. Just a rotten unfortunate accident.

This was when I suddenly realised that the woman Georgie had run off with was probably my Mother, and later found this to be true. I very nearly collapsed. But contained myself, better than a medal winner on an Olympic rostrum, the tears were at the ready, but I was not.

Having been associating with this lot for some time now, I knew exactly what, where or when something should or should not be said.

I had a nice few questions for my Father, and he wasn't gonna be particularly chuffed about what was coming his way. But now was not the time, to worry about his feelings, the selfish fucking bastard!

*

To some extent, it is a little bit like those sick jokes that circulate by text when something disastrous happens or someone dies. You know, Phil Everley died so I got tickets for the Everley Brothers Farewell Tour, half-price. What did Nelson Mandela get for Christmas? Ronnie Biggs!

The fun thing I hope about this book, is that it may end up a bit like the Alcoholics Anonymous Bible, everyone has their favourite story, whether good or bad and I hope you have yours.

There are in fact many many more tales to tell, and many more character's to introduce you to, but to write a book the size of War & Peace on a first attempt is a bit optimistic. Even though the material is quite special, another edition of similar material is ready and waiting for the printer's press, as you finish reading this.

Of course this is a second edition as the first has completely sold out, and I can proudly state that there are two more editions available if you have enjoyed things so far. Making these stories a trilogy after all, so maybe the War & Peace reference in the first edition wasn't so far of the mark after all!

Of course I'm not finished yet and The Epilogue does not pull any punches, but there's no surprise there, is there. Even near the end I can still manage to fit the same word in one sentence three bloody times. It's a knack!

Without trying to be melodramatic, my own personal story, now, equally evolves alongside this bunch of reprobates, scoundrels, scallywags or whatever you wanna call them, like a Barbara Taylor Bradford novel in itself, and when this story fully unfolds, it will go down in the annals of British, as well as Brighton History!!

*

WATCH THIS SPACE!

Epilogue.

So, as not to unravel the heart of the story, the very end is quite special, and so, here we go!

My first interrogation was that of Grace, but before I began this, I made sure I was in full control and was not going to lose my temper or place the blame on her. To make sure of this I had confided briefly with Steve, Jules and Tracey about what had appertained and they were all of the same opinion. Grace would have been acting on my Dad's instructions, lifetime loyalty, all the things they would have shared over the years, blah, blah, blah.

Anyway they agreed I should approach her in a mature way and get as much information as possible, before confronting my Father. They had also grown to value Grace's friendship over the years, and now was not the time to make hasty decisions without all the relevant knowledge. It's so nice to have good friends around when you need them.

My meeting with Grace was quite sedate and it was like she knew what was coming, before I had even opened my mouth. I had probably given the game away over the phone with my tone, or just the sight of me when I opened the front door for sure. (Double barrelled rhyme, even at such, a troubled time!)

She explained nearly everything, but could not go into explicit details of major events, as this would be down to Dad, and after all, it was his responsibility. There would not be any point keeping schtum for nearly four years and then blurting it all out in one go, that would just be ridiculous.

She began by explaining that she and Barney often made trips to Brighton years earlier when he had things to take care of. This explained why a few of the other wives had given her the courteous nod of acknowledgement, when being at the same events recently.

It was not like she knew them intimately, but the wives were left to their own devices whilst the men sorted out all the gory details before any socialising began. It was, however quite hollow for Grace, as they very rarely stayed long, after the business was taken care of; and only stayed overnight if there was a hiccup on some other issues that Barney needed to sort out.

It was all quite cold as far as she was concerned and didn't have a clue what it was all about anyway, if the weather was lousy she'd rather have stayed home, it was strictly business.

Then there was the matter of her best friend, my Mum. This had been one of the most traumatic things she had ever had to experience. Worst of all, there was nothing she could do, to stop, or help her, when she needed her most.

She had at first spent a lot of time looking after me, but my Dad insisted he could take care of things and did not wish her to get too close. The fact was he was scared stiff, that I might blame him when I was older, if I grew up knowing the truth.

Less said about that part the better, it was for him to explain and let's not get carried away. I agreed.

Next on the agenda, there was the issue of not being able to be totally honest with me for all this time, even though I had opened my heart to her. Going back to the time my Father first suggested our arrangement, he had insisted, that if she took on his proposal, it was imperative that I was not to be made aware of the murky past.

It turned out that Dad was quite the control freak. Considering the initial reason, and resulting consequences of my Mum's actions, when you stop to think about it, it's no big surprise.

*

I went to visit my Dad, after George's funeral, with, of course Grace, who was now deemed a co-conspirator, but still forgiven.

I had called my Dad as soon as the penny had dropped. Purely, out of respect, and had pre-empted him that, Grace and I, were firmly in the picture, and that I, needed to be filled in on the finer details.

Therefore my Father, and I met. Can't say that it was the best time for the pair of us, but what the heck, what could you expect!

We discussed a few matters that had come up over the past few years, but nothing was of too much significance, so then decided to crack on with the case in hand. I just needed another day to prepare myself, in order to face the facts in a sensible and sober state, in my own familiar surroundings.

*

Quite disturbingly it was also time for Steve to take the 'Big Bird' across the ocean and begin his new adventure. I drove him to Heathrow with his sister and found it very emotional. I had missed my monthly period and was not in a very pleasant place.

How could I stop such an energised and optimistic person from following their dreams?

It was not an option for me. So when we kissed farewell, it didn't even faze him for a moment and even though totally oblivious as to the circumstances, he knew he would see me again sometime.

*

We met in my flat, just two days later. After all, my Dad was my Dad, and nothing was going to interfere with that.

He said, in a very solemn voice, that what he was about to tell me, was not for anyone else's ears. He had just found out that, although now brown bread, the soppy little prat that I had been having an ongoing, working relationship with, was a no-good, two-bob-bit, piece of shit, and as far as he was concerned, a right rotten wanker.

He was, however, prepared not to interfere too much with what had been going on, and would therefore be prepared to continue to give me his full support, even though he was glad he was dead.

He understood that my work was not finished on this project, even though he had some vague idea. Grace had refused to give him all the answers to his many questions, so don't think she has been disloyal. Grace and I had already discussed this, so things were fine on that count, and I was actually familiar with more of what had occurred than he realised, so for now I'd keep my cards close to my chest.

Well, I was none too impressed, I can tell you!

The thing is however, my Dad then proceeded to tell me The Truth, The Whole Truth, and Nothing but The Truth, as far as he knew it.

Good luck with this one I s'pose!

*

My Mum had had a very bad case of post-natal depression when I was born, something that was now treatable, but back in those days, no one understood the condition or gave any consideration to it, or had any inclination of how to help.

Dad included.

Then, out of the blue, some lively, cocky little runt, one of them 'Knockerboys' from down Brighton way, had impressed her and whisked her off of her feet down to the South of France, with delusions of grandeur and promises of life and a future without any problems.

He loved her dearly, but not being a prat, decided not to have the arsehole mullered, and accepted that these things sometimes happen.

He then realised that he was himself in some way to blame, by not involving her in his life, or sharing the spoils of his own ill-gotten gains. If he had, maybe things would have been better. Hindsight is a splendid thing, but no good till later, as we all know.

He obviously decided to do the best he could, to raise me on his own, despite the attempts of his friends to get outside help. His mind was made up and that was exactly what he had done.

*

He then drove me out to Shoreham Airport, where he had a relatively small Aircraft Hanger all of his own. We looked in each other's eyes and just started to laugh.

It was crammed full of old tables and chairs, rugs, sewing machines, cabinets, copper, paintings, clocks and God knows what else.

I knew instantly what the whole game was all about. It was also at this point that we decided I was to become a partner in the Family business, but I insisted that there was to be no 'Cat Burgling' in my schedule. We laughed a lot that day.

He then explained about how, when he found out about Mum, he had decided to do everything he possibly could within his power, and proceeded to ruin every single solitary one of those horrible little supposed 'Antique Dealing' little bastards down in Brighton, and destroy them!

His plan was not complicated. He would simply buy up all the properties made available, and at a later date, when the kids decided to do the right thing, he would tell them to take a hike.

Of course during this process he had made a small fortune. All the new kitchens and bathrooms were purchased on dodgy or stolen credit cards from places like MFI, at around 10% of cost price of course, and charged at the going rate.

He was always three steps ahead of the competition, or any other cocky little prats for that matter. On top of that, all the old furniture was put into 'Storage', and then replaced with 'Brand New' stuff that was also added to the 'Bill', at no extra cost, because he was just a nice bloke.

He enjoyed mentioning the sincere gratitude heaped upon him, when the lady of the house thanked him so much, for getting rid of all that wooden furniture that was so awkward to polish, and how much easier it was to just get a damp cloth and wipe down the Formica tops and plastic upholstery on the new chairs. Often with a very personal and private 'Thank you very much indeed.'

He had, of course, made all the deals seem reasonable to the punters, but on the backhand, had stolen everything from underneath them.

Everything was written in stone, not one single property was ever to be passed on to family, and once the 'Tenant' passed away the property was reverted back to the 'Landowner'. Magic!

This was when Grace had told me not to press my Father on the issue of Georgie's Mum's house.

If you recall, I'd promised George I knew someone who could help, but once my Dad knew who's home it was, the whole scheme of things had become a harsh reality.

My Dad had had his revenge, but none of this had reaped any reward till now. Now that the 'Home-owners' had started to die.

He explained that he and Barney had been best pals, down Brick Lane way, as kids since they were at school. They were in the Army together, and then joined forces together once again, when they came out. 'The Kray's' took over in the East End around that time, and so they made themselves a separate entity, but still worked with them should the opportunity present itself.

He was of course 'Bob The Burglar' and he and Barney ran 'The Bethnal Green Berets', with the full support and co-operation of The Kray Gang.

He had been approached about the 'Great Train Robbery' job, but had decided to give that one a miss, as he was not to be the one calling the shots.

He had strict rules, he and Barney were proper muckers, and the rest of his crew were well disciplined, reliable and trustworthy, all having done their National Service. He had to be in control, and that was why he'd never got a tug, and no one was in a position to grass him up.

Being of a reputable nature and 'A Right Couple Of Geezers', they had built up a sound reputation for themselves. The trouble began of course when I was born. Mum went on the turn and when she took a 'Funny Turn' as he put it, everything went pear shaped.

The arrangement was quite simple, when there was a 'Clue' that couldn't be cracked, and there was still a shit load of goods available under the roof, it had to be 'Screwed', and that was all there was to it. These 'Clues' came from all over the place, but 'The Cream', always came from them slippery little sods we know as 'Brighton's Knocker's'.

The reason for this was quite simple, they were the greediest most selfish bunch of bastards that ever walked the face of the earth, and if they couldn't weasel or squirm themselves in, then no one could. So, whoever's gaff it was, didn't really matter, coz they woz granite anyway, had it coming and deserved it!

Once my Dad had found out about Mum and some Hector from Brighton running off to the South of France, he had gone berserk. Especially when he found out that the saucy git had met her as far back as 1966, in one of his own bloody Clubs in London for Christ's fucking sake.

Then of course was the tragic accident.

When he had mentioned, in the past, how he may have killed himself, he was actually referring to murdering someone and therefore robbing me of his care and attention all my life.

Now that just wouldn't have been fair now would it?

ALL BET'S WERE OFF!

AND HE WASN'T HOLDING ANY PRISONERS!

My Dad then proceeded to explain, how he and Barney, went over all the clue's they had pending at the time, and prepared to negotiate the most bizarre string of robberies ever to be conceived, in their living memory!

Quite simply, my Dad, evaluated each and every single job proposal, studied through a fine toothcomb, all the information available, and just went for it!

He felt dishonoured, so then felt more than welcome to give as good as he got. Hence, he showed Barney the logbook of jobs to be done.

There were about 27, and told his mucker that they could all be done over the next two months, and the usual 40% cut for the knockerboys, would not be forthcoming, 'Do what you fuckin' like with your share, please yer'self'. He had told him, and Barney played it straight and told no one, not even Grace.

*

NOW, why have I taken so long to publish this book?

I buried my Father two months ago, and had promised him, at that time, back in 1986 that not one single one of these tales would be told, till his dyin' day, and he was safely put in the ground.

That was many years ago and there have been so many more interesting stories gathered over that time and from before.

I've now got an Empire to run and a few other distractions that make good reading too. Everything in my life is crystal clear and untouchable by the powers that be. I am reputably one of the richest independent Women in the country and don't owe a dinar in Tax. Kosher all down the road and can't be touched.

That does not of course give anyone the right to question where my wealth originates from and I'm not telling!

Oh well, Whatkanyadoo? Whatkanyasaay?

It's only a fucking laugh anyway, innit?

*

A Little Extra, for no extra, By Stevie Martin.

I Owe You One Micky Dawes.

Once it became common knowledge that Micky Dawes was not only ready, willing, and able to buy all and anything that they were lucky enough to get their hands on, the new found army of Brighton's Knockerboys did not have to think twice where to deliver their booty on a Friday afternoon. He also paid cash on the nail, with no questions asked.

Monday mornings would see platoons of Brighton Knockerboys, on the outskirts of Brighton at The Robin Hood junction on the A23. In homage to the great board game of Monopoly 'To Get Out of Town', many of whom, who would at a later date 'Go straight to Jail' in a similar fashion, for certain indiscrepencies that would inadvertently be curtailed.

Back out onto the road once again, to engage in their next great adventure and expedition to secure unwanted, unneeded, unnecessary and certainly underpaid for goods, from anyplace, anytime, anywhere.

There is a slightly tongue in cheek private joke slipped in there, but once you read all three books, you will surely smile, if not laugh out loud. To this day I still can't replace real words with text message styles like LOL. Why can't people just simply say what they mean? Any way there's no need to get back on the old soapbox again, let's just get on with the story at hand shall we?

Yes of course we should.

So there he is Micky Dawes, with his 'Big Yard' in Upper Gardner Street, in The North Lanes, all plotted up and cash always at the Nelson Eddie.

The smartest or should we say slipperiest, of the Knockerboys, always managed to get back into town on a Thursday and 'cash up'.

However of course, unsurprisingly, as is often the case in many instances of grand human enterprises, the bulk of the Knockerboy community regularly, like rats deserting a sinking ship, converged back into Town after three o'clock on a Friday, like clockwork.

Half the time they actually had a clock or two loaded on the motor anyway. Grandmother, Grandfather, Mantelpiece or Rolex, any time piece was succilient to their derisive activities and powers of persuasion in order to obtain such valuable goods, at any cost, but always for the very minimum exchange of cash, of course.

The amount of furniture, porcelain, ornaments and God knows what else, was absolutely staggering. But always a man of his word Micky was willing to buy it all, lock stock and all smoking fucking barrels. Next generation Knockerboys were already getting in on the act, with the likes of Fingers, Steve and Shane Wadey standing in line waiting to get served up, it was fucking phenomenal.

Try saying that out loud four times quickly!

With such vast amounts of produce coming his way Micky was always well prepared. But, one monumental and unforgettable week, I think it must have been an Easter or Christmas Bank Holiday or something, for some strange reason, he ran out of cash.

The specific dates or exact details are actually quite irrelevant as to what was about to appertain. Never one to miss out on an opportunity, or possibly even not to let someone down out of the kindness of his heart, he construed a revolutionary payment method. The IOU.

I thought you didn't like writing in text message style I hear you think, well this is one of those exceptions to the rule. Who's writing this anyway?

Soo, one little gang of our merry men had a blinding Dining Cain with twelve matching Lord Mayors. I told you that the Glossary was there for a reason didn't I? This particular one was by Johnstone, Jupe & Co.

It was absolutely stunning, today it would fetch about £220,000, but the hammer wouldn't come down for less than a bottle. The seating arrangements were worth another thirty bags in today's money, but our dear old friend Micky was happy to part with three grand there and then, what a blinder? The deal was done and everyone was happy as Larry. Then came the crux of the matter and possibly a deal breaker. He didn't have any cash left!

"I'll tell you what I'll do," he explained to the leader of the pack, "Howsabout, I write you an 'I Owe You'. Now, you know me boys, my word is my bond, and if I say I'm gonna pay you an hat-trick then I'm gonna. This here is a ticket stating that I will part wiv the nelsons as soon as the Bank opens Tuesday morning. Whaddayasay?"

The appropriate designated dealer did not utter a single solitary word; he just nodded his nut and shook his hand. This deal, which had been struck on a whim and a prayer, was of course honoured, and so a new way of doing business was born.

An IOU from Micky Dawes was now akined to a recognised currency, all of it's own.

The main reason for mentioning this particular strategic phenomenon will now become crystal.

I myself was holidaying, with a girlfriend, on a delightful and lovely little Greek Island called Santorini one year. Having a lovely time and enjoying meeting plenty of lovely people that I have never seen or spoken to ever since. Repetitiveness in the same sentence is one of my pet hates, but, I just can't help myself, I love you and nobody else!

Dining on stuffed peppers and beef tomatoes my companion and I struck up conversation, one evening, in a delightful beachfront restaurant with an elderly Scottish couple at the neighbouring table. It wasn't long before the waiters were asked to join our tables together, and within an hour three more tables were attached to our ensemble.

Jock was intrigued to hear that I hailed from Brighton, and was already familiar with the South Coast resort.

"Lit mee tel'ya theese sunny-boy," he said drunkenly, but with a blissful smile on his boat, " Aah, woz in ma bank wun daay, an diss cocky leetle bastad cums in wid a poxy scruffy leetle scrap a paeper an sez ta mee..."

"Sez ta mee, mind ya. Dinna ya worry abaat it."

"Sez ta mee. Cannyeee cash tiss pleeze missta? Aah teks a lookatit, annit sez, it sez mindya, it sez, wood ya beleevee?"

Now in a loud high-pitched voice, and seemingly with a dangerously high blood pressure to go with it,

"'I OWE YOU TREE HUNDERR'RED POWNDS' tree hundred fockin pownds. I fuckin looksatim and sez, watsdiz, wot am I gonna fockin do wit a poxy 'I OWE YEW'?"

"Anyway, da fellah looks me street in de eyes an sez, are you saying dhaat Micky Dawes's credit is no goot in Bonny feckin' Scotland. Aah tells'ya he woz indeeed a bonny lad."

"Aah deceeded ta spick ta ma managaa." Pausing briefly for a deep breath and swig of his wine, my newfound Scottish friend continued. He was also revelling in the fact that he now had an attentive audience hanging on his every word, as I had done earlier, and he was loving absolutely every minute of it.

"An he sed ta phone da guy. Sooo. Ah phone da guy. Wheel, afta dat call, aah goes back ta ma coontaer and pays da guy oot. Dat Micky fockin Dawes woz a fockin magishan. Aahs fahgatten eggsactly wot he said, buut, let me tell ya diss, he certainly convinced me that his credit was goot, and I belieeeved him. Acourse, the IOU woz honoured wittin two working days. But aah'l tell'yadiss, we don't make a habit of it, but steel ta'disday, nute wun of oure employees ever'r'r hesitate if someone comes into our branch wit a Micky Dawes IOU. Aah dinna suppose yuse knows da fellah diz yah?"

With an incredulous look on my face, I declared that of course being from Brighton I was indeed fully aware of, and knew Micky Dawes personally. I was also more than prepared to vouch for him.

The sweaty was well impressed and ordered liqueur coffees all round, despite my protestations he also insisted on paying the bill for our meal. Micky Dawes even from pastures far and wide and away with the fairies, you still took and continue to take care of many 'Brightonbeautiful' things.

There were of course many disputes and altercations over the years, but never ever, were there any insinuations that Micky Dawes was nothing other than a good honest to goodness businessman.

He certainly stuck a lot of money in a lot of pockets, but never had to pick-a-pocket or two himself.

Oh, and by the way, the mystery man at Gaffer Dawes's wedding, the one that got tied to a Volvo roof-rack, bought the biggest round of drinks the whole day and slung someone out of a window?

That was of course myself.

The Eddie Dawes incident was severely exaggerated, as when I questioned him about his bullying of a dear friend of mine Nicky Sargent, he lunged straight at me and only with a bit of skilful footwork, a trip, slip and a tip, with a clip round the ear'ole for good measure, did he go out of the window.

As stated it was a lovely sunny day so the window was open and it was only on the ground floor anyway. No harm done, but slightly embarrassed, he just went home a little bit earlier than he had expected!

Yours Sincerely

Stevie Martin

The Glossary.

This is not to condescend anyone who has decided to give this Publication a chance, Thank-You So very much, I really mean it.

But some of you may not be familiar with all the tiny idiosyncrasies that brings the whole thing together, and by just taking five minutes to browse through some of these unfamiliar terms you will feel more 'involved' and don't be for one second deterred from referring back to this page to understand exactly what is going on. This also, hopefully, makes sure you don't get fed up by reading something that you don't quite understand, and put the book away till another day, that rhymes dunnit'. That's just a little private joke between us!

It's just the couple of pages, so stick a bookmarker in for quick and easy reference, so please, just relax and enjoy!

Sherbet/Shant	= *Alcoholic beverage*
Jubilee	= *E as in Ecstasy*
Treacle as in Treacle Tart	= *Sweetheart*
Rattley	= Female Companion
China as in China Plate	= Mate
Danny as in Danny La Rue	= *Clue*
Whistle as in Whistle & Flute	= *Suit*
Karked / Karking	= *Dead / Dying*
Jamboree	= *Tea or Coffee*
Harvey Smith	= *Two Fingered Gesture*
Billy Goats	= *Notes*
Tommy Cooper	= *Unexpected Sudden Death*
Bish Bosh	= *Nosh-Food / Dosh - Money*
Sky Rocket	= *Pocket*
Holy Ghost	= *Toast*
Boat as in Boat Race	= *Face*
Cossers / Gavvers	= *Police*
Drum / Gaff / Kenna / Kennel	= *House / Dwelling*
Ricket	= *Mistake*
Haggerty	= *House Clearance*
Scoombers	= *Moulsecomb Council Estate*

Hawkers	= *Whitehawk Council Estate*
Chored	= *Stolen*
Pony as in Pony & Trap	= *Crap / Bad*
Goonered	= *Sacked*
Naused	= *Messed Up*
Cattled	= *Flabbergasted*
Schtum	= *Mouth Shut*
Mivvi	= *Ice-cream Filled Lolly*
Smudge	= *Painting/Picture*
Mullered	= *Killed / Murdered*
Lord Mayor	= *Chair*
Cain as in Cain & Abel	= *Table*
Drum as in Drum and Bass	= *Place*
Mincers as in Mince Pies	= *Eyes*
Crust as in Crust of Bread	= *Head*
Oxford as in Scholar	= *Dollar 5/- (25p)*
Tom as in Tom Foolery	= *Jewellery*
Dustbin as in Dustbin Lid	= *Kid*
Muddy as in Muddy Water	= *Daughter*
Norman as in Norman Hunter	= *Punter*
Currant as in Currant Bun	= *Son*
Hubble Bubble	= *Trouble*
V.AT.	= *Vodka & Tonic*
Vera and Philharmonic	= *Gin & Tonic*
Sweaty as in Sweaty Sock	= *Jock / Scotsman*

Bottle = 2
Carpet = 3
Dinar = Shilling (5p)
Ching = £5
Cockle = £10
Score = £20
Half a Spot = 50
Spot / Ton = 100
Monkey = 500
Bag as in Bag of Sand = 1000